MOONLIGHT AND FIREFLIES

SPRING LAKE SERIES
BOOK 1

PENELOPE BELL

DEDICATION

What is a Godwink? According to the internet, it is an event or personal experience, often identified as coincidence so astonishing, it is seen as a sign of divine intervention, especially when perceived as the answer to a prayer. From my own personal experience, a Godwink can be a person.

I had been writing for decades and published two coffee table books, containing my short stories, poetry, photography, and bits of wit and wisdom. I had many stories in my head, some of which I did manage to put on my computer, thinking "one day," I just might publish one of them.

"One day" came, and I finished a story about rising above a life of hurt and tragedy. Yes, some of the events within the book did indeed happen to me. Encouraged by family, I started making contact with several authors who were in my area, A L Jackson, Nikki Lynn Barrett, and Barbara Hinske, in particular. I needed their input about how to get my book published.

Nikki suggested I attend an author signing not far from my home in North Scottsdale. While there, Nikki introduced me to Cheryl Maddox, an awesome Author's Assistant. Nikki told Cheryl what genre I wrote, and Cheryl suggested I contact her after the signing, and she would give me a lead for a publishing company.

That was the beginning of a beautiful relationship. Through the Dragonfly Ink Publishing company, I connected with editor Sandy Ebel (aka Sandy Kaye.) I had no idea the relationship would grow into such a strong friendship.

Sandy has been with me from the first book, every step of the way. Her invaluable guidance and expertise are such that I sincerely doubt I could have done five books, let alone one, without her in my corner. I've learned so much from Sandy, and although at times, I cringe when I see editor marks, she has helped me enhance so much of the story flow in each book.

Sandy, you have been my Godwink since day one. I thank you from the bottom of my heart for your undying encouragement and professionalism.

Love, Penelope

"Your direction toward your destiny will never be altered, and your course will never be corrected if you are still sitting by the side of the road. You must stay in motion—and stay alert for God's winks."

— SQUIRE RUSHNELL

PROLOGUE

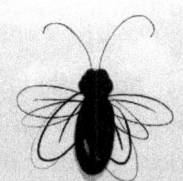

The early May rain formed rivulets on the windowpane, blurring the view outside. Absently lifting her hand, Nikki McKay traced the little streaming paths downward with her long slender finger against the glass, her emerald-green eyes focused on the wet train. A deep sigh escaped her lips as the oppressive atmosphere outside gained momentum within her.

Sophia McKay stood at the family room doorway, taking in her daughter's air of distraction. Her grimace conveyed her concern, and a worry line creased her almost smooth brow.

A flash of lightening silhouetted Nikki's petite frame. The similarity in appearance to her mother ended there. Nikki had the vibrant burnished copper hair and verdant green eyes of her father, Sean, and his Gaelic ancestors. Sophia was of Italian descent with dark wavy hair and luminous brown eyes with abundant dark-fringed lashes. Nikki's parents were constantly teasing each other that Nikki had inherited her passionate nature and fiery temper from the other parent, depending on the situation.

Another bolt of lightning zigzagged across the sky, followed by a crack of thunder so close to the house, Sophia jumped. Looking at

Nikki, she was quick to notice the mounting storm had no effect on her transfixed daughter. No response, no reaction—nothing.

Sometimes, life wasn't fair. It was about how much someone could take and survive.

Sophia stepped into the room far enough to be in Nikki's peripheral vision. "Quite a storm out there, but they're predicting it will let up soon," she said as she clicked on a table lamp.

Nikki only nodded.

"Your father had to read two stories to Christopher before he'd fall asleep."

At the mention of her little boy, Nikki perked up.

"I'm pretty sure Dad is wrapped around Christopher's little finger and would have read him a dozen stories if he asked."

"You've got that right! Two peas in a pod, I'd say." Sophia relaxed, seeing a spark in Nikki's eyes and a smile appear on her lips. Nikki's four-year-old son, Christopher, was the shining light in her life.

"Nikki, you need to get some rest. You have a long drive ahead of you tomorrow."

"I'm truly not tired yet." Turning away from the window, Nikki shook her head and adopted a cheerful attitude for her mother's benefit. "Guess I'm keyed up about the trip."

"Nikki, you're my daughter, and I know you like a book" Sophia raised an eyebrow. "So, don't try to fool me with the carefree act you're putting on. It's not working."

Nikki looked pensively at her mother and found comprehension. There was a silent plea for help in Nikki's gaze and loving concern in her mother's eyes.

"Your father and I talked things over as soon as we heard about Peter's accident." Sophia stressed the word "accident." "You and Peter were living apart for over a year, and before that, you weren't really living as man and wife for at least a year." Sophia paused as if weighing her next words. "I know what I am about to say may upset you, more than you are now, but it still needs to be said. In your six years of marriage, only two of those years could be described as happy, owed to the fact you had a positive attitude, believed your husband was who you thought he was, and you were pregnant with Christopher."

Nikki started to interrupt but held off when she saw her mother's look of determination.

"Honey, listen. Your father and I were just as taken in as you were by Peter's charm. When he showed signs of never attaining emotional maturity, and we saw the bad choices he was making, not only for himself but for you as well, we knew he had some serious flaws. Flaws that cause relationships to crumble. Although he was four years older than you, his immaturity was evident.

"You gave him so many chances to change his ways and grow up. He made promises he could never keep. Your father and I kept wondering how many times you would turn the other cheek. We didn't want to interfere, but it hurt seeing him taking advantage of you and betraying your trust. It was a one-sided marriage and could never have survived."

Nikki turned back to face the window. Although the storm had abated somewhat, the patter of rain against the glass was a steady beat. The rhythm was as calming as knowing she had such a supportive relationship with her parents. During her most trying times, they were there, only offering their advice when she asked for it, even when the plea was a silent one.

Nikki's father, Sean, entered the room, followed closely by Nikki's bounding Irish setter, Barney. Sean took in the scene with a knowing look.

"What time do you figure on leaving in the morning, Nikki?" he asked, trying to relieve some of the tension.

Nikki turned from the window.

"Oh, I want to get an early start. As a matter of fact, I'll take Barney out now before bed since the rain has let up, then I'll turn in." She left the room, motioning to Barney to follow, and missed her parents' concerned looks. Picking up a hooded windbreaker in the hallway, she pushed her arms through the sleeves, tucked in her long copper-colored hair, and zipped it up tight.

"Come on, Barney, like it or not, it's time for a walk." The Irish setter peeked his head around the corner and resignedly ambled toward the door. "A little rain won't hurt you."

His big brown eyes gave away his feelings. Galloping through the lawn sprinkler was fun. Walking in the rain was not, especially when lightning and thunder were part of it.

Nikki stepped out under the overhang and walked toward the sheltering tall pine trees dominating the garden.

"Stay under the trees, Barney, and you won't get as wet." Glancing around, she thought how silly it would sound to someone if they overheard her talking to her dog as if he understood what she said.

A while later, after wiping dry four paws and two feet, she returned to the den. Her father was sitting in his favorite easy chair with a newspaper in hand. Peeking over the rim of the glasses propped on the end of his nose, he quietly folded the paper and put it down.

"Come here, Nikki. I think it's time we had a little chat." He patted the sofa next to his chair for her to sit down.

"Dad, Mom and I have been through this, and I—" she replied as she plunked down next to him.

"Please," he cut her off. "I'll try not to lecture or go on about the past. What's done is done, and nothing can be changed." Taking her hands in his, he went on. "You have the future to look at now. Don't spoil it by dwelling on the past and what might have been. Your mother and I know you did your absolute best in the worst of situations. You need to realize it too. There's a little boy upstairs who is counting on you to be there for him. The past is purely that... the past.

"Your mom and I are glad you're getting away for a while to the lake house. You need time to sort things out, and I'm sure you will. I know you plan on fixing things up at the cabin but try to do something you really love to do for yourself... like your writing. Remember, if you need someone to talk to... other than Barney," he added with a glint of amusement, "you know we're only a phone call away."

"I'll remember. I'll check on Christopher before I turn in." She realized she'd been holding tight to her father's hands as if drawing strength from his spirit. Rising from the sofa, she kissed his cheek and gave him a hug. Stepping back, she smiled. "Thanks for taking on the burden of watching Christopher for a couple of weeks."

Standing, he put up his hands in protest. "Burden, my foot! Christopher is a joy to your mother and me. It brings back memories of you at that age. And since your mom and I now have more than enough time on our hands with the first-quarter tax season finished, we can really enjoy him. So, don't worry about him. He's in good hands."

"Oh, I know, Dad. I really do."

They looked at each other with deep understanding.

"Okay, off to bed with you. I'll lock up and turn out the lights."

Smiling, she turned and made her way up the stairs and down the hallway to the room that became Christopher's bedroom when they moved into her parent's home two years ago. Squeezing silently past the partially opened door, she tiptoed to his bed. She grinned when she noticed the difficulty in determining where Christopher was among the myriad of stuffed animals.

Looking down at him, she wondered how much of the past would affect his future. She vowed to herself never to subject him to anything traumatic, no matter what the cost. He wouldn't be cheated anymore. Although incredibly young at the time, Christopher had witnessed too many arguments between Nikki and Peter. Christopher had a father who only acknowledged his existence when it was convenient or beneficial in some way.

Nikki had to be both mother and father to Christopher. Peter had never accepted responsibility but had wanted to reap any rewards. He used his marital status as a stepping stone to move up the corporate ladder, and the bonus of having a child increased his upper management promotion chances within a family-oriented corporation.

Nikki shook her head to get rid of unpleasant memories. She was moving forward, not backward.

Christopher had a few more weeks of preschool left, after which they would all spend the summer together at the lakehouse. Hopefully, by the time he arrived with her parents, she would have the house back in order, opened for the season, and her head together to start a new life for her and Christopher. One with all the happiness they deserved.

Bending over, she softly kissed Christopher's cheek and tucked the blanket around him, then tiptoed out of the bedroom.

1

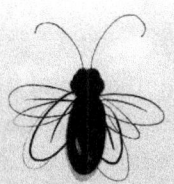

Sunlight streamed in through the window, spilling distorted patterns on the bed. Nikki rolled over and squinted at the bedside clock. It was only six o'clock, and the house was still quiet.

She'd left the window open a crack, so rain wouldn't come in during the night, and the sweet smell of wet grass breezed in to refresh the spirit. Stretching languorously, she decided today would be the first day of the rest of her life.

Springing from the bed, she grabbed her robe from the side chair and quietly laughed to herself at how her mother blushed when she found out Nikki slept in nothing but her birthday suit. A quick stop in the bathroom, and she headed down to the kitchen to get a cup of coffee. As she passed Barney, who was lying on "his" rug in the hallway next to the foot of the stairs, she smiled. Sleeping on his back with his head turned to the side and his paw thrown over his ear, he looked like a character out of the Sunday comics.

"Character." That's the word for him, alright, she mused, shaking her head. She was debating whether to take Barney out when he made the decision for her when he entered the kitchen and angled toward the back door. His soulful eyes and cocked head could never be ignored.

After letting Barney out to do his business, Nikki grabbed a yogurt and blueberries from the fridge and settled down at the kitchen counter. It wasn't long before a thump at the back door let her know Barney wanted back in. Opening the door, Barney dutifully stood on the throw rug while she wiped his feet. A lick on her cheek was his thank you.

"You're such a good boy, Barney." His jowls turned up, creating a smile.

Nikki returned upstairs and slipped into the bathroom to shower. Thirty minutes later, she descended the stairs dressed in jeans, an oversized sweatshirt, and sneakers, with her radiant red hair in a braid down her back.

Her mom was standing at the kitchen counter, pouring a cup of coffee. They exchanged morning greetings, then both exaggeratedly sniffed the coffee aroma. They weren't morning people until after their first cup of coffee—another inherited trait.

"Christopher up yet?" Sophia asked, handing a steaming cup of coffee to Nikki.

"Nope. I looked in, and he's blowing zzzs. When I checked on him during the night, he was turned upside down in bed. I turned him back around, and he didn't even stir. I'm surprised he's not up now. Normally, he has a built-in rooster alarm."

"Probably because things have not been exactly normal lately. First, the news about Peter, the rushed memorial service, then the confrontations." Sophia noticed the grimace on Nikki's face. "I hope you aren't taking any of Peter's family's comments seriously."

"No, I'm not. I can't blame the Foresters for being angry at losing their only son. As far as them accusing me of contributing to his death, it was truly Peter's own doing. He always drove recklessly—the need for speed, whether it came with an engine or a pill bottle. If both, it was a lethal combination."

"Pamela, Peter's sister, was a no-show. Her parents made a big deal of her being in Europe, and said due to her obligations, she wouldn't be able to attend the service. However, there was another couple with them at the service. They were very distraught as well. I didn't recognize them from any previous Forester gatherings."

"I noticed them as well. I don't have a clue who they were."

"Your father checked the newspapers and online this past week for any mention of Peter's obituary or his memorial service and couldn't find anything, let alone anything about the accident. Seems strange for a high-profile family not to have anything mentioned in the news. They never seemed to want privacy before."

"It doesn't matter now, does it? Whatever they do, it's their choice. I have my own choices to make, and my first choice is to make the best possible life for Christopher and me. I wasted too much time and energy trying to salvage something never meant to be saved."

Understanding what Nikki was saying, her mother nodded.

Sitting down at the kitchen island, Nikki proceeded to "pollute" her coffee—as her father would say—adding brown sugar and cream to her cup, then took a donut from a bakery box and dunked it.

"Emily Post doesn't live here." Nikki smiled

"Oh, by the way, your brother said he would swing by here with his brood so the kids could spend time together."

"Brian is one in a gazillion. I'm lucky to have him as my brother... even though he was such a pain in the butt growing up." Nikki had been thinking a lot about her brother lately. Especially in comparisons. Brian was reliable and took his marriage and fatherhood seriously. Without neglecting his own little family, he still had time to help his "little sister."

"I'll go on up and check on Christopher." Rising from the table, Nikki took her cup to the sink and washed it.

"Are you sure you don't want something more to eat? It's a three-hour drive."

"No, I'm fine, Mom. You know I'm not a big breakfast eater." Turning, she left the kitchen and proceeded up the stairs to her bedroom. Pausing at Christopher's door, she listened for sounds of stirring. A slight rustling of the sheets brought her into the room. Barney had found his way into Christopher's room and was nestled on the floor at the foot of the bed. Christopher rubbed his eyes with his small fists.

"Morning, Sweetheart," Nikki whispered as she sat on the edge of the bed. "Did the Sand Man put more sleeping sand in your eyes than usual?"

"Guess so. Is Barney up, too?"

"He sure is, and he's here."

At the mention of his name, Barney leapt on the bed and showered Christopher with wet, sloppy kisses. Christopher broke into giggles as he buried his face into Barney's neck. It was hard to tell at times where Christopher's head was since Barney's coat was the same rusty brown color as Christopher's hair.

"I'm quite sure Grandma has plans to make you scrambled eggs and pancakes, so you better hustle and get down there."

Christopher tossed back the covers and headed for the bathroom as Barney raced to the hallway and down the stairs to the kitchen. The mere mention of food in any form was music to Barney's ears. A few minutes later, Christopher entered the kitchen. Sophia gave him a hug and lifted him onto a stool at the kitchen island.

"Eggs and pancakes for you, sir?"

"Yes, please!"

When Sophia served him his plate, his blue-green eyes lit up and crinkled, displaying a bridge of freckles across his face. The "bottomless pit" devoured his breakfast while Barney waited patiently next to the stool for a stray morsel to fall to the floor.

"I'll go up and get my bags together," Nikki said.

"Do you need help, Nikki?"

"No, I'm not bringing up much since I have clothes there."

"Oh, that reminds me. Your father put some groceries in your car to take with you, just some munchies and things."

Just "some munchies and things." Probably enough to feed a small army for a month.

"Thanks, Mom. I'll get settled in, then run into town for fresh produce and perishables."

Half an hour later, she returned to the kitchen. Her father and Christopher were sitting across from each other at the island, debating what came first... the chicken or the egg?

Walking over to Christopher, she tousled his copper hair and leaned next to him. "You be a good boy for Grandma and Grandpa." She hugged him close and gave him a kiss.

"Ugga-mugga, Mommy," Christopher grinned.

"Ugga-mugga, Christopher," she repeated as they rubbed their noses together.

"I'll miss you heaps, but it won't be long until preschool is over, and we'll be spend the whole summer at the lake. You can call me, you know." He nodded.

"He'll be fine." Sophia gave Nikki a hug and a kiss. "Of course, he'll be spoiled more than usual." It was Nikki's turn to nod.

Sean helped Nikki with her bags and loaded them into her SUV. Barney followed and jumped into the passenger seat as if he owned it. Before she got into her car, her father gave her a bear hug.

"Take it easy driving. No rush. Make sure you call your mother when you get there, or she'll worry." Sean paused and grinned sheepishly. "Me, too."

As she stepped onto the running board, she looked up at the window and saw her mother and Christopher waving. Waving back, her eyes blurred with unshed tears.

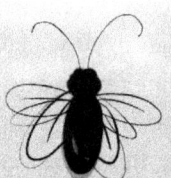

2

Forty-five minutes into the three-hour trip, the suburbs behind her, Nikki kept heading north. Barney curled up his large body on the front passenger seat, resigned the trip would be a long one, and he might as well catch a catnap... pardon the expression.

She'd be crossing the state line soon and get farther away from the recent events troubling her. Niggling thoughts invaded her mind.

Was Peter's accident her fault? Had he been intoxicated? She'd been told where and when it happened, and from what she knew, the weather had been fair and the road dry and in good condition. It happened at two in the morning. Did their marital status cause him to drink more heavily than normal? Maybe if she had given him one more chance.

"Oh, stop it, Nikki!" she mumbled.

She had given him plenty of chances, although she knew she hadn't loved him anymore and wondered if she ever had. She doubted if he ever genuinely loved her or had known what love was. She had been a convenience to him. Why she married him? Her close friends were all married... happily married. Was it the reason she'd accepted Peter's proposal? To be married like her friends? When she met him, she was in her late twenties and teaching at a local high school. He was charming, to be sure. Looking back, she realized he'd been *too* charming.

Peter had grown up in an atmosphere completely alien to Nikki. Where her parents had struggled financially at times when she and her brother were growing up, Peter's parents were very well off. To them, money and material things were their only goals. They were too busy socially and in business to give their children what they really needed—time and love.

Peter and his sister, Pamela, had no responsibilities and almost no supervision, except for nannies, who gave their charges anything they wanted to keep their positions. Should the children complain about restrictions imposed by a nanny, she was soon replaced. Their parents thought giving them the material things they wanted would be enough. How very contradictory it seemed for people who were quite shrewd in business sadly to so lack in the parenting department.

Peter had grown up unable to make responsible and logical decisions. He'd had his father's innate gift of charm and his mother's calculating attitude whenever he wanted something bad enough. However, he had no common sense or ethics.

In his estimation, everything and everyone had a price. Even when they'd argued, he thought a bouquet of flowers or a piece of jewelry was all he needed to get back into Nikki's good graces. He'd been wrong... so wrong. All those years, all those arguments—what a complete waste of time....and love.

Deep down, she knew her parents were right. She wasn't at fault for Peter's death. She'd done her best, but it never had been good enough to change him. It had been up to him to make changes inside himself, no one else, and he paid the ultimate price for choosing not to make those changes.

She had been terribly mistaken in thinking a child would encourage him to change his ways and accept responsibilities. Christopher was a blessing, but to Peter, a child was a steppingstone up the company ladder. Appearances of a happy little family increased his chances of promotion. In private, Peter was absent. He missed Christopher's birthday party because of a golf date. Schmoozing with clients was more important. Peter's father was well connected and sent him plenty of leads for new clients. Nikki suspected those new clients owed Peter's father and were more than willing to level the debt by adding to Peter's client list at the brokerage. Entertaining those clients was the catalyst for the final split.

Nikki's longtime friend Lynnette was out with her hubby, Jim, for an anniversary dinner when she saw Peter with a young woman. Lynnette knew there were marital issues between Nikki and Peter and debated whether to mention it to Nikki. A couple of days later, Nikki and Lynnette had a lunch date, and when Nikki mentioned Peter had been out of town on business for the past week on business, Lynnette felt obliged to tell her. Nikki hadn't been surprised. In fact, she'd looked resigned.

She had her suspicions—too many times.

Upon his return from his so-called business trip, she confronted him, and he didn't deny it. He'd been proud he snagged, as he put it, a beautiful young woman. His words had been so hurtful. Nikki remembered the times he would show her off in public when she was pregnant with Christopher but in private, he demeaned her for losing her svelte figure. After giving birth, she worked hard to get back to her pre-pregnancy form, but there was no getting rid of those womanly curves gained from giving birth. His comments had made her feel worthless and unattractive.

She was tired of the derision. Tired of his excuses for not being with her and Christopher. Tired of his lies and irresponsibility. And tired of his cheating. Their marriage had been long gone, and it hadn't mattered to her if their marital issues had stained his reputation at the company and ruined any chance of climbing the corporate ladder.

She'd been finished.

When Nikki was pregnant with Christopher, they purchased a house with funds from the sale of his high-end condo. Being fed up with his actions, she moved out of their house and moved into her parent's home. Retaining a lawyer, she started the process of ending her old life and starting a new one.

It had been years since then. The legal separation still hadn't been granted because Peter kept coming up with reasons to stall it. Only now, with Peter's death, there was no need to finalize the separation. It was a moot point. However, there was the issue of the house. Although she was still on the title, she wanted no part of it. She suspected the purchase of their house had been funded not only by the sale of his luxury condo but also by his parents. When the time came, she'd deal with it.

For now, she had dreams of the life she would share with Christopher, which mattered above all else.

Nikki set the car audio system to a station playing her favorite type of music and brushed the negative thoughts out of her mind and replaced them with Christopher and how much fun they would have at the lakehouse this summer.

The scenery became hillier, and the surrounding farmland was lush from the abundance of spring rains. Even the corn was showing signs of being more than "knee high by the Fourth of July."

Exiting the main highway, she accessed a state route headed west, and felt the tension leave her body. Her hands unclenched their tight hold on the steering wheel. The atmosphere always soothed her when she was surrounded by rolling farmland, grazing cattle, and a patchwork of spring crops. She lowered her side window to inhale the fresh air, cleansing the senses and raising the spirits.

Barney lifted his head as if enjoying the scents, then quietly returned to his circular position.

She was only fifteen minutes from her destination, and her anticipation was growing. As she reached a crest on the road, her breath was taken from her as it had so many times before at this point. There was her refuge, her end of the lake she called her home away from home.

Spring Lake was in the shape of a chubby dogleg, six miles long and two miles across. In some spots, it was a bit wider due to bays. Its depth was approximated at two hundred twenty feet. The shoreline measured about twenty-six miles, with several beaches, boat launching sites, and marshes. Towering sandstone bluffs were popular for diving into the crystal-clear waters, especially around Seminary Bay, so named for the retreat started there in the early 1900s. It was said the students attending the seminary would find God as they were pushed from the top of the highest bluff.

She could count on one hand how many times Peter had joined her at the lakehouse. He had found it boring and made excuse after excuse for not coming.

This was one of the best times of the year to be there. The summer crowd wouldn't arrive until Memorial Day weekend. Quite a few of the lake homes weren't year-round homes, so they didn't have air-conditioning, although it was rarely needed.

Fortunately, the McKay home on the lake was considered year-round. It had a fully functional HVAC system and a well-and-septic system. The water cistern was below the freeze line, and the large propane tank was kept filled. Sean McKay was adamant about keeping everything in working order. He had inherited the lakehouse from his parents, who inherited it from his paternal grandparents. Sophia and he had put a lot of time and effort into renovating it over the years. The only issue was getting to it in the winter.

Maggie and Hammy Hardy lived year-round in a lakehouse down the road and kept an eye on the property when the McKays weren't there. Hammy made sure the driveway was snowplowed in case someone ventured up in winter. Nikki was sure her dad had contacted the Hardys to let them know she would be arriving.

As she crossed over the inlet road, she took in the beauty of the lake and its clear, spring-fed waters. Fishing enthusiasts had already staked out their spots in the hopes of bringing home dinner.

She glanced over at Barney. He'd slept most of the way or at least he pretended to. He only squinted open his eyes when he heard the rustling of a candy bar wrapper or a Crunchy Cheetos bag opening in the hopes of snagging a loose crumb or two. Now, he seemed to sense where they were and sat up in his co-pilot seat, taking in the view.

Nikki turned off the lake road and up onto a winding drive through and around a stand of towering trees. Sean McKay vowed to keep as many of the trees as possible as they cleaned up around the property over the years, making sure to transplant saplings where needed. Nikki noticed how much those little saplings had matured over the last ten years.

She parked next to the garage, which was higher on the hill than the house. She'd open the garage later after she unloaded and car and brought everything down to the house. It was obvious Hammy had been there and cleared the debris from the sloping flagstone walkway.

Smiling, she remembered last year when Christopher rode his little Hot Wheel down the walkway on the hill. He'd squealed as he raised his legs and gravity took momentum, then he would struggle to pedal his way back up. Of course, Grandpa Sean would come to his rescue and carry Christopher and the bike back up the hill, to his grandson's delight.

As soon as she jumped out of the SUV, Barney let her know she forgot something.

"I didn't forget you." Nikki circled around the car and opened the front passenger door. let Barney leapt out of the vehicle and raced to his favorite tree to relieve himself. While Nikki took things out of her car, Barney surveyed the area with his nose to the ground, sniffing and huffing. His ears perked up at the sound of a small motor coming over the hill from back.

Maggie and Hammy Hardy crested the hill in a retrofitted golf cart with a small trailer attached to the back.

"Hey, Nikki!" they shouted over the roar of the motor. They pulled up to where Nikki was standing. Hammy turned off the motor, and he and Maggie greeted her with bear hugs. "Welcome back, Sweetheart! You're looking mighty fine!"

"Oh, thank you! I'll bet my dad called to tell you I was on my way up."

"He sure did," Maggie replied. "Actually, he called us yesterday and again this morning, right after you pulled out of their driveway."

Sure enough, Nikki's cellphone dinged with a text from her mom.

Mom: *Maggie texted she saw you pull in. They should be greeting you soon.*

Nikki smiled to herself. Her folks had been hesitant to get mobile phones years ago, but now, they were techier than she was.

Nikki: *They're here now.* She added a heart and a smiley face.

"Looks like it'll take about three trips down to the house." Hammy was already loading the mini trailer with what Nikki had brought with her.

"Trust me, Dad was the one who packed everything in there. Poor Barney had to sit up front with me. Although I'm sure, he didn't mind."

"How's the munchkin doing?" Maggie asked. "I'll bet he's grown like a weed since last fall."

"He has indeed. I have a hunch he's inherited flipper feet like his Grandpa Sean and his uncle Brian. He's already outgrown his shoes a couple of times."

Hammy had already made it down the hill with the first load, placing everything on the porch and unlocking the back door. Nikki and Maggie grabbed a couple of things out of the car and walked down the stone walkway. By the time they got down to the house, Hammy had already started back up the hill for another load.

"I sent Hammy over here yesterday to get the water heater turned up. The pilot on the stove is relit, and the refrigerator and freezer are ready for you to fill up."

"You two are amazing friends. I don't know what we would have done without you."

"Nikki,"—Maggie took Nikki's hands in hers—"I know you have been through a lot... more than most realize. Please know we'll always be here to help, no matter what. Now, enjoy yourself while you're here. Relax. Christopher is in good hands and will be joining you in a couple of weeks. Take the time now to do whatever you want to do. Do whatever makes you happy."

When everything was unloaded, unpacked, and put away, Maggie and Hammy headed back to their lakehouse down the road. When they asked Nikki to join them for dinner, she declined, saying she was tired and would be going to bed early, but asked for a raincheck.

There was some cleaning, sweeping, vacuuming, and dusting to be done, but it would have to wait until tomorrow.

As darkness fell, the moon shone brightly, casting its spell over the lake. Walking onto the deck, she sucked in the cool, damp air of spring and the scent of the forest. A silence enveloped her, not even a night owl could be heard. It was as if time froze, a moment of reflection.

A moment of rebirth.

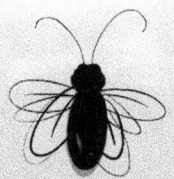

3

Sleep had come quickly, a deep, restful sleep, absent of the dreams she had been having over the past year. When she awoke the next morning, she stretched languorously. Disgruntled groans came from Barney, who didn't appreciate being disturbed from his spot at the foot of the bed.

"What are you complaining about, lazy bones?"

He cocked his head and waggled his brows as he skittered up close to her hand, so she would stroke him. Patting his head and scratched behind his ears, his left foot tapped in pleasure.

"You are so freaking spoiled, Barney."

As if understanding what she said, his jowls turned up in another of his signature smiles.

Nikki pushed back the covers and shivered in the cool air. She hadn't reset the thermostat and had left one of the bedroom windows open a crack. When her feet hit the floor, she hustled to the bathroom.

Barney repositioned himself in the warm spot she had vacated and let out a sigh.

Ten minutes later, Nikki was washed and dressed in jeans, a bulky sweatshirt, and her favorite old sneakers, and her long red hair was pulled up into a ponytail. At first glance, she looked like a teenager, no makeup of any kind to cover the freckles of her telltale Irish heritage.

"Come on, Barney, shake a leg. Breakfast time."

That got his attention. He bounded off the bed and followed her down the stairs. Nikki unlocked the sliding door accessing the main floor deck, and Barney shot out in search of his other favorite tree.

Nikki noticed the heavy fog on the lake, making the shoreline invisible. The gentle lapping at the water's edge echoed up to the house. She wondered how soon the sun would burn off the haze. She had work to do outside, and it looked as if it would have to be done in the afternoon.

After making breakfast for Barney and herself, she started getting the interior of the house in order. Originally, the house was a two-story with a basement. When her parents renovated it, most of the basement wall facing the lake was dug out, demolished, and reinforced, and a large, enclosed room was added on. A deck was added on top of the new addition, which was accessed through a sliding glass door on the main floor. The basement was totally refinished, complete with new laundry facilities. The basement addition had a fireplace, a large living, a dining area with a small kitchen, and a full bathroom. Her parents also added a new HVAC system.

The main floor had a living room with a brick-faced fireplace, a large country kitchen, and a good-sized dining area, as well as a full bath and a bedroom. The top floor contained three bedrooms and two baths. Two of the bedrooms faced the lake and shared a narrow porch with a staircase leading down the side of the house. Sophia had insisted on modernizing the bathroom plumbing but was adamant about keeping the wainscotting panels and trim.

The boathouse had been rebuilt. It had been infested with termites and critters, so the only choice was to tear it all down and start from scratch. During the construction, the Hardy's housed the McKays' Bayliner at their place, while the small aluminum dinghy was brought up on shore and covered with a tarp. The new boat house had ample room for the large boat and the dinghy with room to spare for a jet ski.

The property had a one-of-a-kind L-shaped cement pier with a fiberglass-and-wood extension jutting out into the lake about twelve feet to accommodate tying up a boat. The only property on the lake with a cement pier, Sean was grateful his grandparents had the foresight to put it in when they did.

All in all, it took almost six years to complete the cleanup, renovations, and additions. As Nikki surveyed the house, she appreciated the arduous work and time her parents had put in.

Gathering her cleaning supplies, she started on the top floor, cleaning the bathroom and making up the beds. Last fall, they had stripped the bedding and bath linens, laundered them, and stored them away. Next, furniture was dusted and polished, windows and sliding glass doors cleaned, cobwebs removed, and curtains shook out. Floors were washed and carpets vacuumed.

It was almost one in the afternoon when she finished the top floor and main floor. She made a list for herself of things she noted needed repair and several places that needed touch-up painting. She knew she'd have to check the boat house for repairs as well. She hoped whatever she needed for the repairs she would find in the garage.

Barney joined her as she trotted down to the boathouse. The side door stuck, so she gave it a good yank and fell on her backside. She turned to Barney.

"Don't you dare smile."

He lowered his eyes and looked down, but she knew he was really laughing.

She flipped on the light switch in the boathouse, but no light. Grabbing a flashlight stowed on the shelf near the door, she clicked it on. Spooky spider webs gave her the shivers. As she ran the beam of light across the walls and roof, she aroused a nest of swallows. They fluttered around, finally coming back to their nest high in the rafters. Every boathouse had at least one or two nests. The swallows gained access through the roof air vents, and depending on the season, they shared their shoreline residence with bats. Although Nikki wasn't fond of those bats flying at night, she knew they served a purpose keeping the mosquito population down.

She opened the circuit breaker box. Crap! A packrat had chewed on a few wires. It had happened once before, and she knew how to fix it but was sure she'd need some supplies from town. Flashing the beam of light over the boat and the dinghy, everything looked fine, but she'd need to fix the light first to be sure.

Making a quick trip back up the hill, she remotely raised the garage door and held her breath as she flipped on the light switch. It worked! Everything was in order, her dad's workbench area neat and organized. She checked her list and found some of the items she needed.

"Barney, we're headed to town."

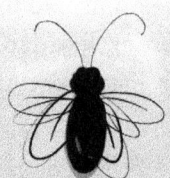

4

Washing off the dust and dirt from the boathouse, she coiled her ponytail, pinned it, and added her old baseball cap. The cap had been a gift from her dad when he took her to her first major league baseball game. When Peter first saw her wearing it at the lakehouse, he commented how pitiful she looked when she wore it. She shook her head at the memory. He was clueless, but then, again, she had been, too... about him.

She grabbed one of the protein bars she'd brought with her, a bottle of water, and her "hobo" bag.

"Barney, let's go!"

As she passed the entrance to the road down to the Hardy Lakehouse, she saw Hammy trimming some trees and slowed to a stop.

"Hammy, need anything from town?"

"Nope. All good. Be safe. There's a storm a-brewin'."

She gave him a thumbs up and continued to town. Her first stop was the hardware store. Motioning to Barney to follow, Dan Burke warmly greeted them. Dan's family was one of the founding families of the area, going back hundreds of years. He was also on the town council and knew everything that was happening in the area.

"Nikki! Heard you were in town. Welcome back!" Dan reached under the counter and pulled out a dog biscuit and offered it to Barney. Barney looked up at Nikki, and she nodded, which produced his infamous smile. He carefully took the biscuit from Dan's hand and chewed it up in seconds.

"Hey, Dan! Glad to be back. How's the family?"

"All good. Grandkids are growing like weeds. I heard your little guy is doing the same. Looking forward to seeing him and your folks soon."

"News travels fast, doesn't it?"

Dan nodded. "What do you need?"

Nikki showed him her list.

"Ah... another packrat left you a problem. I'll get what you need. The old wires were quite tasty to the critters. The new ones have a different wire wrap, which tastes terrible. Not that I tried to chew on them." He laughed.

Nikki joined his laughter.

She roamed around the store aisles to see if there was anything else she might need. Barney dutifully stood near the door, waiting patiently and secretly hoping Dan would share another treat with him for being such a good fur buddy.

Nikki added a few more items to her purchase, then checked out. Dan came around the counter and gave her a hug, and Barney got another biscuit. He smiled again before inhaling the biscuit and woofing it down.

"Bye, Dan. I'm sure we'll see you again soon."

"Take care, Nikki. There's a spring storm moving in."

Nikki loaded the purchases in her SUV and told Barney he'd have to wait in the car while she went into the grocery. The smell of rain permeated the air, and the wind had picked up quite a bit. She grabbed her cap as a gust of wind almost blew it off. Taking it off and shoving it in her hobo bag, her ponytail whipped in the wind, and the band holding it broke. Her copper tresses escaped and flew wildly about her. She hurriedly shut the hatch on the car and tried to pull her hair back to see as she made a dash into the grocery store. Barney watched her from the car window.

"Well, look what the wind blew in! Hi, Nikki!" Linda Lee, the owner and manager, greeted her.

"Hey, there. A wee bit windy out there, Linda."

"So, it seems. Heard on the news it would 'come a cloud' soon."

Nikki loved that turn of phrase. There were so many of those country phrases she found endearing, while Peter had considered them unsophisticated.

Getting a grocery cart, she started down the aisles, checking her list as she went along. A rather tall, good-looking gentleman was ahead of her in line at the deli counter. He looked out of place, wearing awfully expensive "city clothes," so she assumed he was only passing through town. His jet-black hair was longer on top, so it fell on his forehead in a slight curl. He gave Nikki an obvious once over and winked. She tried to ignore him, but he was in her direct line of sight with the display. His aftershave or cologne seemed so out of place here in Spring Lake.

"Who's next?" the butcher called out.

"Please, let the little lady go on ahead," the man said. "It'll give me a chance to admire the view a little longer."

She felt a wave of red spread across her cheeks. Blushing was something she had hoped she would outgrow, but it seemed to be a permanent feature. Besides, she wasn't the naïve girl of years ago, succumbing to the false charm and double meanings. A vision of a viper came to mind.

Dropping her package into the cart, she went to the produce department and chose fresh fruits and veggies, avoiding the stares of Mr. Obnoxious. She finished with the rest of the grocery shopping and headed to the checkout.

Just her luck, Mr. Obnoxious was again in front of her at the one and only open checkout line. With a ridiculous flourish and an outlandish bow, he waved Nikki ahead of him and stepped back with a smug smile.

She nodded back as a courtesy, but was thinking to herself, *"You're barking up the wrong tree, Buster."* She paid the cashier and rushed out of the store, noticing Mr. Obnoxious was moving in on the young cashier, full tilt.

She could hear Barney's welcoming bark as she got to her car. The wind had increased, and once again, her hair flew wildly about her as she loaded the bags of groceries into the back of the SUV. Back in the driver's seat, she pulled down the visor and looked in the mirror.

Retrieving her baseball cap from her hobo bag, she pulled a brush out of the center console and did her best to tame the errant tresses. She pulled her hair back, twisting it tight as she jammed her baseball cap firmly on her head.

"A few more stops, Barney, then we'll head home."

Home.

Yes, the lakehouse was home to her. Other than her family, for many years, the lakehouse had been the one stable thing in her life. She wondered what her life would be like living there permanently, year-round. She had her teaching degree and could homeschool Christopher. She also had a minor in journalism. Maybe she could work at the local newspaper or the library. Her mind drifted to all the "what-ifs."

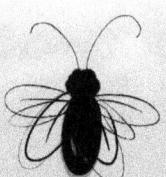

5

D riving down Lake Street, the main street in the town of Spring Lake, she passed by the little shops, which had been owned and operated by townsfolk for decades. The small-town atmosphere was to her liking. Annie's Antiques, What-In-Yarn-Nation, Dr. Walker's Animal Hospital, and Morton's Diner, to name a few, were all mainstays in Spring Lake. The town supported the activities in and around Big Spring Lake, and vice versa.

Nikki pulled into a parking space at McConnell's Bait and Tackle Shop next to the marina. The boats tied up to their berths on the dock rocked and rolled with the wind.

"Stay here, buddy. I won't be long, " she told Barney as she exited her car. Keeping her head down into the wind, she struggled with the shop's door until it finally opened enough for her to squeeze through.

Big Steve McConnell looked up to see who entered, and a smile broke out on his face.

"Well, I'll be damned. Look who's here. Suzie, come out here."

A petite blonde with a pixie haircut poked her head out from the back room.

"Holy Shit! Nikki!" She ran to Nikki and gave her a hug.

It warmed Nikki's heart to be greeted so kindly by everyone she saw in town.

"How are you two doing? The boys?"

"Oh, they're great. All three are now taller than me."

"Honey, everyone is taller than you," Big Steve commented.

Suzie threw him a stink-eye.

"How long will you be here?"

"Through the summer, maybe longer... depending. Mom and Dad are coming up with Christopher in a couple of weeks."

Suzie gave her a side glance. "You definitely are more than welcome to stay around here as long as you want."

"What can we get you, Nikki?" Big Steve asked.

"I noticed our fishing and tackle supplies have dwindled, and the fishing line is old and ready to break. Don't want to lose a big one. I made a list."

Nikki showed it to Suzie and Big Steve.

"On it."

While Suzie and Big Steve gathered up the items, Nikki roamed down the aisles. She found a child's rod and reel in a package and put it on the counter.

Suzie noticed it and smiled. "So, you're finally gonna teach Christopher to fish, huh?"

"Sure am. I think he'll enjoy it."

"I'll bet you'll need a larger size vest than the old toddler one."

"Wow, you're right." As Nikki was about to head down one of the aisles, Suzie stopped her.

"I'll get it. How much does he weigh now?" Nikki told her, and Suzie moved to where the vests were displayed. In less than a minute, she laid a vest on the counter. "This one's on me. Need to protect our babies, no matter their size or age."

"Thanks, Suzie."

Big Steve put her purchases and the vest in a couple of canvas totes.

"You need help out to the car, Nikki?"

"Nope. I'm fine. I'm sure Barney is eager to sniff out the bags."

At the mention of Barney, Big Steve reached under the counter and plopped a couple of dog biscuits in one of the totes.

"In that case, let's give him something to sniff that he'll like."

"Thanks, Guys! See you soon."

"Try to make it over to the Morton's Marina Restaurant and Bar this weekend," Suzie called out as Nikki reached the door. "It's been renovated, and there's live entertainment."

Nikki nodded as she juggled the totes and her hobo bag. Holding the life vest tight to her chest blocked her vision a bit. She had made it outside and was turning to head for her car when she hit a solid object. At first, she thought someone had moved a brick wall in front of her. One of her bags fell, and the other was sliding off her arm when two iron clamps grabbed her arms. Her breath had been knocked from her, and she was trying to figure out what had happened.

"Why don't you watch where you're going, kid?" a deep voice bellowed.

Kid? Was he talking to her? Undoubtedly, he saw the questioning look she gave him.

"What's the matter with you? Don't you understand English?"

By this time, the numbness from the impact was wearing off, and she took in the towering and massive figure before her. He was well over a couple inches taller than her father, who stood at six foot four, and he had to weigh in at over two hundred twenty pounds. Clad in a plaid flannel shirt, heavy-duty work boots, and fitted jeans, he reminded her of what Paul Bunyan would look like. As she drew her eyes up the expanse of his chest to his face, the picture of a lumberjack was complete with his blonde shaggy hair and face scruff. It didn't help when her eyes lowered to the tuft of golden hair poking out from the top of his shirt. When she raised her eyes again, her attention was drawn to his fiery liquid amber eyes, but the look he gave her was far from warm.

As a matter of fact, his whole demeanor was one of icy rudeness. She gazed at his mouth, which was set in an uncompromising line, and found it to be sensual... too sensual. She licked her lips. Her awkward appraisal was deep but swift and must have thrown him off for a while.

"Damn it. What's the matter with you? Did you get knocked senseless?" He shook her by her shoulders, and her baseball cap fell off, allowing her hair to tumble around her in flaming glory.

He stumbled back in surprise.

Her predicament and his rudeness had gotten her fiery temper up. She'd had enough of this overbearing clod.

His brows had drawn together in dismay and stared unbelievingly at first, then, still holding her firmly by her shoulders, gave her a thorough assessment of his own. She felt his eyes penetrating her very being. Never had she felt so completely exposed with so many clothes on. Her blood turned to ice, then sizzled. She could feel the crimson color extend from the top of her head to the tips of her toes.

She finally found her voice and bit out a scathing tirade.

"I beg your pardon, sir, but why didn't you watch where you were going? And, yes, I understand English, and no, I'm not senseless, simply stunned. It isn't every day a brick wall runs into me, and if you were any kind of a gentleman, you would apologize for your rude behavior and help me retrieve my fallen packages."

At the beginning of her oratory, his expression almost softened, but nearing the end, the icy glare of contempt was back. A muscle twitched in his jaw, betraying his clenched teeth and the temper he kept in check. He released her shoulders as if they were burning his hands.

Nikki held her breath, awaiting his fury with her own. He turned silently, gathered up her bags, and abruptly shoved them into her arms.

"It will be a cold day in hell, miss, before I'll apologize to you or any other woman for my ungentlemanly behavior." He brushed past her and stalked into the tackle shop.

Suppressing the desire for a retaliatory verbal attack, she pulled herself together and continued toward her SUV. She was surprised Barney hadn't gone into a barking frenzy when he saw her having words with the Neanderthal. As she loaded the bags in the back of the car, she yelled to Barney in the co-pilot seat.

"Gee, Barney, what a great protector you are."

He cocked his head to the side as if to say, "Gee, Nikki, you handled it just fine. You didn't need my help."

Nikki shrugged, closed the back hatch, and hurried into the car as the wind splattered raindrops sideways onto the windshield. She sat there, watching the drops skitter across the windows and onto the hood of her car. Barney was staring at her, and she was sure he could tell her feathers were ruffled. His brows were raised to their highest point.

"Sorry I yelled at you. Not your fault some people have no manners. Speaking of..." Nikki leaned over the back of her seat and yanked one of the totes toward her, digging around until she found what she was looking for. She waved the dog biscuit in front of Barney. "Forgive me?"

His big brown eyes moved away from the biscuit target and focused on Nikki, then he licked her hand and glanced back at the biscuit.

"Good Boy! Thank you, Barney. At least you have manners."

The biscuit was gone from her hand in a nano-second.

The next stop was the combined pharmacy and liquor store. Nikki mused at the irony.

Whatever ails you... your choice.

"Barney, you need to stay here... too wet and windy."

As if understanding what she said, he nestled back down into the co-pilot seat.

She made a mad dash for it and barely reached the door at the same time as someone else. Recognizing the shock of shaggy red hair, hazel eyes, and an all-encompassing smile, she broke out in a huge grin. The automatic doors opened, and they both entered the store, shaking off the droplets of water from their clothes onto the floor mat.

"Tommy, how are you?"

"Just fine. Had to drop off a winch I repaired at the marina and figured on picking up a six-pack while in town. I heard you were coming up."

Nikki was amazed at how word traveled so fast in Spring Lake.

"Yep, for the summer at least."

He looked at her pensively for a moment.

"Everything okay at the lakehouse? I don't really get up to your end of the lake much, but if you should need something, let me know."

Tommy Caldwell was a renaissance man of sorts. Although only twenty-eight, there wasn't anything he couldn't fix and always had an extensive list of people wanting his expertise. Of course, his good looks also kept him in demand among the female population.

"I sure will. Mom and Dad are bringing Christopher up with them in a couple of weeks, and I want to make sure everything is cleaned up and in working order for them."

"Seriously, Nikki, I'm only a phone call away."

"Hey T.C!" the young cashier at the register called out to Tommy. "How ya' doing? Going to Morton's this weekend?"

Tommy nodded in reply.

Nikki smiled to herself. There was no doubt in her mind Tommy never lacked for female companionship.

After bidding Nikki goodbye, Tommy headed for the beer aisle, and Nikki headed for the wine aisle. After choosing a couple of bottles of her favorites, she went to the pharmacy area and picked up some first aid supplies to restock the house. She was sure splinters, skinned knees, and all sorts of scrapes and bumps would occur over the summer.

She was about to check out when she remembered something else and rolled her cart back to the liquor department. The nights were still cool, and memories of her parents snuggled up in front of the fire pit near the water's edge, sharing a butterscotch schnapps made her smile. As she and her brother Brian got older, they joined them in the evening ritual.

Her hand reached for the bottle, and the overhead lights illuminated the gold wedding band she still wore, and the shiny surface glinted brightly. If only her marriage had had the same sparkle. Several times, this past year especially, she'd felt like taking it off, but then Christopher came to mind, and in an effort to allay any comments from Peter's family, she kept it on.

"I'll not have to worry about them anymore," she whispered quietly to herself. Setting her chin at a determined angle, she slipped the ring off and dropped it in her hobo bag.

Adding the schnapps to her shopping cart, she went to check out.

After battling the wind and rain again while loading her packages into the back of the SUV, she hurriedly hopped back in the car. Barney eyeballed her with a questioning look.

Treat?

"Sorry, Barney. No more treats."

He snuffled and laid back down.

Pulling away from the curb and halfway into the main traffic lane, she heard the roar of a car engine speeding around the corner behind her, bracing for the inevitable as the jeep sideswiped her left front bumper. She hadn't realized she had her eyes tightly closed and her teeth clenched until her car door was abruptly pulled open, and there stood the Nordic giant.

"Lady, what are you? My own personal nemesis? Didn't you see me coming before you pulled out? Typical woman driver. You—"

She had reached the end of her tether.

"That does it! You, ignorant, chauvinistic pig. I'd already pulled out when you were turning the corner, like a bat out of you know where."

She exited her car on shaky legs to survey the damage. Neither of the vehicles had more than minimal damage—slight indentations, scraped paint and chrome. Setting her chin at a defiant tilt and determined not to back down, she turned to face the Nordic giant— the spitfire sapling challenging the towering oak. Their eyes clashed, and a silent declaration of war was communicated. Before more words could be spoken, another voice interrupted their thoughts.

"Excuse me, but can we be of help?" It was Mr. Klein from the gift shop across the street. He and his wife were dressed in hooded raincoats and under an umbrella, wearing worried expressions.

"Sure, you can be of help if you saw what happened, and you could tell this lady I wasn't at fault." His words were punctuated tersely, sarcastically emphasizing the word "lady".

Nikki was taken aback by his inference and stood with arms

akimbo and feet planted firmly apart, the appearance of someone ready for a fight. Except she was drenched, and her copper tresses were plastered to her face and down her shoulders.

"Well, I don't like to disappoint you none, young man, but my wife and I saw what happened," Mr. Klein spoke up. "Nikki had already pulled into the road, and you came hightailing it around the corner. We heard you clear into the store. We thought for sure, with the wet pavement and all, you might have lost control or flipped over going so fast."

He looked at the Kleins, then back to Nikki and if confirming some sort of notion, he nodded.

"All right. If *Nikki* would be so kind to accept my name and insurance company's information, I'll make sure the damage is taken care of."

Nikki knew she would certainly look like a fool if she didn't accept his offer but also realized he hadn't actually made an admission of guilt or apologized.

Turning away and reaching into his jeep, he extracted a clipboard and pencil. He quickly wrote something down, tore the sheet of paper from the pad, and handed it to Nikki with a glare that could have frozen the equatorial jungles.

Mr. and Mrs. Klein, feeling the awkwardness of the situation, excused themselves and drifted back to their store.

Nikki took the high road.

"Thank you, Mister...." She glanced at the paper he'd given her. "Mr. Heath Winters. I'll notify my insurance company, and they'll handle the rest. I can't say it's been a pleasure dealing with you... because it definitely hasn't." Nikki turned on her heel and got into her car, leaving the reprehensible Mr. Winters standing in the wind and rain as she left.

She buckled her seat belt with a smug smile. In her rearview mirror, she watched Mr. Winters walk back to his jeep, his fists clenched to his sides.

She nodded to Barney. "Next time, if there is one, I won't be so nice."

She debated on stopping at the gas station on her way back to the lakehouse but decided to wait. She was looking forward to getting back and unloading the bags, bringing in only the perishables and leaving the rest in the car parked in the garage until the storm let up. She was chilled to the bone and was in dire need of a soothing hot bath.

6

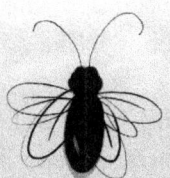

With the perishable groceries safely secured in the refrigerator, freezer, and cabinets in the kitchen, Nikki ran water into the footed tub in the bathroom next to her bedroom. She was mumbling to herself.

Barney was obviously concerned. He followed her closely as she stowed things away, then up the stairs to her bedroom and into the bathroom. He could sense she had been upset and wanted to stay by her side, which included lying down next to the tub.

Flashes of lightning illuminated the skylight in the bathroom. Nikki settled back into the steaming water, feeling the tension leaving her body as the warmth enveloped her. The wind roared and the heavens poured. Listening to the sound of the rain on the roof, its rhythmic beat lulled her into a sleepy state. The thunder, almost muted now, indicated the storm had moved off, and the drumming of rain had lessened.

She was sure there would be cleanup around the outside of the lakehouse the next day, broken branches and debris tossed around by the wind, but it would have to wait until tomorrow. Today was fraught with inspection of the house and grounds, errands, and of all things, encounters with the best and worst of humanity.

When the bath water cooled, she rose and dried off. Wrapping herself in her pink chenille robe and donning a pair of bunny slippers, she went down to the kitchen to make dinner. She was surprised when she looked at the clock and realized how late it was. She'd had nothing substantial to eat all day.

Surveying the contents of the cabinets and refrigerator, she opted for a bowl of thick and hearty soup. She emptied the jar of soup into a saucepan and lit the burner. Breaking off a chunk of the loaf of sourdough bread she had purchased, she broke it into smaller pieces and placed them in a large bowl. Tea sounded good, so she set the kettle on the stove.

Not forgetting her furchild, Nikki put fresh kibble in his bowl and topped it off with some meat broth she had in the fridge. He smiled up at her.

"Go ahead, Barney. Don't wait for me."

He buried his nose and lips into his bowl, only coming up for air every so often to lick his face.

When the kettle whistled, Nikki poured the hot water into her cup, dunked the tea bag of her favorite blend of caramel peach, then let it steep for a while. Pouring the hot soup over the bread pieces in the bowl, chicken and vegetable aromas wafted into the air. While the tea steeped and the soup cooled a bit, she checked to make sure the living room fireplace flu was open, then lit the logs. Slowly, they ignited and dispelled the chill in the room.

Nikki settled down on the leather sofa with her soup and tea on a tray. When she finished, she pulled her mobile phone out of her pocket and called her parents. It rang three times before a voice near and dear to her answered.

"Hi, Mommy!"

"Hi, Honey! So, Grandma and Grandpa have you answering their phone now."

"Only when they tell me it's you. Is Barney there? I miss him."

"Yes, he is. He misses you, too...right, Barney?" Barney chimed in with a loud bark. "See, he misses you too, Christopher."

"And I miss you, Mommy."

"I miss you lots! What did you do today?"

"Grandpa and I put holes in jars... the lids... so they can breathe."

"Who can breathe?"

"The lightning bugs... the fireflies."

"Oh, I see."

"And Grandma helped me paint pretty stuff on the outside... on the glass. Are they there yet? The fireflies?"

"No, not yet, but they'll be here when you're here this summer."

"I'm going to catch lots of them."

"I'll bet you will."

"Grandma wants to talk to you now. I love you, Mommy."

"I love you, too, Christopher. Have sweet dreams tonight. I'll call you tomorrow."

Sophia took the phone and made sure Christopher was out of earshot.

"How are you doing up there?"

"I cleaned the inside of the house, checked around the property, including the garage and boat house. The packrats got into the electrical again. I ran a couple of errands in town and picked up the things to make repairs and replenish any supplies we needed."

"Well, if you need any help with the repairs, there's always Hammy or Tommy."

"I know, but I think I can handle it, and if I need help, I know who to call."

"Anything unusual happen in town?"

"Boy, nothing happens that doesn't get passed you." Nikki rolled her eyes, knowing someone had spilled the beans about the fender bender. "Nothing major, Mom. The guy gave me his name and insurance information."

"It seems Mr. and Mrs. Klein saw the whole thing. They told Maggie, and Maggie told Hammy, and Hammy called us. They said you were okay except for the fact you were spitting fire at a giant of a guy, and they thought it was funny because he looked like he was essentially afraid of you."

"In fact, I ran into the Nordic giant twice today. The first time wasn't with the car, though. I physically ran into him outside a store. He was so rude and condescending. Then he blamed me for the car accident when it clearly was his fault. When the Kleins came to my defense, he backed off and gave me his information, but in no way did he accept blame or apologize. A complete knuckle-dragger. I gave him a piece of my mind."

Sophia snickered. She could well imagine her daughter standing up to a Neanderthal with fire in her eyes. It had been a long time since she'd seen her daughter with such gumption. It came from what she'd experienced over the past several years. Now, Nikki wouldn't take crap from anyone. Sophia wondered if it would be a suitable time to tell her about the visitor they had today. She went for it.

"Nikki, we had a caller today, a gentleman representing Peter's estate and his insurance company."

Nikki felt a chill up her spine.

"What did he want?"

"He wanted to talk to you specifically. He wouldn't share much information with us. We told him you were out of town and wouldn't be back until maybe September. He wasn't happy but asked us to relay his name and information to you and requested you contact him. He said he's more than willing to see you wherever you are."

"To be honest, Mom, I really don't want him coming here and disrupting my life. I plan on vegging out and doing what I can to move forward, not backward. Anything to do with Peter is going backward. I'll call or email him, but that's all."

"I totally understand, Honey." Sophia paused, debating on whether she should tell her the rest.

"Mom? What else... there's something else, isn't there?"

"Yes." Sophia took a deep breath. "He let it slip that Peter wasn't alone in the car when it crashed. There was another fatality."

The chill Nikki felt now turned to ice.

"Who?"

"Don't know. The man hustled out of here when he realized he'd blundered. I'll snap a photo of his business card and message it to you."

"Thanks, Mom. And thank you for running interference for me. He doesn't know where I am, does he?"

"We didn't share any information as to your whereabouts."

"Good. The last thing I need up here is another moron to deal with."

"Nikki, please relax. Put the bad behind you. Soon, Christopher will be with you, and you'll be catching fireflies together. Take some walks. Go fishing. Maybe do some writing. Your dad and I loved the stories you used to write."

"Thanks, Mom. Give dad a hug for me, and tuck Christopher in with a story, a big hug, and a kiss."

"I will, Nikki. Sweet dreams to you."

Nikki rose from the sofa and carried the tray into the kitchen, cleaning up the dishes and pan, then went to the sliding door to the deck.

"Barney, last chance before I call it a night."

He ambled over to her and peeked out. The rain had slowed to a light mist, but large droplets fell from the trees. Deciding he better do his duty now, he crossed the deck and raced down the stairs in search of one of his favorite spots.

Nikki leaned against the door frame. Tree frogs croaked, making their presence known, and a gentle breeze caressed her face. Instead of waves breaking on the shoreline, there was gentle lapping. Barney returned and sat down on the door mat. Nikki ran a towel down his back, then wiped each of his paws.

"Good Boy, Barney!" Nikki reached over to the corner of the kitchen counter and lifted a lid on a jar. "Here you go." She flipped a biscuit to him, which he snarfed, then he smiled with the biscuit hanging out of the side of his mouth.

Locking up, they headed upstairs to bed. Barney sacked out on the fuzzy throw rug beside the bed, but Nikki knew full well by morning, he would be on top of the bed.

She washed up and sank under the covers. She was about to turn out the side lamp when she changed her mind. She opened the drawer of the nightstand, pulled out a large notepad and pen, and wrote.

Once upon a time...

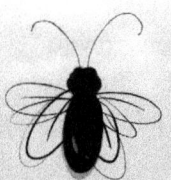

7

Her night was laden with dreams. Dreams of Heath Winters. Dreams spurred on from the memories of their chance encounters. She came wide awake and stared at the ceiling. The encounters frightened her and aroused her at the same time. She remembered the feel of his strong, firm hands grabbing her as she almost fell backward. All too soon, she remembered the anger in his eyes, and she flinched. She shook her head to dispel his contemptuous look.

Why would he be in her dreams? If nothing else, he'd be a nightmare. Can you imagine having to live with someone with such a big chip on his shoulder?

Nikki rolled to her side and came face to face with a very wet nose. A tongue darted out to give her a lick.

"Oh, Barney! You've got morning breath. Yuck!" If Nikki didn't know any better, she saw hurt in his eyes.

"Come on, Buddy, rise and shine." She tousled his head and jumped out of bed. Barney launched himself right behind her. Straightening the bed covers, she found her notepad and put it on the nightstand for her next round of writing.

After freshening up, she got dressed in her standard lakehouse attire, a pair of jeans and a sweatshirt, opting to pull her hair up in a topknot. She looked around for her baseball cap but couldn't find it. Figuring she'd left it in the car, she headed downstairs. She had her work cut out for her today and hoped to accomplish quite a bit of it before dinner. She wanted a quiet evening and some time to do more writing.

Eating a quick breakfast, she went to the garage, making several trips back and forth to the house with yesterday's purchases. She sorted through them and put most away, leaving out the tools and supplies she needed to make repairs.

The first order of business was the boathouse light. All in all, it took thirty minutes to fix and test the electric panel. She left the boat house, trying not to disturb the swallows nesting high in the rafters. She wanted to make sure the double tracks for the boat launch were secure and didn't shift during the winter. Raising the lakeside overhead door, she was pleased it moved smoothly. A cool, refreshing wind blew through the boathouse. Nikki looked out onto the lake and spotted a few fishermen trying their luck in their boats. Looking at her watch, she shrugged.

"Why not?"

She grabbed a rod from the rack and checked the line. It wasn't as bad as the others. Opening the tackle box, she chose a bobber and a lure, snapping them onto the line. Barney was sunning himself on the cement pier, watching her movements. When she walked out to the end of the wooden pier, he sat upright in a protective stance. She noticed his position and called him.

"No, Barney, I'm not going swimming, just fishing. Water's probably too cold right now, anyway."

Barney laid back down but kept an eye on Nikki.

The lake water level was high in the spring, especially after the big rain. Normally, she sat on the edge of the pier and dangle her feet above the waterline, but the water was only a couple of inches below the surface of the pier, so dangling was not an option unless she wanted to freeze her feet.

Nikki cast her line out about twenty feet. The weighted lure sank beneath the crystal-clear water, drifting about two feet below the red and white bobber. She didn't care if she caught anything. It was the peace and tranquility she sought. Swallows soared, and bees buzzed around the flowering spring plants growing along the shoreline.

She sat down cross-legged on the pier, and Barney moved next to her. Holding the rod in her right hand, she stroked his head and back with her left hand. The sun warmed her into a sleepy relaxed state. She turned to stretch out her legs, then nestled with her back against Barney.

The drone of fishing boat motors echoed around the lake. Scooting down, she raised her knees up to support the rod, and rested her head on Barney, who seemed to be fast asleep.

A nearby fisherman cruised by, causing ripples from the wake of his boat. Barney opened his eyes to surveil the intruder. The boat slowed almost to a stop, then moved away once Nikki's bobber was spotted. A good fisherman didn't encroach on other's territory.

A few minutes later, her bobber shook, and her rod was almost torn out of her hand.

Nikki sat up abruptly and tried to get to a standing position as quickly as she could. Barney scurried to the end of the pier and anxiously watched Nikki. Reeling in her line, the noticeable catch battled her all the way. She hadn't brought a net down to the pier, so she would have to take a chance and haul it up onto the pier. As she got it close, she reached out, grabbed the line, and swung it over. Barney watched the two-pound bass flopping around, not sure if he should grab it.

"Leave it, Barney." Nikki bent down and carefully removed the hook from the fish's mouth.

"Grow up, Mr. Bass. Maybe I'll see you later." See reached over the edge of the pier and released the bass, sending him on his way. It was obvious she had gained the attention of a few of the fishermen in the vicinity when they moved their boats into the area, hoping to stake a claim and make a catch.

Motioning to Barney to follow her, she started back to the boat house. On her way, she noticed a couple of large clumps of lake weed and debris on the launch tracks in about a foot of water. Her waders were at the house in the basement storage area.

She took off her sneakers, then stepped off the shore near the boathouse and cringed at the chilly water and sloshed through a foot of water. Yanking the weeds and debris from the tracks, she tossed them onto the shore, then made sure the tracks hadn't become misaligned. Her toes were numb as she hurried back up to the cabin, sliding all the way in the wet grass. She reached the sliding door and dried her feet, then Barney's.

Putting on her bunny slippers, she pulled some ground beef out of the freezer to thaw. Meatloaf or burgers were on the menu for later. For now, she made herself a sandwich with cold cuts from the butcher. With lunch over, Nikki headed back out to pick up the debris left by the storm. Barney followed her as she moved a wheelbarrow around, collecting the branches and the storm's rubble. The rumble of a motor vehicle caught her attention as Maggie drove over to her.

"Hey, Nikki! Did you have plans for dinner? Hammy and I are going to Morton's for dinner and would love for you to join us."

She knew the meat she had taken out could be used the following day, so she accepted the invitation.

"Sounds good, Maggie. What time?"

"How about five-thirty? Happy Hour! We'll pick you up around five, okay?"

"Works for me. See you then."

Maggie tooted the horn on her souped-up golf cart and went on her way.

"Barney, I'm going out tonight, and you need to stay home and guard the house, but I promise to make you something special for dinner." At the mention of dinner, it didn't really matter where he was.

Nikki dumped the load of debris in a compost pile on the side of the garage and went back to the house to clean up.

She felt grungy and desperately needed a shower. The warm water eased the soreness in her muscles tender from lack of use. Hauling the wheelbarrow around was playing havoc with every inch of her body.

Wrapping herself in her favorite chenille robe and donning her bunny slippers, she prepared Barney's favorite dinner ahead of time —looked chicken bits, green beans, and kibble. She warmed it up, then spooned it into his bowl. A supreme look of pleasure came over his face, and he woofed it down in no time at all. Nikki opened the sliding door for him to do his thing.

She stood out on the deck, gazing at the lake. It was four in the afternoon, and boaters were still out and about. Pulling her phone from her pocket, she noticed a message from her mom, a photo of the business card. In no mood to call the guy, she scrolled back to place a call to her parents.

"Hi, Nikki!" her dad answered. "All is well, I imagine."

"Yep, sure is. Got the boathouse switch fixed, then cleaned up after the storm, added to the compost pile, and did some fishing. Caught a bass but released it to grow up some."

"Good for you. I'm looking forward to doing some fishing when we get up there."

"Reminds me... when in town yesterday, I saw Big Steve and Suzie, and picked up a child's rod and reel set. They gave me a new vest for Christopher, a gift from them to him."

"How awesome! They're good people."

"Tell Mom I received her message. I'm not in any hurry to call the guy. I'll wait until Monday. I have another call to make then as well."

"The insurance company of the guy who hit you?"

"Yes, but I'm sure the damage is minimal. The guy was a total jerk."

"I've heard."

"I'm heading out to dinner tonight with Maggie and Hammy, so it will probably be after Christopher's bedtime when I get home to call. Is he available now?"

"He just walked in the house with your mom. They were in the backyard doing who knows what. He wanted to dig worms to take to the lakehouse, but we told him it was too soon. He was disappointed, so your mom was trying to get him to help her plant seeds. Here's Christopher now."

Nikki heard her dad call out to Christopher.

"Yay. Hi, Mommy! We were in the garden. Grandma showed me how to plant seeds."

"What kind? Flowers or vegetables?"

"All kinds. Merry Golds, sunny flowers, pumpkin... and some others."

"Maybe Grandma could bring some seeds up here, and you can plant them around the lakehouse."

"Okay, and we can plant them together and watch them grow this summer."

"We sure can, Honey. Mommy is going out with Miss Maggie and Mister Hammy for dinner, and it will be past your bedtime when I get back. I'm sending you big bear hugs and sweet dreams."

"Sending you my bear hugs, Mommy."

"Love you, Christopher."

"Love you more, Mommy."

Nikki's heart ached to hold him close. Although she knew he was in good hands, she missed him immensely.

Her mom came on the line. "Dinner with the Hardy's tonight?"

Nikki knew the lake grapevine was in hyperdrive.

"Yes. They're picking me up at five, so I best be getting ready."

"Well, enjoy yourself. Relax. You're in good company with people who care about you."

"I know, Mom, and I appreciate them so much. I'll check in with you tomorrow... although I know you'll get a full rundown from Maggie."

"Yes, I will!" Sophia laughed. "Good night, Nikki."

"Night, Mom."

Nikki smiled as she clicked off the call.

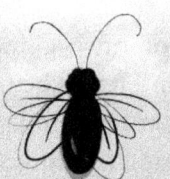

8

Nikki's long flaming red hair cascaded across shoulders and down her back. Dressed in casual jeans, an emerald cowl-necked long-sleeved sweater, and mahogany half-boots, Nikki listened for the sound of Maggie and Hammy's jeep in the drive. She made sure Barney had one more trip out to his favorite tree, then locked the sliding door when he returned. She left a lamp on in the living room and a light above the kitchen sink. There was a motion detector light outside the back door, which illuminated the flagstone walkway up to the garage. Giving Barney a pat on his head, she told him she'd be back soon. She saw him amble over to his special rug near the fireplace, knowing full well he'd move to the leather sofa after she left.

"Be a good boy, Barney." Peter always ridiculed her for carrying on conservations with Barney as if he was human. She thought to herself how much more of a conversationalist Barney was than Peter.

Seeing the beams of headlights cresting the hill, she grabbed her jeans jacket and hobo bag. As she locked up, she heard the beep of the jeep and moved up the walkway.

"Hey, Nikki! Welcome aboard."

"Thanks for the invite. I'm looking forward to seeing the place. Heard it was renovated."

"Yep, practically all new inside. The owner secured a loan from an investor to fix the place up, and it was done up well," Maggie responded.

"The menu is the same, with the addition of a couple of new things," Hammy put in his two cents worth. "They've already had to increase the staff, and it's not even summer yet."

The trip into town was short but finding a parking space took a while. Once they were inside, they were greeted by a bunch of townsfolk who were "old timers," like the Hardys. Most recognized Nikki and gave her hugs.

Her glowing red hair stood out in a mass of graying or balding heads. One would be blind to miss it, and it wasn't missed. Leastways by the dark-haired gentleman sitting in a back booth.

No sooner had Maggie, Hammy, and Nikki been shown a table and sat down, the man got up from the booth and placed a hand on Nikki's shoulder. She jumped, turned around, and came face to face with Mr. Charming from the grocery store.

"Hey, Red! Remember me?"

Nikki hated it when people called her Red. Maggie and Hammy were very aware of it and cringed, waiting for Nikki's fiery response. When Nikki opened her mouth to reply, she caught sight of Heath Winters entering the restaurant, and to the surprise of Maggie and Hammy, she went speechless. Feeling the squeeze of Mr. Charming's hand pressing her shoulder, she came to her senses.

"Yes, I remember you, and by the way, my name isn't Red." Nikki thought her reply would put him off, and he'd leave, but the opposite happened.

"Well, why don't you tell me your name? My name is Lance... Lance Winters."

Nikki's head jerked up.

"Careful, Lance," a voice from behind her boomed. "Nikki McKay has a blazing temper to match her hair and a razor-sharp tongue."

"So, you two are acquainted." Lance stepped back, releasing his hold on Nikki's shoulder. "I see."

"You could say that. We've run into each other on occasion."

Nikki sat quietly while Maggie and Hammy gave the impression they were enjoying the banter.

"Don't we have some business to attend to?" Heath asked Lance.

"Um... right. I have a table in the back."

Lance turned back to Maggie and Hammy and nodded. To Nikki, he only said, "Later, Red... I mean, Nikki."

Maggie and Hammy waited to see if smoke appeared out of Nikki's ears or nostrils. Even when she was a little kid, no one dared stir her ire. They remembered how some kids had tried to bully her brother, Brian, at the marina, and as small as she was, she'd turned into a fierce fire-breathing dragon, causing the bullies to run for their lives. Later, her father, Sean, admonished her for her actions, but secretly, he was very proud she stood up to them. It didn't matter to Nikki that she had been younger, outnumbered, and outsized. She would do anything to protect those she loved.

A waitress came to their table, handed them menus, took their drink orders, and left. Nikki had resumed her calm demeanor and surveyed the menu.

Hammy, the consummate jokester, leaned over to Nikki. "What looks good to you, Red?"

Maggie hauled off and hit his arm. "Don't you be starting something now, Hampson Hardy."

Nikki broke out in laughter, not at Maggie's reaction, but that she used Hammy's formal first name, which he hated. Soon all three were knee-deep in laughter. When the waitress came to take their food order, they were still choking back laughter and wiping tears from their eyes. Relief was felt around the table.

While Maggie and Hammy chose salads and that night's house special night, prime rib, Nikki opted for the Cajun shrimp in an aioli sauce as an appetizer and broiled walleye. The server brought them three draft beers.

Occasionally, another restaurant patron and longtime local would stop by the table to say hello. None had said anything about Nikki's late husband Peter or extended their condolences. It appeared everyone knew the circumstances and left well enough alone. Any time Peter had been at the lakehouse, he didn't socialize or try to make friends. His mind was always on what was happening three hours away in the big city.

Nikki commented her walleye was done to perfection. Hammy told her the chef was the same, but they had added two new sous chefs to keep up with the demand. She looked around and noticed every table was filled, and there were people waiting for tables.

"Business is certainly booming."

Frank Morton made the rounds of the tables, making sure his guests were pleased with their meals. When he came to their table, he clapped Hammy on his back.

"So glad to see you tonight. How was your dinner?"

"It was great. Done exactly how I like it... just short of walkin' and talkin'. And the grilled onions and mushrooms were out of this world."

Frank nodded over to Nikki. "How was your walleye, Nikki?"

"It was great, Frank. My compliments to the chef. And the place looks terrific."

"I'll tell the chef. I can't take credit for the renovations, though. My silent investor did it. He designed it and contracted it out."

Maggie commented they had been at the restaurant for lunch the week before and how nicely even the ladies' room was decorated.

Nikki excused herself to use the restroom and let Frank, Maggie, and Hammy carry on their conversation.

Entering the restroom, she noticed how it had been expanded. A large, gleaming white stone counter with three basins lined one wall. Three regular stalls and one handicap stall filled the wall opposite the sinks. The lighting had been updated, and the floors were a pale gray stone.

A speaker system had been added, and Nikki could hear what the evening entertainment must be. She finished up and stepped out into the hallway only to run into the Neanderthal Winters again.

This time he backed away and held up the palms of his hands in a surrendering action.

Nikki felt a tingling run up her spine, and her breath caught. She turned quickly... much too quickly and lost her balance. His hands grabbed her shoulders to steady her, only to release her as soon as she found her footing.

She swallowed hard and squeaked out, "Thank you," and continued down the hallway, missing his troubled look.

Returning to the table, Maggie didn't miss Nikki's flushed appearance.

"Nikki, are you up for dessert? I am. They have a wonderful selection." Before Nikki could make up her mind, Maggie waved the server over and asked for the dessert menu. Within a minute, each was handed a dessert menu.

Nikki still could feel Heath Winters' touch. Closing her eyes and shaking her head to come to her senses, she took a deep, cleansing breath. Maggie took note and wore a sneaky smile. She'd seen Heath get up from his table and walk down the hallway to the restrooms. It was obvious Nikki and he had crossed paths, and the encounter was disconcerting Nikki.

The server returned to take their orders, and all three chose the key lime cheesecake.

"We had a very interesting conversation with Frank while you were gone."

"Oh? How so?"

"About three years ago, a young man rented an old home on the far end of the lake," Hammy explained. "He liked the property so much, he bought it, gutted the house, redesigned it, and basically, rebuilt it on his own. Got the exterior finished in time for the winter and worked on the interior during those months. When spring came, he did the landscaping, including regrading the road, and added a wraparound porch. Last fall, he tore down the old boat house and took out the old rundown pier, then rebuilt both. Then he disappeared for a bit."

"He became a hermit until he bumped into Frank at the bait and tackle shop," Maggie picked up the story. "He overheard Frank talking to Big Steve about maybe selling the restaurant. It needed repair, and lenders were scarce. Seasonal businesses are difficult to finance."

"But the restaurant is year-round," Nikki protested. "There's plenty going on in the winter, skiing, snowmobiling, ice fishing. When the lake freezes two feet thick in February, there's the Trout Derby. People come from all over for the event."

"Bankers still consider it seasonal. This guy was all gung-ho about investing. He told Frank when he was a kid, his family came up here one summer. He'd loved it and never forgot about it."

"Is the guy still around? It would seem he made a wise investment."

"Frank said he is, but he keeps to himself. Rarely comes to town except to pick up supplies. He and Frank do business at his house, never at the restaurant. He wants to maintain his 'silent investor' status. He's a mystery for sure."

Their cheesecake arrived, and all three ordered coffees. Then Hammy stopped the server and pushed for Nikki to get Coffee Keoke, a concoction of hot coffee, brandy, Kahlua, and crème de cacao, topped with whipped cream.

"Come on, Nikki. It'll relax you. Besides, you're not driving."

Nikki relinquished, sensing Hammy was probably right. She did need to relax.

"Great! Three Keokes, please." A few minutes later, the server brought the three Keokes for Hammy, Maggie and Nikki.

One sip and she knew she would sleep well that night. She looked cross-eyed at the whipped cream on the tip of her nose.

Maggie laughed.

"I should snap a photo of you and send it to your mom. She's been worried you wouldn't relax up here."

"Oh, I'm sure Christopher would get a bang out of it." Nikki quickly wiped the whipped cream from her nose with her napkin. "He's always doing it with his cocoa."

At the mere thought of her son, the true love of her life, Nikki went silent, and tears formed in her eyes. Oh, how she missed him. Missed his hugs. Missed his wet sloppy kisses.

Maggie recognized the emotional reaction. Lord knows how many times she felt the same thing, even though her children were grown and living out of state, she missed them and her grandchildren. She reached over and patted Nikki's hand.

"Soon, Honey. He'll be with you soon. You'll have the place all fixed up, and you'll be able to spend a wonderful summer together doing all kinds of fun things."

"I know." Nikki swiped a stray tear on her cheek. "I think about it all the time. I have some ideas what we'll do when he gets here."

Finishing their desserts and spiked coffees, Hammy suggested they move to the open bar area, where music had been playing, and allow those waiting to take their table. Nikki and Maggie nodded, rose from their chairs, and headed for the bar area while Hammy settled the dinner bill. Nikki couldn't help but look back over her should to where Heath and Lance were seated, but someone else now occupied the table. A flash of disappointment crossed her mind.

She wondered if Heath and Lance were brothers. They certainly didn't resemble each other, and their personalities were so different. Heath was moody and never seemed to smile, while Lance was outgoing and engaging. Both were very attractive in their own way, although the permanent scowl on Heath's face was very detracting. While Heath was blonde with warm amber eyes and rugged looking, Lance had jet-black hair and was polished. She couldn't say what color his eyes were. He seemed to keep them hooded when he looked at her as if he didn't want her to see inside his soul. Her mother always said you could tell what was in a person's heart and soul by their eyes.

What did that matter to her? She had no interest in either of them —the one with the chip on his shoulder or the slick, smooth-talking one.

Frank directed Nikki, Maggie, and Hammy to a high-top table with views of the lake and near the dance floor.

"So, what will you have? It's on me."

Before Nikki to say anything, Hammy ordered another round of Coffee Keokes.

"Hammy, are you looking to get me drunk tonight and have your way with me?" Maggie teased.

"Mags, I'll have you drunk or sober." He leaned over and gave her a kiss.

"You old fool." She said as she pretended to punch him in the shoulder.

Nikki loved to see the repartee between them. It reminded her of her parents. She and Peter never had that... never the kidding or the innuendos lovers have.

Their drinks were delivered, and Nikki wondered how the heck she was going to drink it and be able to walk steadily to the car.

"Not to worry, darlin'," Hammy said when he saw the look on her face. "If need be, I'll carry both you and Maggie out!"

That set off a chain of laughter as Maggie told a story of how she had twisted her ankle getting off their boat, and Hammy had to carry her up the hill to their house. It took him three tries because he kept falling. Nikki's jaw hurt so much from laughing.

The band started playing a two-step, and Hammy suggested Maggie dance with him before she wouldn't be able to. Again, the love punch to the shoulder. They walked hand-in-hand to the dance floor. Nikki watched them and was surprised to see how agile they were. They were in sync with each other. She could tell they'd danced together for many years. Another one of those things Nikki missed having with Peter.

The scent of an overpowering cologne assailed her nostrils. Nikki turned to her left and looked into the shaded eyes of Lance Winters.

"May I have this dance?"

She was about to decline when he continued.

"I feel I owe you an apology for my behavior. I certainly didn't mean to offend you. I was overwhelmed by you when I saw you at the grocery store. My stepbrother, Heath, reminded me I come on too strong at times, which puts people off. I would take it as an honor and a show of forgiveness if you would give me the honor of a dance."

Nikki was thrown off-course. She didn't want to be rude after hearing his apology, so she nodded. Lance took her hand and led her onto the dance floor.

Nikki was pleased it was an upbeat number. A couple of minutes later, the band switched to a slow romantic song, and she made a move to leave the dance floor. She resented it when Lance held tight to her hand as if to pull her in close for the slow dance. Another hand removed Lance's hand and took hers.

"I think I owe Miss McKay an apology for not being more welcoming when we met."

Lance looked surprised and relinquished. "Of course, Heath."

Nikki could sense an underlying tension between the stepbrothers.

She didn't want to add to the tension, and she gracefully accepted Heath's hand as they moved into the center of the dance floor.

He gingerly placed his right arm and hand around her waist while she positioned her left hand on his right shoulder.

Nikki expected him to say something to her while dancing, but he was quiet—eerily quiet. She felt him tremble as if this was the first time he'd danced with a woman. When she looked up at his face, his eyes were on her, wide open and molten lava. He took her right hand and brought it in close to their bodies. He smelled of the outdoors, fresh and earthy. His breathing was heavy, and when he moved her hand over his heart, she looked deep into his eyes and fell into his soul. She saw something she never expected.

He finally found his voice, but it wasn't what she imagined she'd hear.

"My stepbrother is out of your league. My advice to you is to steer clear if you don't want to get hurt. He chews up innocent girls like you and spits them out."

Nikki was dazed, as if she had been doused with a bucket of ice water.

"It's for your own good. I know what he is capable of, and you certainly don't want to get mixed up with him."

She finally came to her senses.

"I'm not some young schoolgirl, Heath Winters, and I certainly don't appreciate your implying I am. I can handle myself and don't need you to tell me who I can or cannot be friends with. I can make my own choices. If I didn't know any better, I'd think you were jealous of your stepbrother for his charming ways... ways you seem to lack."

They had stopped dancing and were standing on the dance floor, having a whispered conversation ill-suited for the place and time.

Recognizing their situation, she turned away from Heath and walked back to the table, where Maggie and Hammy were sitting. Heath disappeared from the dance floor.

The Hardy's were wondering what happened out on the dance floor. When she returned to their table, Nikki had fire in her eyes and chugged her Keoke. Setting her empty Irish coffee cup on the table and looked up at Maggie and Hammy.

"The gall of that man... basically telling me I'm so naïve, I can't take care of myself or know who I should be friends with."

"We saw you dancing with Lance, then with Heath. Okay... what exactly did he say?" Maggie asked.

Nikki told them practically verbatim.

"It appears this guy Lance is what some would call a player," Hammy piped up.

"Player or not, it's up to me who I should play with." Nikki realized as soon as the words were out of her mouth, they came out all wrong. "I mean..."

"We know what you meant." Maggie reached over and put her arm around Nikki. "You're smart enough to know who you should be friends with. Heath doesn't know you, so who is he to judge whether you're capable of discerning a genuine friendship?"

"You're right, Maggie. He doesn't know me or my past. Sure, I've made mistakes, but I've learned from them. I don't intend on getting involved with either Heath or Lance. Heath is arrogant, self-righteous, and irritates the heck out of me. Lance has characteristics reminding me of Peter... a smooth talker with no substance."

"No one is devoid of character flaws," Hammy pointed out. "Some have more than others. You need to weed through them to see which ones have more importance than others. Of course, then there are those of us who have no flaws."

"You think you're flawless, Hammy?" Maggie nudged him in the side. "Wait. I'll get my list." She made a move to reach into her purse.

"Now, Mags, you know you married me because I was perfect."

"A perfect asswipe at times."

Nikki laughed at their amusing tête-à-tête, knowing full well how much they truly loved each other.

As they left the restaurant, Nikki couldn't help herself and looked around for Heath and Lance but didn't see either of them.

After Hammy and Maggie dropped her off, they waited to make sure she got into the lakehouse safe and sound. Nikki waved from the doorway. Barney greeted her with energetic tail wags.

"Okay, Barney. I know you need to go out."

She walked through the kitchen to the deck sliding door, opened it, and Barney jetted out.

Nikki stood on the deck, relishing the serenity. Night owls hooted, crickets chirped, and water lapped softly at the shoreline. Deciding to walk down to the pier, she went back in the house for a battery-operated lantern to guide her way down the hill. She knew as soon as she neared the boathouse, the motion-sensing light would kick on.

Barney finished his business and joined her when she was halfway down the hill. She carried the lantern in front of her to watch where she stepped. The quarter moon shed minimal light through the trees. About thirty feet from the boathouse, the light triggered and illuminated the area, including the cement dock and wood pier.

Her father had insisted on installing the lighting system after hearing about boathouses being broken into in the middle of the night. Although everything was insured, they felt being proactive would be prudent. If there were intruders, the light would alert them and their nearby neighbors. She knew the light would stay on for a few minutes before turning off, so she hurried onto the dock and walked to the end of the pier.

After settling cross-legged and switching off the lantern, Barney claimed a spot next to her and laid down. The motion-sensing light on the boathouse turned off after a few minutes.

Beyond the canopy of the trees, the moonlight shone brighter, its reflection across the water magnified. Barney moved closer and set his head in her lap, and she stroked it lovingly. The sky was pitch black except for the half moon and the star-studded Milky Way. When a shooting star crossed the heavens, she gasped in awe.

"Make a wish, Barney!"

All she wished for was a happy life for her and Christopher. Nothing more. Nothing less.

Out on the lake, the running lights of fishing boats moved almost silently across the lake, indicating they were outfitted with secondary electric motors, a low hum was their only sound. They were quiet enough not to scare off fish coming to the surface to snatch their nighttime dinner of insects skimming across the water. Occasionally, there was a splash from a fisherman casting his line or a fish snapping a meal.

A fishing boat cruised too close to the boathouse and set off the light. It blinded Nikki for a few seconds as she turned toward the boat. The fisherman reversed his boat and pulled away, but not before his running lights had flashed across her on the pier. She shielded her eyes and stood up. Barney assumed a protective stance and barked.

"It's only a fisherman." She patted his head. "Let's go back to the house. We both need some sleep." The temperature had dropped, and Nikki drew the collar of her jacket close, thinking it would be a good night for sleeping.

The boat had motored farther out but was still within sight of the pier and the flaming-haired woman with a lantern walking up the hill with a dog. It coasted awhile outside of the range of the light's motion sensors.

Watching.

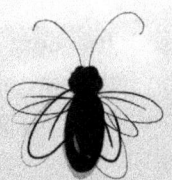

9

Morning dawned bright and chilly. Curled on her side, Nikki peeked her head out from under the covers, one eye squinted open, the other shut tight. She wasn't sure if it was the two Keokes she had at the restaurant or the fresh air from last night's excursion on the pier, but she'd slept deeply, although her dreams were extraordinarily strange.

A faceless person handed her an envelope. She attempted to accept it, but it kept getting farther and farther out of her reach. There was writing on the envelope, but she couldn't make it out.

Breathing a deep sigh, she put her arm out to her side to scratch Barney's ears, but he wasn't there. How odd. She kicked back the covers, then she swung her legs over the edge of the bed, quickly noticing how cold it was. Going to the bathroom to take care of her morning routine, she threw on her old pink chenille robe and bunny slippers and headed for the stairs.

Reaching the main level, she called out, "Barney...where are you?"

A low "ruff" came from the kitchen, where he sat at the sliding door, looking out. He looked at Nikki, then back outside. Something or someone had caught his attention. A squirrel on the deck or a raccoon? She looked out and didn't see any critters except for the birds pecking away at the feeder she filled the day before. She unlocked the slider, and Barney took off. She watched him head for the dock.

"Crap! Hope we didn't get burglarized last night."

She had zonked out as soon as her head hit the pillow. Now, she was worried she didn't see the boathouse light go on or hear any noises. Pulling her pink robe close against the chill, she padded onto the deck and down the stairs. The grass was slick with dew, and she almost fell on her ass a couple of times.

Barney was out on the pier sniffing at something. When she reached him, she saw a rope tied to the dock. She pulled on it, and a floating fish basket came up. When she brought the basket up onto the dock, inside were about four good-sized bass.

"Hammy!" She looked over at Barney. "Appears our buddy did some night fishing after we got home. We're all set for dinner tonight. I should have Maggie and Hammy over."

Barney sniffed at the fish hopping around in the basket and dejectedly walked away. Fish were not his favorite thing to eat.

Carrying the basket up the hill to the house, she removed the fish and set them in the laundry room sink. She covered them with ice she took from the spare freezer in the basement. Picking up her cell phone, she called the Hardy house, and Maggie answered after the first ring.

"Good morning, Nikki! Did you sleep well after those Keokes?"

"I did. I walked down to the dock last night, and I'm sure the cool air added to the deep sleep. I didn't hear Hammy down on our dock dropping off the fish."

There was silence.

"Maggie? You there?"

"Yes... but I don't know what you're talking about. Hammy didn't go fishing last night. He crashed as soon as we got home and woke up about an hour ago."

"Well, who would've left me fish out on the dock?"

"The Fish Fairy? Maybe one of the folks in town. They all know you're up here alone. Steve or Tommy... it could be any of them."

"Anyway, I have four beautiful bass. Would you and Hammy like to join me for dinner tonight?" Barney barked. "Barney would like it."

"Sure, Nikki. I'll bring my cranberry-apple coleslaw you like so much. Okay?"

"Perfect! I have some Yukon potatoes. Will six o'clock work for you? I thought we could eat on the deck. The weather is looking good today."

"Six o'clock is fine. See you then, if not before."

Nikki was sure one of the townsfolk had dropped off the fish.

AFTER BREAKFAST, Nikki showered and put on a clean pair of jeans, a sweatshirt, and sneakers. There were still things on her list to do around the lakehouse and the property. The boathouse windows needed cleaning and cobwebs needed to be knocked down without disturbing the nesting swallows.

After washing the windows and removing the rest of the dust and debris from winter, she looked wistfully at the boats. One was an old nineteen-foot Bayliner inboard/outboard her father had inherited and kept in tip-top shape. Her mom renamed it Bella Fortuna. It was used for fishing and skiing, while the other was a small aluminum dinghy with a small engine and an electric motor, used primarily for fishing along the shoreline. She was anxious to winch the boats out of the boathouse to air them out and clean them. No telling what critters may have set up residence in them over the winter.

Tomorrow would be a good day to start on them. For now, she needed to finish up in the boathouse, check the tracks one more time, and make a phone call. A phone call she didn't want to make but felt obligated to, anyway.

Her mother had texted earlier that the gentleman, who had stopped at their home a couple of days prior, had called to see if her parents had let Nikki know he was trying to reach her.

It played on her mind until she took off her work gloves and stomped up the hill to the house, leaving her tasks for later. She scanned her phone for the photo her mother had sent of the man's business card, then punched in the number and listened to it ring. She was about to hang up when it was answered.

"Trey Westin here. How can I help you?"

"Mr. Westin, this is Nikki McKay. I understand you want to talk to me."

"Yes. It's vitally important we meet to discuss your late husband's estate."

From the sound of it, he seemed surprised and eager to hear from her. She could envision him sitting up straighter in his chair.

"I'm not sure what there is to discuss. Peter and I were finalizing our separation documentation prior to his death. The separation hadn't been granted or recorded yet, but we weren't living together."

"Yes, but you still were his wife and heir since he never changed his will or the trust."

"What trust?"

"A trust established years ago, before he met you. You didn't know he had a trust?"

"No, I didn't. He never spoke about it to me. Besides, I have no interest in his estate. While alive, he made it clear he wanted no part of a relationship with me or our son, for that matter."

"Even if it would benefit you and your son?"

"I imagine if he had anything of value it had a hefty mortgage on it."

"The house was free and clear."

She was surprised, then it dawned on her. His parents more than likely funded the money for the house when Peter purchased. He'd shared no information about its purchase or where any of the funds came from.

"Were you aware of the trust fund his grandparents set up for him?"

Nikki vaguely remembered his parents talking about his grandparents but always derogatory terms.

"No, I didn't know. Peter was always tight-lipped about anything pertaining to his estate and assets. I figured he'd eventually share the information. Six years... he never told me. I didn't want him to think I was after him for his money if I pushed."

"I really think we need to meet face to face to discuss this. Can we please get together? I'm willing to come to wherever you are."

"Give me a day to think about it." Nikki's mind was going a mile a minute. "I'll call you tomorrow."

"Well, all right." Mr. Westin sounded disappointed. "Tomorrow, then. Goodbye."

Nikki clicked off the call. She didn't want him to come to the lakehouse but was curious what he wanted to tell her. Since he was so insistent about meeting, she'd have to come up with a compromise. Driving to the lakehouse, she'd passed a turnoff to a much larger town than Spring Lake. The town and its large population warranted its own police department and fire department instead of depending on the county or volunteers. Kingston was a forty-minute drive from the lakehouse.

She'd call Westin back tomorrow and arrange a time and place, preferably somewhere public, yet where a private conversation could take place.

Deciding it was a good time to break for lunch, she remembered the ground beef she had in the refrigerator and decided to make burgers for her and Barney. She hadn't yet checked the grill on the deck and remembered one year, a furry critter had taken up residence under the burners during the winter. Had her father not noticed before he ignited it, they would have had a mess on their hands. Her brother, Brian, removed the squatter safely and cleaned up the grill before they could use it.

Nikki carefully lifted the lid. Not seeing any indication of a potential resident, she checked under the burners. All good. All clean. Of course, she noticed her dad had tightly stuffed tinfoil into every nook and cranny around the edges of the grill lid and the fuel line openings to prevent any future trespassers. Smart man.

Firing up the grill to heat up, she went back in the house to get the burgers ready. She pulled two frozen buns out of the freezer and zapped them in the microwave for less than a minute, then sliced tomatoes and onions and opened the pack of sliced provolone she got at the deli.

Barney remained nearby, watching her every move.

Nikki carried a tray out to the deck and set it on the table near the grill. Opening the grill lid, she laid two slabs of sliced red onion on the grate. She mixed up the ground beef with seasonings and egg, formed patties, and set them on the hot grate as well. They sizzled, sending out the most pleasant aroma Barney could imagine.

Nikki returned to the kitchen and brought out two plates, flatware, napkins, and a bag of chips. She checked the onions, moved them to a plate, and flipped the burgers. Next, she brought out a pitcher of ice-cold lemonade, a tumbler, and a bowl of water. Barney's bowl, to be exact.

Checking the burgers, she put a slice of cheese on each one and closed the lid, then sat on the picnic bench and looked over at Barney.

"You're drooling, buddy."

He raised a paw and set it on her knee. He knew something special was coming.

Nikki went to the grill, opened it and placed everything on the tray, then brought it to the table. Preparing a plate for Barney first, when she set it down on the deck, he dove in headfirst. She put her meal together and sat down to enjoy it, listening to the sounds of nature and the engine noises emanating from the fishing boats offshore. As the temperatures warmed up, the skiers, tubers, and jet ski enthusiasts would populate the lake.

More and more, she was thinking about moving here. The big city had lost its appeal. Sure, it was nice to go downtown to see Broadway musicals or join the crowds at professional sports venues, but the peace and quiet of the lakehouse were what she desired. The townsfolk caring, hardworking people who would go out of their way to help anyone. Yes, she had friends back in the burbs of the big city, and they were good people, but it seemed they were being outnumbered by those who weren't. Besides, if there was something special happening, she could always make the three-hour trip and spend a long weekend with friends and family or attend an event.

Spring Lake would be a great place for Christopher to grow up.

When she finished up her lunch, Barney had already gobbled his down and was soaking up the rays sunning himself on the deck... a lazy afternoon.

After Nikki cleaned up their lunch dishes and the kitchen, she rolled the wheelbarrow down to the firepit. Charred logs were all that remained from last fall when the family had sat around the fire pit in the six dark-green Adirondack chairs her grandfather had made. The bottom of the five-foot diameter pit was lined with several inches of coarse sand, and the pit itself was bordered with large rocks.

Barney had followed her down the hill and continued trotting down to the pier, lying down to catch more rays. *Lazy bones.*

Nikki put on her heavy-duty work gloves, then, one by one, she lifted the charred logs out of the pit and placed them in the wheelbarrow. Moldy leaves had filled the gaps between the logs, so she scooped them out with a large garden trowel and added them to the stack of logs destined for the compost pile.

After making the trip up the hill to dump the wheelbarrow, she straightened and stretched. Muscles not normally used were complaining. She swiped at an errant lock of hair, which had escaped from her ponytail.

"Looks like you're pretty handy."

Nikki swung around toward the voice, her stance defensive as she held the metal trowel.

"Whoa! Sorry to scare you. Simply wanted to visit with you."

Lance Winters stood there in his city attire, looking so out of place, it was comical.

"Normally, people call before they visit. What do you want, Lance?"

"Now, that is a loaded question." The innuendo was clear.

"I'm quite busy, as you can see. If you don't mind, I need to get back to things."

He took a few steps toward her and reached out. She backed away only to run into the edge of the wheelbarrow.

His hand reached into his pocket, and taking out a handkerchief, he handed it to her. He motioned with his finger at the side of her face. Nikki took the handkerchief and swiped at her cheek. A smear of black soot soiled the linen.

"Oh! Sorry. I'll launder it and get it back to you."

"No need. I have plenty... unless, of course, you can deliver it to me in person this evening at dinner. Will you join me for dinner, Nikki?"

Damn, this guy was slick.

Lance recognized the look she gave him.

"Nikki, I can well imagine what my stepbrother said about me. Suffice it to say, I tend to be somewhat over the top, and at times, people find me too aggressive, which is a total misinterpretation of my intentions. When I see something or someone I like, I do my best to make it, or whoever, a part of my life. It's simple. I like you and find you extraordinarily attractive and witty. So, will you join me for dinner this evening?"

Her grandmother's words rang in her head. If words were honey, there's those who speak a whole hive. Careful you don't get stung listening to them.

She smiled inside, remembering those words and equating them to Lance.

"I already have dinner plans this evening."

"How about tomorrow night?"

She took a deep breath.

"Lance, I'm not in the market for a relationship... with you or anyone else. Moreover, my ex... my husband recently passed away, and I need to get my life together for myself and my son."

He kept looking at her with those hooded eyes.

"I'm sorry to hear of your husband's passing. I assumed since you aren't wearing a wedding ring, you were single." Switching gears, he said, "It must be difficult for you to maintain all this property on your own now."

"Why would you think that?" she asked, distracted by the sound of a nearby motorboat echoing from the lake.

"The property title shows the property is in the name of the McKay trust, with you listed as trustee."

Nikki shook her head in disgust. Was this what it was all about? He had checked the county records of the properties around the lake and found her name listed as trustee of the family trust. For as smart as he thought he was, he obviously hadn't investigated more thoroughly. If he had, he would have found she, along with her parents and her brother, were all trustees of the estate trust that owned the property.

"In other words, Lance, it's not me you want in your life but this property." The emerald green in her eyes turned to fire.

"No! You have it all wrong. I want to help you... in case you want to unload the burden of the property or possibly turn it into something profitable. A Bed and Breakfast maybe, or—"

She held up her hands to stop him from saying anything further and digging himself a deeper hole.

"You need to leave. NOW!" She pointed toward the road on the hill.

"Nikki, I—"

"NOW!"

She stood with her hands on her hips, her jaw clenched, her eyes boring into him as if they'd shoot fireballs at him.

He looked as if he was going to say something but thought better of it. Backing away, he turned and walked briskly up the hill in his Italian loafers, occasionally slipping on the wet grass.

A few minutes later, she heard him rev the engine of his Mercedes and speed away, kicking up gravel all the way to the blacktop access road.

She wondered where Barney had been during the altercation with Lance and called out to him. He came bounding up the hill to her with something in his mouth.

Nikki was surprised when Barney got to her and sat down, holding her baseball cap in his mouth.

"What the..."

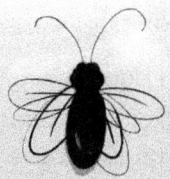

10

Nikki finished the cleanup of the firepit and the surrounding area, wondering where Barney had found her baseball cap. A mystery for sure.

Gathering her tools and the wheelbarrow, she traveled up the hill to the garage. It was past four, and she wanted to take a hot bath to soak her strained muscles before preparing dinner for Maggie and Hammy.

Forty minutes later, she was in the kitchen, cleaning and filleting the bass and setting them in the refrigerator in a glass Pyrex dish to chill and ready to be fried. She scrubbed six Yukon Gold potatoes, sliced them into small pieces, then rolled the pieces in a bowl with olive oil and seasoning. Spreading the potatoes out in a square glass dish, she covered them with plastic wrap, ready to be zapped for eight minutes in the microwave. Quick, tasty, and easy.

Maggie was bringing her awesome cranberry and apple coleslaw. The meal was complete except for the dessert. She sliced fresh peaches in a bowl, sprinkled brown sugar, cinnamon, and nutmeg on top, and added vanilla, carefully stirring to ensure the peaches were all coated. Taking a sauté pan from the cabinet, she set it on a lit burner. Dropping two tablespoons of butter in the pan, she rolled it around, then added the peaches and simmered them at low heat.

Barney raised his head and sniffed the air. Something good with cooking, and he was hoping it would be on his menu, too.

Nikki went to the bar in the great room and opened a cabinet. Spying what she needed, she brought two bottles to the stove. Adding a couple of ounces of dark rum and a splash of peach schnapps to the sauté pan, it blended with the contents and sent up a heavenly aroma. Barney drooled. Nikki turned off the burner and set the pan aside to be warmed up later.

Reasoning the marinated potatoes could be cooked ahead of time and kept warm, she placed them in the microwave to cook and went about setting the redwood table on the deck. Forest green stained bamboo placemats were set out with dark brown rustic ironstone dinnerware and flatware with thick Lyndon olive wood handles, or as her dad would say, "man-handles."

Wine and beer were chilling in the fridge, if Maggie or Hammy preferred either.

Sitting on the deck, she called her folks, knowing it would be too late to talk to Christopher after dinner. She wanted to hear his sweet voice and catch up on what he'd done during the day. After a brief conversation with her mom, she talked with Christopher and listened to his rundown of the day's events. After wishing him sweet dreams, she disconnected the call.

At five-thirty, taking the fish filets out of the refrigerator, she coated them with a batter she had made, then gently lowered them into a pan of hot oil. She took a large oval platter and laid a layer of toweling on it, and as the filets rose to the top in the oil, indicating they were cooked, she took them from the pan with a slotted spoon and laid them on the platter. Removing the last filet from the pan, she was covered the platter and was placing it in the warming oven when she heard Maggie and Hammy arrive.

"Welcome to Nikki's Diner!" she greeted them at the back door.

"Hey, Sweetie! We've been looking forward to this all day!" Maggie replied while handing Nikki her covered container of coleslaw.

Hammy scooted around her and gave Nikki a hug.

"Come on in. Supper is pretty much ready. I'm keeping it warm, so we can have a few minutes before we sit down. How about something to drink?"

"How about I make you something special," Hammy responded. "I'm pretty sure you have all the ingredients I'll need."

"Oh... the Hammy Hottie." Nikki knew what he was talking about.

His grin confirmed her guess.

"Extra spicy Bloody Mary coming right up."

"How'd you know I would have everything to make it?" Nikki asked as Hammy went about throwing the ingredients together.

"Your dad always has the makings, and he happened to mention on the phone that he sent you up here with all the add-ons and add-ins."

"Figures. It's his favorite before-dinner drink. Although with everything in it, it's more like an appetizer. Celery, pickle, olives, lemon..."

"Let me know if it's too hot or not hot enough." Hammy handed her a large beverage container.

Taking a sip, the liquid settled on her tongue, then down her throat. She gasped and coughed.

"Wow! I'd say it's hot enough." Her eyes watered.

"Want me to thin it down a bit?"

"Nope, it's fine, just takes getting used to." Nikki took another swallow and found it was better or else her mouth had become numb from the Tabasco Chile pepper sauce.

Nikki turned on the sound system and adjusted the speakers on the deck to a soft music background.

Maggie asked if she had company earlier.

"I guess you saw the car at the top of the hill. It was Lance Winters. He came uninvited."

"That's not right." Maggie frowned. "Didn't anyone teach him manners?"

"Same could be asked about Heath, too."

"May I ask what he wanted?"

"It appears he came to charm me and ask me to dinner. Of course, I said no... especially when I found out his ulterior motive."

"Ulterior motive?" Hammy asked.

Nikki nodded again.

"Mr. Slick, as I now will refer to him, checked the county records and assumed I was a single lady who owned this property and needed some help either in selling the property or developing it into a money-making venture."

"Oh, my God! He investigated you and the property?"

"Yes, but what I don't understand is his interest in the property and how, if he's such a hotshot wheeler-dealer, he didn't find out the property is in a trust and has four trustees, not just me. Anything to do with the property has to be decided by a majority vote of my parents, my brother, and me."

"Are you sure it's the property he's interested in, not just you?"

"Positive. He tipped his hand when he brought up the county records and the trust. Why would anyone delve into those records if they were only interested in going out with me?"

Maggie and Hammy agreed.

"I didn't hear him pull up the drive when he arrived, but I sure heard him leaving. You must have sent him running with his tail between his legs," Hammy said.

"Hopefully, he'll think twice before he approaches me again."

Barney jumped up from his sacked-out position on the deck and took off for the dock.

"Hmm. Seems something stirred him up." They rose from their chairs and went to the railing.

Barney stood at the end of the wooden pier, not barking but his tail was wagging.

There were several boats in the area, more than likely angling for a catch. It was dusk, one of the better times of day to fish.

"Must be one of our neighbors or townsfolk he knows."

Maggie and Hammy helped her bring the covered dinner platters and Maggie's special coleslaw out to the table. Nikki lit several lanterns and placed two on the table and four others around the deck.

"Would either of you like beer or wine with dinner?"

"I'll take a beer," Hammy replied. Maggie and Nikki opted for beer as well.

Barney joined them up on the deck, and Nikki put out his bowl of kibble.

As night fell, the crickets sang their songs, owls hooted, and the lake slapped at the shoreline. All three were lost in their own thoughts as they sat on the deck enjoying their dinners.

"Nikki, what're you thinking about?" Maggie asked.

"How beautiful it is here. You and Hammy have been living here year-round for decades. What made you do it?"

Maggie looked over at Hammy and let out a deep sigh.

"The first time we came here, back in the dinosaur days, we fell in love with the lake and the property. At first, it was a weekend getaway, only a small shack. By the second year, we knew we had to build a real home for us and the kids. Two years after that, we made it our permanent home. Every time we came here, it was harder to leave. We didn't find joy like this anywhere else... the joy of knowing you're surrounded by the most beautiful of God's creations. And the people here are special."

"There were some rough spots, mind you," Hammy added. "At times, we have harsh winters, not often, but it happens. You prepare for it, so when it does happen, you're ready to ride it out."

Nikki couldn't help but think how preposterous it would have been for Peter to move here.

"Are you thinking about moving here?" Maggie looked quizzically at Nikki.

"It's been crossing my mind... a lot lately. A new beginning for Christopher and me." Nikki thought of the call she had to make the next day. "There are still some issues I need to discuss with some guy representing Peter's estate and insurance."

Seeing the concern on Nikki's face, Maggie patted her hand. "If you ever decide to move here, we'd be here to help any way we can." Hammy nodded in agreement.

Nikki was moved by her words and gave her a hug.

"How about dessert? I made something special."

"Hell, yes!" Hammy said. "I knew I smelled something incredible."

While Nikki went into the kitchen to tend to dessert, Maggie and Hammy cleared the table and set the dishes on the kitchen counter. Hammy scraped the plates while Maggie rinsed and loaded them into the dishwasher.

Barney must have sensed something good was coming and wagged his tail.

Nikki set out three large bowls and spooned large scoops of vanilla ice cream into each. She heated the sauté pan until it sizzled, then split the contents between the three bowls.

"Wow, it smells and looks wonderful," Maggie commented.

Hammy inhaled deeply. "Rum! I smell rum." He breathed deeply again. "Peach schnapps, too!"

Nikki smiled.

"I swear, Hammy, you have the nose of a bloodhound," Maggie teased.

Nikki placed the bowls on a tray to take out to the deck.

"Anyone up for coffee... or anything else?" Nikki winked.

"I'll take a pass. Between the Bloody Marys and the beer, I'm good. Besides, there's probably enough rum and schnapps in here to give me a buzz tonight." Maggie dittoed his response.

Nikki had put a scoop of ice cream in Barney's bowl and lovingly watched him dive in. As he slurped the ice cream, the bowl moved around the deck.

"Did you ever find out who gifted you with the fish?" Maggie asked as they devoured the Peach Foster and ice cream,

"No. I figure it was probably Tommy from the marina or Steve McConnell from the bait and tackle shop."

"I saw Steve McConnell out the lake early this afternoon. Frank Morton, too."

"Could be any of them. Whoever it was, it was a nice gesture. Another mystery."

"Another mystery?"

"Yeah. Strange thing. I misplaced my baseball cap the other day. You know, the old raggedy one I usually wear. Last time I remember wearing it was in town when the storm hit. I looked for it later but couldn't find it. Then, this afternoon, right after Mr. Slick left in a huff, Barney comes up from the lake with the cap in his mouth."

"That is strange."

After Maggie and Hammy left, Nikki sat in one of the deck double lounge chairs. The temperature had dropped, so she huddled in a large, heavy woolen throw, a glass of tawny port on the table beside her. Earlier, she'd dimmed the lanterns on the deck so they only slightly glowed.

Barney jumped up and sprawled out on the other side of the lounge chair.

"Comfortable, Barn?"

He snuffed loudly and nuzzled into the wool blanket.

Sipping her port wine, she watched the mesmerizing running lights of fishing boats skimming almost silently across the lake's surface. A waxing crescent moon hung in the sky.

Nikki wasn't sure how long she had been asleep, but she was jostled awake when Barney barked and jumped down from the chair. He ran to the edge of the deck near the stairs leading down, looked back at her, then toward the lake. At the same time, the boathouse motion detector switched on the light, illuminating the dock and the boathouse. Barney was on high alert in a protective stance. He stood at the top of the stairs as if a statue, placing himself between Nikki and any intruder. His eyes pierced the darkness between the boathouse and the lakehouse.

The sound of a boat motor starting up reverberated from the water's edge, then the thunderous rumble of full throttle.

Nikki peered out but could only see the undulating waves the boat had caused from its wake. A fisherman who drifted too close to shore?

"Easy, Barney. Come here, Boy."

The lights at the boathouse clicked off.

Barney looked at her, then into the darkness. Nikki called him again and patted the seat next to her. He trotted over, leapt onto the chair, and threw his body over her lap in a shielding position.

Wrapping her arms around him, she hugged him tight. When he

looked up at her with his serious big brown eyes, she could see into his very soul, and she smiled.

As Barney gazed into her eyes, he saw the same thing and lifted his jowls to smile his special smile.

11

Nikki was in a deep sleep when there was a pounding on the backdoor, and she heard her mobile phone ringing. Groggily she reached over to get it off the nightstand and remembered she'd left it charging on the kitchen counter.

She jumped out of bed and was about to run down the stairs when she realized she should put her robe on. Pushing her arms through the sleeves and tying it around her waist, she hurried down the stairs, wondering who would be calling this early and who the hell was pounding on her door. She grabbed her phone and answered.

"Hello!"

"Nikki, are you okay?" her father's asked.

"Yeah, I'm fine. What's going on?"

Nikki glanced over to the back door, and Heath Winters stood there, looking upset.

Her dad was talking a mile a minute the way he did when he was keyed up about something.

"Dad, slow down."

As he began again, slowly this time, Nikki walked over to the door and pointed to her phone and waved it at Heath through the glass.

She raised her index finger up, indicating he should wait a minute, and he looked more upset. He placed his hand up on the door frame, leaned against it and rolled his eyes, then looked down and shook his head in disgust.

Her dad explained he had received a call from the County Sheriff Doug Hansen and a deputy Lou Parker, and there had been several break-ins around the lake last evening. Lake houses had been broken into, but mostly boathouses had been burglarized. One homeowner caught the thieves in the act in his boathouse, but after assaulting him, they got away.

Nikki kept an eye on Heath outside the door. Barney wasn't barking at Heath, only whimpering and whining as his tail whipped back and forth. Having faith in Barney's judgment, she unlocked the door, allowing Heath to enter, and put her phone on speaker.

"The homeowner gave a good description of the robbers. All young kids... teenagers looking to steal boating and fishing equipment and sell it online or at a pawn shop... probably for drug money. Several other areas nearby are experiencing the same thefts. Have you noticed anything strange or worrisome up there?"

Nikki so much wanted to say something snarky about Mr. Slick, aka Lance Winters, but felt it out of place with Heath standing an arm's length away.

"Not really. Barney and I heard a boat close to shore late last night, but when the boathouse lights went on, whoever it was left the area. There were quite a few night anglers on the lake last night. Who got broken into? The Hardy's?"

"No, but the boathouse on the other side of Hammy and Maggie did."

"I'm sorry to hear that. I've always felt safe and secure here. Things are changing."

"The deputy has a feeling these teenagers aren't from the area, more than likely from a larger metropolitan area. He figures with Memorial Day coming up and more people at their lakehouses, they'll move on to look for other places to rob."

"How's the homeowner who was assaulted?"

"Shaken up but all good. He told the deputy there were three of them. Although there may be another as a lookout."

"I hope they catch them soon. If they keep getting away with it, no telling if they'll move on to bigger and more dangerous things."

"I'm sure Hammy and Maggie will get in touch with you and give you more details. Please be careful, Honey. If you don't feel safe there, come back home."

Home.

In her mind, this was her home now, and no one was going to make her leave it.

She looked at Heath and noticed his eyes narrowed with a question.

"I'm fine, Dad. Besides, I've got Hammy and Maggie nearby, and I've got the best watchdog in the world."

"And you have Sweet Karma."

Nikki knew what her dad was referring to.

"We'll call you later today. Love you."

"Love you, too, Dad. Give Mom and Christopher a hug for me."

Nikki clicked the phone off and looked at Heath, who now looked more relaxed.

"Not quite neighborly pounding on my door early in the morning and wanting to get in."

"I was worried about you... concerned, I mean. A woman all by herself with God knows what kind of miscreants playing havoc with the property owners here."

"I can take care of myself, Heath Winters."

"I'm sure you can, Nikki McKay." He looked at her pensively. "I'm sure you can."

Realizing she was standing there barefoot, in her pink robe, and probably looking a fright with her red hair disheveled from sleeping, she excused herself.

"I'll be right back. Barney, stay here."

She ran up the stairs, taking two at a time. Walking into the bathroom, she immediately took in her appearance in the mirror.

"Yikes!" she whispered.

She combed out her hair and tied it up in a topknot, then washed her face, brushed her teeth, and swigged some mouthwash. Entering her bedroom, she undid her robe and threw on a pair of pink sweatpants and a white sweatshirt. Forgoing her usual pink bunny slippers, she slipped on her sneakers and rushed down the stairs.

Heath stood in the kitchen, leaning against the counter and enjoying a cup of coffee.

"Well, make yourself at home, why don't you?"

"I assumed you'd offer me one."

"You and your stepbrother appear to assume too much... and wrongly."

"Lance?" Heath looked puzzled.

"Forget it." Nikki waved her hand in dismissal. "Now, why have you darkened my doorstep this morning?" She had mixed feelings about him being there, looking so comfortable.

Heath seemed amused by her caustic tone. Turning, he opened a kitchen cabinet, pulled out a coffee cup, and filled it, then handed it to her. "Here... I think you need this more than me. Are you always so grouchy in the morning?"

"I'm only ill-tempered when someone wakes me up pounding on my door."

"Good to know."

What the hell did he mean by that?

She looked at the coffee cup he shoved into her hand. "I put brown sugar and cream in mine." As she moved toward the refrigerator to get the cream, he blocked her way.

"Please, allow me. After all, I was the one who disturbed her Royal Highness."

He was becoming more infuriating by the second. She was trying to come up with some sassy comment.

"One or two?"

"What?"

"One or two... lumps of brown sugar?"

"Oh, two." She stopped herself from saying please or thank you. He was the one with bad manners, not her

"You're welcome." He handed the cup back to her. "I think you were going to say thank you, right?"

Nikki rolled her eyes and moved to the other side of the kitchen island, maintaining a distance between them.

"Are you going to tell me or what?"

"Oh...why I'm here?"

"Yes!" She looked exasperated. "Why are you here?"

"Let's sit down. You look frazzled."

Here he was in *her* house, making *her* coffee, and inviting *her* to sit down. She ground her teeth as he led her to *her* sofa. Audacity was the first word that popped into her mind.

Barney followed them into the room and obediently laid down at Heath's feet.

What the hell?!

"Let me start at the beginning."

"*Please* do," she snarked.

He smiled as if facing a petulant child.

"I received a call from the county sheriff and a deputy in the middle of the night... well, around four in the morning. It was right after a homeowner heard noises at his boathouse and went down to check. He doesn't have the lighting system you have, so he was able to sneak down there in the darkness with only a flashlight. He heard whispers and things being moved around. There was a lookout in a boat on the far side of the boathouse, who didn't see the owner coming. Opening the boathouse side door, the homeowner shone his flashlight on them. I can imagine they crapped in their pants. Two of them took off through the opened overhead, which faced the lake, while the third one threw a heavy-duty wrench at the homeowner, striking him on the side of his head, then rushed past and knocked him down. All three hopped into the waiting boat and took off."

"And the owner?"

"He's okay, only bad cut on the side of his head. I think his pride was wounded since he couldn't catch one and turn him in. Said they were all around males around sixteen."

"The owner is lucky." Nikki shook her head in dismay. "His injury could have been much worse."

"You asked why I'm here."

"Yes."

"The Sheriff got another report of a theft, which must have happened an hour earlier, from the owner, elderly neighbor Mr. Jensen. He lives next door to the Hardy's. The Jensens had turned in early, but they have an old dog who needs to be let out during the night. When Mr. Jensen opened the door for the dog, he noticed their boathouse door was open. Mr. Jensen was sure he had closed it, and when he checked, he could see someone had been in there. Most of his fishing rods and tackle were missing.

"Mrs. Jensen called Maggie Hardy to let her know. She was worried about her husband, who was so upset about the break-in and losing his fishing equipment. Hammy Hardy went over there to be with them and to calm Mr. Jensen down."

Nikki was still waiting to hear why Heath came to her home.

"When the Sheriff called me to tell me about the thefts, I hopped in my car to check on the Jensens. I felt bad about him losing his things. When I got there, Hammy was sitting with Mr. Jensen, who was still totally shaken up. Mrs. Jensen's concern for her husband was written all over her face. Hammy pulled me aside and told me he was going to stay there for a while and asked if would I mind looking in on you to make sure everything was okay."

"Ahh... so Hammy asked you." Nikki smiled. "Of course. He and Maggie have always watched out for my family and me, and he knows I'm here alone... except for Barney."

Barney's ears twitched, hearing his name.

Nikki took a sip of her coffee.

"Obviously, Hammy called my dad as well."

Heath nodded in agreement, then rose from the sofa.

"Another cup?"

"Yes, please," she answered, holding back her sassiness. Watching as he moved about the kitchen, he looked up to see her staring at him. She abruptly looked away.

He brought the fresh cup to her and joined her on the sofa again, only closer. His proximity was troubling, although Barney didn't seem to mind. Once again, he was lying at Heath's feet.

She kicked off her sneakers and drew her legs up, tucking her toes under her.

The silence was deafening.

She had a gazillion questions running around in her head, but she picked one.

"When did you move to Spring Lake?"

"Several years ago."

Hm. He offered no more information.

"Been here before... in Spring Lake?"

"Yes." He realized he was being evasive, but his personal life was off limits in so many ways. He changed the subject. "Are you hungry?"

"What?" She certainly didn't expect him to ask her that. "Are you going to cook in *my* kitchen now?"

He shrugged.

"Heath Winters, you are what some would call a weird duck. You come over here to check on me, make me coffee, then when I try to make conversation, you put up a wall."

He sat quietly, obviously trying to come up with an answer to appease her.

"I'm a very private person, not at all like my stepbrother... but I am honest. What you see is what you get. I have a very small circle of friends, probably can count them on one hand."

"Why?"

"Personal reasons, and by that, I mean no more questions."

"I'll tell you what, how about you ask me a question, then I'll ask you one. If you don't want to answer, simply say *off limits*."

She could tell his curiosity was piqued.

"Okay. Me first."

She was about to debate whose turn should be first but relinquished.

"Have at it, Mr. Winters."

"We'll start with an easy one. How old are you?"

"Thirty-three... almost thirty-four. How old are you?"

"Thirty-six. Married? Engaged?"

"No. Recently widowed."

He seemed surprised by her answer.

"What about you... are you married or involved?"

Who could be partnered with an irritating curmudgeon like him?

She saw his slight hesitation.

"No... never married." Evading again, he reached down to pat Barney's head, trying to throw her off-course.

"How old is your dog?"

"Barney is seven, but at times acts like he's still a puppy."

She smiled warmly at Barney.

She added, "He's my best friend. Do you have pets?"

"No, not now. I did when I was young, though. Kids?"

"Yes, my son, Christopher." There was her smile again. "He's four and the love of my life."

She saw a look of wistfulness come over his face. What would it be like to have a connection with someone and consider them the love of their life? Maybe he had once.

"I take it you don't have children, Heath."

"None. Are you a working mom?"

Nikki almost laughed out loud.

"All moms work, some at home and some outside of home." She wanted to be totally honest with Heath. "I have a teaching degree and taught for six years before I had Christopher. My plan is to go back to the things I love to do. Teaching... or writing. I was a high school English teacher and the administrator for the school's newspaper and yearbook."

"Writing?"

"Hold it, Buster. My turn to ask a question. What do you do... other than run into people either with your body or your car?"

He grinned at her sarcasm, then rubbed his forehead in an obvious delaying tactic to come up with an ambiguous answer.

"I'm a carpenter of sorts... kind of like a handyman."

"Oh! I'm sure there's plenty of people around the lake who use your talents."

"Is that a leading question?"

It was her turn to shrug.

"Yes, I've done some jobs around the lake, if that's what you're asking."

Listening to their back and forth, Barney's eyes went from Nikki to Heath as they spoke, a verbal tennis match.

She remembered something from what he told her earlier. He must live around or near the lake. Otherwise, why would the Sheriff have contacted him?

"Back to what I wanted to ask before...writing? What kind?"

"Yes. I love to write. Poetry, fiction, short stories, romance, mystery, and more recently, kid's stories. Christopher was my inspiration. During college, I published a book of poetry." She was intentionally giving him more information than he asked, hoping he would do the same.

As she was about to ask another question, her stomach growled.

"You're hungry. Come on. We can *both* cook something up in *your* kitchen." He took her hand, pulling her off the sofa, and electric shocks traveled up her arm. When she looked into his eyes, he turned away.

Did he feel what she felt?

Releasing her hand, he walked toward the kitchen, with Barney following him.

What gives?

Nikki raised her hands in disbelief and joined them in the kitchen.

Heath opened the refrigerator, pulled out several things, then went through the cabinets.

"I thought this was going to be a *we* thing, that *we* were cooking."

"Okay,"—he stepped back from the counter—"what shall *we* make?"

"Bacon, eggs, and grits."

"Grits?" He made a face.

"Don't knock it until you try it, especially how I make them. You work on the bacon."

"Yes, chef!" He saluted her and opened the bacon.

Thirty minutes later, they sat on the deck, enjoying their breakfast of bacon, eggs, savory grits, fresh fruit, and more coffee. Barney enjoyed his scrambled eggs and bacon.

"Well?"

"Well, what?"

"The grits..."

"Oh... I like them."

She raised her cup to her lips and murmured, "Told you so," before taking a sip.

"I'll help you with the dishes before I leave, but I also want to check around your boathouse for any signs you might have had unwanted visitors."

"You think they might have tried..." Nikki expression was serious.

"If they did, the light would have scared them off when it switched on. It covers all the way past the end of the pier."

"How do you know that?"

There was his infamous shrug again.

The Fish Fairy? The baseball cap?

She'd look like a fool if she asked if it hadn't been him.

Nikki, Heath, and Barney walked down to the boathouse after cleaning up in the kitchen. All was good, nothing disturbed in or around the boathouse.

As he pulled out of the drive, he waved and called out, "See ya' around Barney... you too, Nikki."

Smart ass!

She brushed off a pang of regret at his leaving.

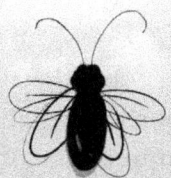

12

Nikki called her parents to fill them in on everything... well, almost everything. Until her mom asked about Heath. *How did she...* Maggie must have noticed Heath's vehicle parked on the drive and how long he was there and mentioned it to Sophia.

"Isn't he the same guy you ran into in town? I think you called him a Neanderthal," Sophia asked.

"He ran into me... both times, Mom. And yes, he's one and the same."

"It was nice he looked in on you, Nikki."

Nikki could sense her mom was reading far more into it than there actually was.

"We had coffee, then went down to check around the boathouse to see if anything was amiss. If anyone had tried, the security lights would've discouraged them."

Sophia knew her daughter well enough to grasp Nikki was leaving out a lot. Sophia was a firm believer in Godwinks and hoped this was one.

"You alluded he was ill-mannered and bad-tempered. Seems he might not be what you first thought. Am I right?"

"He's... complicated. I was grateful he stopped by, even though he pounded on my door so early this morning. I thought by engaging him in conversation, I'd get to know him better, but he's very evasive when I ask him questions. Not sure if he's hiding something, or he values his privacy to the nth degree."

"What did Barney do when he was there?"

"Hah! Barney followed him around and sat at his feet." Nikki looked over at Barney. At the mention of his name, he lifted his head. 'You talkin' about me?'

"Barney has good instincts. Maybe when you met in town, Heath might have been having a bad day. We all have them."

"Barney has his instincts, and I have mine. Heath Winters is carrying around a chip on his shoulder about something."

Sophia knew better than to pursue the conversation and moved on to talk about Christopher and what he was doing in preschool.

Ending the call with her mom, Nikki went upstairs. She hadn't showered yet, so she headed into the bathroom. Tomorrow, she would work on the boats. Today would be for relaxing and maybe catching a nap out on the deck later. After showering and dressing, she straightened the bed. Her writing pad on the nightstand coaxed her. Picking it up, she read the notes she had jotted down previously. Not liking what she wrote, she tore the sheet out of the pad and crumpled and tossed it in the nearby waste basket.

Bringing the pad with her downstairs, she made herself another cup of coffee. She smiled as she remembered Heath preparing her cup earlier. It was kind of him to check on her, even though it was at the request of Hammy. Maybe her first impression of him was all wrong, and he simply was a very private person who'd had a bad day they met. She's certainly had some bad days, particularly when it had something to do with Peter or his family.

Peter's sister Pamela caused several adverse issues in their marriage. She preyed on Peter's inabilities, inciting him against Nikki. One such provocation was when Peter and Nikki married, and she opted to keep her maiden name while teaching. She would change it later when they had children. Looking back, she wondered if she had delayed changing her name to Forester because of her instincts about Peter—his irresponsibility and his lack of commitment.

When Christopher was born, he was given his father's last name, Forester. Peter kept pushing Nikki to change her name. She'd stalled him, but Pamela had kept provoking.

Since Peter was dead now, she had no plans to change her last name. However, there was no way was she would change Christopher's last name from Forester. If she did, the proverbial shit would hit the fan with the Forester family.

Nikki sat on the chaise lounge on the deck with her pen and pad in hand, Barney nestled beside her. She tried to juggle the pad on her lap, hold her pen and reach for her coffee.

"Barney, I should have brought my laptop with me. It would be a lot easier."

His eyes twitched as if in agreement.

She set the pad and pen down on the deck beside her and pulled out her phone.

"Hi, Mom! Could you remember to bring my laptop with you when you drive up in a couple of weeks?"

There was silence.

"Mom?"

"I might as well tell you."

"Tell me what?"

"We were going to surprise you and come up next weekend. We'd drive up on Friday afternoon and come back here on Sunday afternoon."

"Mom, that would be great!"

"Your father doesn't have any meetings with clients on Friday, and Christopher gets out of preschool at two, but it's a surprise for him. Plus, it's a break for your dad. Tax season is wrapped up for the first quarter, and he won't have another full load until September for the third quarter."

Sean McKay's tax accounting firm had flourished over the past ten years, allowing him to expand his staff and giving him the opportunity to have some downtime. He could also work remotely when he wanted.

"I'll bring your laptop with us. Is there anything else you can think of you'd need?"

"Not right now, but if I do, I'll message it to you."

"Did you call Trey Westin, the man handling Peter's estate?"

"I spoke to him yesterday and told him I would call him today about meeting up."

"What did you decide?"

"I'll meet with him, but not here at the house or in town. Down the road in Kingston."

"Oh! There's a cute little fifties diner there. Your dad and I have been there. It's right across from the courthouse on the main square."

"I'll check it out online with my phone. Could be a good spot to meet up with him."

"Remember, hush-hush to Christopher about the trip next weekend."

"Will do, Mom. I can't wait to see him... and you and dad, of course."

Nikki disconnected the call and looked up the diner in Kingston on her phone. After reading about it, she scrolled through her recent calls, then called Westin.

"Hello, Westin here."

"Mr. Westin, this is Nikki McKay." She rushed on before she'd change her mind. "I've decided to meet with you."

"Great! When and where?"

"Does tomorrow work for you? Preferably around noon?" She knew it would be a three-hour drive for him and figured they'd have a brief meeting, and he'd need to turn around and head back another three hours to his office afterward.

"Where?"

"The Kingston Diner. I'll message you with the address."

Silence.

"Kingston? It's a long drive."

"You wanted this meeting, Mr. Westin."

"Yes. I'll be there... at the Kingston Diner... at noon."

"See you then." Nikki clicked off the call, and Barney looked up at her. "He must really need to meet with me, Barney, to drive three hours to see me, then three hours back."

Nikki settled back in her seat, lifting her face to the sun. She was happy her folks were arriving on Friday, and she'd have time with Christopher. There were still things she needed to do around the lakehouse and the property, like painting the shutters, cleaning out and repairing the gutters, and rolling the compost, but the house was ready for their visit. She'd tackle what needed to be done most over the next few days and leave the rest to do after they left.

A short while later, Hammy's golf cart was coming down path along the shoreline, with Maggie riding shotgun. They parked on the side of the house and came up the stairs.

"Hey, Kiddo, we heard you're having company this weekend."

"You heard right. I can't wait."

"We thought it would be a good idea to get together Friday night at Morton's for their special fish fry. After the long drive, it would be nice to sit down and be waited on. Your folks haven't seen the restaurant since it's been renovated."

"I had the same idea. I guess I better call and make reservations, though. It was getting pretty crowded the other night. I'll stop in tomorrow while I'm out and make reservations for six guests... for six-thirty, okay?"

"Fine by us. We'll meet you there at six-thirty."

"How's Mr. Jensen doing?"

"Poor guy. I thought he was going to have a stroke. He'd recently cleaned up his boathouse and restocked his tackle. His grandkids are due to come up soon, and he wanted to take them out fishing."

"After Heath heard what happened, he brought a bunch of his own tackle over to Mr. Jensen to use," Maggie piped up.

"No kidding." Nikki was awestruck. Heath Winters was indeed an enigma.

"We have to make a run into town. Need anything?"

Nikki shook her head.

"Out of curiosity, what do you know about Heath?"

Maggie and Hammy looked at one another.

"Nothing much. Keeps to himself mostly."

"Can't keep to himself too much if the Sheriff and the Deputy call him when things happen around here."

"Probably because he does a lot of work around town, and they want him to keep an ear out for any scuttlebutt on who might be burglarizing the houses and boathouses."

Nikki had the innate feeling they knew more than what they told her.

"Where's his place?"

Some hemming and hawing between Maggie and Hammy.

"Just yonder down the lake, I think," Hammy finally answered.

"We better get going, Hammy. Got lots of errands to run. See ya later, Nikki."

They were gone before she could ask more questions.

"Just when you think you know someone, you don't know them," she told Barney.

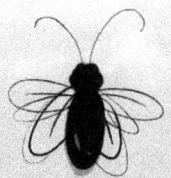

13

Nikki rose early, feeling rested and full of energy. Christopher would be here in a couple of days. Barney picked up on the excitement running through her body.

After showering, she put on dress jeans, a purple pullover sweater, and wedged denim sandals. She fashioned her hair into a twist in the back, with tendrils of loose hair at the sides.

"I don't want sophisticated Mr. Westin to think I'm some country bumpkin," she told Barney.

She had a light breakfast of yogurt and fruit. Feeling guilty at the look Barney gave her, she poured kibble into his bowl and added some beef broth. Nikki remembered yesterday's breakfast with Heath. The man was a conundrum. People appeared to honor his wishes for privacy, including Maggie and Hammy.

Wandering down to the boathouse, there was no sign of anything out of place. She had slept so soundly last evening, she wouldn't have noticed if the light had switched on or if a boat had been at the dock.

It was shortly after eleven when Nikki locked up the lakehouse, hopped in her car, stopped for gas on the state route, and proceeded to Kingston with Barney as her co-pilot. She arrived in Kingston and immediately found the diner her mother had told he about across from the courthouse. After parking and lowering the car windows a bit for Barney, she was about to get out of her car when she spotted Heath leaving the diner. He was with two uniformed men she assumed were the county sheriff and a deputy. They crossed the street and walked up the steps into the courthouse.

Heath Winters was becoming more of a mystery each day.

Nikki exited her car and went into the diner. Trey Westin was already seated and had several folders laid out on the table and rose from his chair when he saw her enter the diner. She guessed him to be in his late thirties. He stood around six feet, had thick dark brown hair, and hazel eyes surrounded by heavy-rimmed glasses. His build was that of a runner or cyclist, not an ounce of fat on him. If her mother got hold of him, she would force-feed him for sure.

"Nikki... McKay?"

"Yes."

He looked relieved. Nikki couldn't help but notice the look of admiration on his face. She saw he was ringless when he reached out to shake her hand.

"Right on time. Would you like coffee or water...?"

"Coffee is fine."

He motioned to the waitress, who was dressed in fifties attire, complete with a poodle skirt, saddle shoes, bobby socks, and snapping her gum.

"What'll you have, folks?"

"The lady and I will have coffee for now. We'll order lunch in a couple of minutes."

"Terrific!" The waitress winked at Trey and went to get their coffees.

Nikki was wondering what his reaction was to the diner. She didn't need to wonder long.

"This place is a hoot! Thanks for suggesting it."

"My mom thought it would be a good place to meet up."

The waitress quickly brought their coffees, then left just as quickly when they weren't ready to order yet.

"Shall we discuss business or eat first? Your choice."

"Business, please."

"Good."

He shuffled the folders around and opened one while Nikki added cream and sugar to her coffee. He took his black.

"We'll start with Peter's trust fund set up by his grandparents. After several disbursements were made from the fund per the instructions of his grandparents and requested by Peter, there is a sizable balance to which any and all heirs of Peter's would be entitled. If Peter had died with no heirs or if his heirs passed before the rest of the disbursements were made, the remaining balance in the trust fund would go to Peter's sister, Pamela. Peter was due a final lump sum disbursement of the remaining balance on his next birthday, July fifth of this year."

Nikki was letting his words sink in.

"Um... how sizeable is this fund?"

"Originally, it was almost two million dollars. Peter had taken several disbursements when they were due him. The remaining balance is somewhere over one million dollars now."

"I'm sorry... could you repeat that?"

He repeated the amount and waited for her response.

"So, let me get this straight. My son and I are entitled to the balance of the fund on July fifth of this year?"

"Yes, so long as you're both alive. Otherwise, it goes to Peter's sister." Trey looked at her to see if she comprehended what he told her.

Nikki nodded.

Trey closed the folder and opened another one.

"Now, as to Peter's personal estate, he had a will and trust prepared prior to your marriage. In both documents, it clearly states if Peter was married at the time of his death, his wife would inherit his assets. Should there be any children born as issue of the marriage and if his wife preceded him in death, the child or children, as the case may be, would inherit his assets. If said child or children were minors, a trust fund would be set up for incremental disbursements at designated ages. Disbursements would be made at the discretion of the named trust administrator. If Peter never married, then his parents are the beneficiaries. It's how he set everything up."

"There's just the house asset as far as I know."

"Peter had the house listed as an asset, as well as a downtown condo he purchased eight years ago. There's also an insurance policy, but it's being held up due to an investigation."

Nikki took a deep breath. Condo? An investigation?

Trey could see she was troubled. "You didn't know about the condo, did you?"

Nikki shook her head. "I'm not sure. He had a condo when I met him. We lived in it for a short while. Then he wanted to buy a house, but he told me he sold the condo to pay for the house." It was so confusing.

Didn't he sell the condo when he told her he did?

"No." She looked him straight in his eyes behind his glasses. "I have no knowledge of a condo. And what investigation?" Nikki could feel her hair standing on end, and she was sure Trey could sense her anger rising to the surface.

"The car accident... the insurance company is fully investigating, particularly since there were other deaths involved."

"Other deaths? Besides Peter's?"

"The woman in the car with him was a couple of months pregnant and died in the crash."

"Oh my God!"

"From your reaction, you didn't know. I thought maybe you might have heard something from Peter's parents."

"No. Since I moved out of the house, and even before, we didn't really communicate. They never seemed interested in developing a family connection with me, their grandchild, or my family."

"I've met them and understand what you're saying. Just so we are clear, I'm representing the trust fund set up by his grandparents and his estate. In no way am I representing his parents or his sister. When I presented them with copies of Peter's estate documents, they tried to get me to disregard them and not contact you."

Nikki closed her eyes. Looking up at Trey, she said, "That doesn't surprise me in the least."

Trey reached across the table and touched her hand. "I've run into all kinds of people, but the Foresters take the cake. I'm here to help you any way I can, Miss McKay, to get what you and your son are entitled to receive."

She felt comfortable with him. He wasn't at all what she had imagined. That's twice she had misjudged someone in the past week.

"Please call me Nikki."

He smiled. "Then you must call me Trey."

Nikki nodded.

"Let's eat." He moved the folders to the side and pushed a menu toward her. "I'm starved, and it smells awesome in here."

Nikki knew he was trying to change the course of the conversation to calm her after hearing the accident details—details yet to be fully investigated. Was there something else to be uncovered?

Nikki ordered a turkey BLT, and Trey ordered the meatloaf. They both ordered malteds. Nikki chose chocolate while Trey got strawberry. Nikki thought for sure he would order a plain vanilla. There she was again... misjudging.

Trey avoided talking any further about Peter's estate. Instead, he commented about the décor in the diner. They discussed the black-and-white tiled floors, the red and chrome soda bar with red vinyl-covered swivel stools, and the wise-cracking, gum-snapping waitresses. Someone put a coin in the jukebox, and Elvis crooned a love song.

When the bill came, the waitress handed it immediately to Trey as if it had been prearranged. He passed his credit card to her, and she brought it to the cashier.

"Thank you... Trey."

"My pleasure, Nikki."

The waitress returned with his receipt. After signing the diner's copy, he laid down a crisp twenty-dollar bill under it. He saw her watching him.

"I always leave cash. Otherwise, if I add it to the bill, the tip is taxed."

She felt a warm fuzzy feeling from him.

"I best be going. Barney, my dog, is waiting in the car, and you need to get on the road. Sorry it's a distance for you."

"It was well worth it to meet you. I'll probably need to meet with you a few more times to finalize the documents. Your mother mentioned you may not be back until September. Next time, I'll arrange an overnight stay here in Kingston."

"Sounds good." For now, at least, Nikki didn't want to say exactly where she was staying.

Trey walked her to her car, where Barney let out a friendly bark.

"I'd better let him relieve himself over in the park. I notice they have dog waste stations," she commented, looking at the park around the courthouse.

"I'll join you after I put these files in my car. I need to stretch some before I head back."

Trey's Lincoln Navigator happened to be parked next to Nikki's SUV.

Nikki clipped a leash on Barney as he jumped out of her car. Trey came to her side and took her arm as they crossed the street. Just in case Barney needed to do more than water the trees, she retrieved a bag from the waste station. Walking through a colonnade into a lush green area with many ancient oaks, Barney was in his glory. Decisions! Decisions! Which one to choose?

She spied parents playing with their children, and Trey noticed her melancholy expression.

"How soon will you see your son again?"

"It wasn't supposed to be for a couple of weeks, but my parents decided to surprise both my son and me and come this weekend."

"But you know?"

"Mom told me today, but Christopher doesn't know. It's a secret." Nikki made a motion as of zipping her lips.

Trey laughed and made the same gesture.

With the long leash, Barney had found several trees needing to be watered. Each time they stopped to let Barney do his thing, they made small talk. Trey spoke openly and freely with her. She didn't have to pry anything out of him.

They walked back through the portico. At the curb, as they waited for traffic to clear, then he guided her with his arm around Nikki's back across the street to their cars. Barney obediently got into his favorite seat.

"Thank you again, Trey, for driving here to meet with me."

"It was a pleasure, Nikki. You're not at all what I expected."

"How so?" she questioned.

"I guess after meeting with the Foresters, I wasn't sure what to expect. It's been a pleasant surprise, though." He took her hand in both of his. "Take care, Nikki. I'll be in touch soon. If you have any questions... or need anything, call me." He reached into the breast pocket of his jacket for his business card and was about to hand it to her. Instead, he took out a pen and wrote another number on the back.

"It's my personal cell phone number... in case you need to reach me after hours."

"Thank you, Trey."

He helped her into her car. She shut her car door, then turned on the ignition and lowered her window all the way.

"Be safe on the drive back."

"I will. Talk to you soon."

Nikki fastened her seatbelt and pulled away with a smile, unaware Heath was watching her from the courthouse steps.

He wasn't the only one.

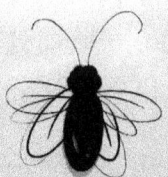

14

On her way back to the lakehouse, she took a side road around the lake and went through town. She pulled into Morton's Restaurant and Bar at the marina and saw Frank near the door.

"Hey, Frank!" she said while giving him a hug.

"Hi, Nikki. What are you up to?"

She used her father's old joke. "Five foot two and not an inch taller."

Frank laughed heartily. "You've got your father's wit for sure."

"Speaking of my father... Mom and Dad are coming up on Friday with Christopher to spend the weekend. I wanted to make reservations for six-thirty for the fish fry if it's okay."

"Sure is. Party of four?"

"Nope. Maggie and Hammy are joining us. So, party of six."

"I guess you heard about the break-ins. Not good press for our town."

"Yes, I heard. Dad called early yesterday, and Heath came by to check on me."

"He did, did he? Heath is one of a kind." Frank seemed to know things about Heath.

"What's his story? He seems so overly tight-lipped."

"Why are you asking, Nikki? Gotta crush on him?"

"Oh, Lord, no, Frank! Curious is all. He runs hot and cold."

He hesitated a moment before responding. "Heath has a lot to be cold about. It's all I'm going to say. You'll have to get to know him better to find out more."

"How can I get to know him better if he's always so incorrigibly evasive when I ask him questions?"

Frank looked at her with kind eyes. "Show him he can trust you. Don't ask him any more questions. Let him tell you in his own time when he knows he can put his faith in you."

By the time she reached the lakehouse, it was late in the afternoon, and the work she needed to do around the exterior of the house would have to wait until tomorrow. She had forgotten to check to see if there was paint for the green shutters on the house. If not, she'd have to call the hardware store in town to see if they carried it in stock.

Sitting at the counter in the kitchen, she punched in the number to call Dan Burke. He picked up the call on the second ring.

"Hi, Dan! It's Nikki!"

"Hello, Nikki! What can I do for you?"

"I've got shutters needing a repaint. They're in pretty good shape, but the color has faded. I think the last time we painted them was over five years ago."

Nikki heard him rustling some papers. "Yep... it was exactly five years ago. I've got the invoice right here in my file. And I know we've got the color in stock if you want to go with the same green."

"Yes. I'm not sure how many gallons I'll need, and I'm pretty sure I'll need some new brushes and pans."

"Why don't you use a paint sprayer? It's a lot easier. I can loan you one to use."

"Are you sure, Dan? I've never used one before."

"Hold on, Nikki." She heard him talking to someone in the store. "Tommy is here. He said he'll bring the paint, brushes, and pans over to you and also the paint sprayer. He'll show you how to use the sprayer. He's an expert at it."

"I hate to impose."

"No imposition. That's what we do here in Spring Lake. We take care of our own. I'll send him with the same amount of paint cans as the last time. If you need more, I have it. If you don't use all the cans, you can return them or keep one for touch-up. Whatever works for you."

"I'll give you my credit card number..."

"Nope. Your dad called this morning. I have his card on file with special instructions to use it while you're fixing the place up. Direct orders from your dad."

It didn't surprise Nikki that her dad would call Dan and probably the rest of the people in town they dealt with to help her.

"When do you think Tommy will drop everything off?"

Nikki heard him talking to Tommy in the background.

"He'll be there early tomorrow morning and said you better have the coffee ready."

Nikki laughed. "Tell him I will, and if he wants breakfast, I'll make it for him."

"Hell! If I weren't tied up at the store, I'd come, too!"

After hanging up with Dan, Nikki walked onto the deck. Barney had returned from visiting his favorite trees and galloped up the steps.

The days were getting longer. The sunlight glittered on the waves rolling up on shore. The lake was fairly calm after all the busy activities on it during the day, but she knew the still waters could be deceptive. As in life, below the composed surface, there could be treacherous currents.

The revelations of today played havoc with her inner peace. Something troubled her, and she couldn't put her finger on it. Knowing Peter hadn't been alone in the car didn't shock her. She had known he was seeing several women, even while they were married —no surprise there—but finding out his companion was pregnant... had it been his child she was carrying?

Remembering what Trey told her about the inheritance and what it could mean for not only her but for Christopher interrupted her thoughts. Whatever she inherited, she would use as backup and put the bulk into an account for Christopher. She knew how expensive college was and wanted to afford her son every opportunity she could when the time came. She was able-bodied and could go back to teaching... or pursue her writing if possible.

Turning from the railing on the deck, Nikki called to Barney, "Time for dinner."

He jumped up from his prone position at her side and followed her into the house.

Later, she placed a call to her folks and talked with Christopher, then told her mom about what transpired during her meeting with Trey Westin. To say Sophia was dumbfounded would say the least.

Ending the call, Nikki went to shower, then climbed into bed, with Barney assuming his place on the floor at the foot of the bed. She plumped her pillows, then took out the writing pad and jotted a few lines. Her eyes quickly drew heavy, so she switched off the lamp and nestled down under the covers.

A few minutes later, Barney hopped up on the bed, resting his head on the pillow beside hers.

A friend forever. A guardian always.

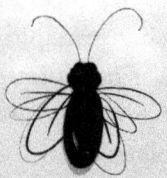

15

Nikki had set her alarm for six-thirty. Tommy was due to drop off her painting supplies early, and she wanted to make sure she had at least one cup of coffee in her before he arrived.

When the alarm sounded on her phone, she had to blink several times before her eyes would focus. Looking to her left and found Barney staring at her. She reached over and stroked his head.

"Hope I didn't disturb you last night. I had a bunch of crazy dreams."

Making her way to the bathroom, Nikki washed up, then dressed in a pair of old denim shorts and a t-shirt. She pulled her hair up into a ponytail, coiled it, and pinned it, then looked in the mirror.

"Not bad for a thirty-something mom. What do you say, Barney?" As if he understood what she asked, he barked once and gave her his legendary smile. Finishing up, she and Barney went down to the kitchen, where she switched on the coffeemaker and pulled the creamer out of the fridge. When she took her first sip from her coffee cup, she let out a deep, "Ahh."

She counted how many shutters would need to be painted and surmised it would take four days minimum to complete the painting.

Nikki pondered her plan of action for the shutters. She wanted to make it as easy as possible without having to move the ladder too many times. She figured she'd attack one side of the house at a time. Since she wouldn't be finished by the time her parents arrived, she'd complete the painting once they left.

Satisfied with her plan, she got up to get another cup of coffee. Pulling out the makings for breakfast, she set about cooking up a storm. Half an hour later, she heard a vehicle come over the crest of the drive. It was Tommy in his tricked-out jeep. He turned into the drive and shut off the engine.

"Breakfast ready? I'm famished!" he called out when he saw Nikki come out of the back door

"Almost ready. Just need you to sit down at the table out on the deck."

"Great!" Tommy grabbed a few of the things from his jeep and jauntily walked down to the house, where Barney greeted him enthusiastically.

"Yeah... I know." Tommy reached into his jacket pocket and pulled out a dog biscuit. "Compliments of Dan."

Barney gave his most pleading look at Nikki. When she nodded, he lifted his eyes to Tommy, who offered it to him. Barney gingerly took the biscuit out of Tommy's fingers. Within a nano-second, the biscuit had disappeared.

"Looks as if Barney's as hungry as you," Nikki joked.

While eating breakfast out on the deck, Nikki laid out her plans on how she would be painting the shutters.

"Nope," Tommy said. "Not going to happen."

"Why not?"

"First of all, the best way to paint them is to get up on a ladder and take each shutter down. Your dad has each of them secured with fasteners on the back. The fasteners simply unlock when you depress them in a certain spot with a long screwdriver. The tricky part is trying to carry a shutter down while on the ladder."

"Oh."

"Then you hang them on a cord."

"What cord?"

"The cord you're going to string from... that tree to that tree," he said, pointing to two trees on the side of the house.

"And..."

"Then you'll lay a plastic tarp down under the hanging shutters." He could see she was puzzled. "Nikki, I brought paint sprayers with me. Dan basically shoved them in my hands and told me to show you how to use them. Once you have the shutters hanging on the cord, you use the paint sprayer. Simple. The paint is fast drying, so by the time we get the next group of shutters down, the first batch can be put back up."

"What's this 'we' you mentioned?"

"I'm doing it with you."

"No, you're not. You have a job. I don't want you to miss work. You can't be helping me, and even if you did, I'd pay you."

"I'm working this coming weekend. Today and tomorrow are my days off. And if you want to pay me, make sure it's with food. You're a great cook."

"Tommy, I can't let you..."

He held up his hands. "You're not letting me. I insist on doing it. A while back, when I was out of work, your dad found out and gave me a list of things to do around here. It's why I know about the shutters. Guess who installed them. Your mom fed me while I worked here. Your folks are very generous, not just with money, but with their care and concern. Please take my help as a thank you. Besides, you want to get the shutters done before they arrive on Friday... right?"

Nikki agreed but told him if something came up and they needed him at the marina, he had to go there.

"Okay. Now let's get to work. We have shutters to paint."

After stringing a cord between the two trees and laying down a plastic tarp under the line, Tommy began his "Paint Spraying 101 Class." Nikki caught on fast. As a well-oiled machine, with Tommy insisting on being the one on the ladder and handing down each shutter one at a time, they got all the shutters from one side of the house ready to hang and paint.

At half-past twelve, they broke for lunch. Nikki made sandwiches, and they walked down to the dock to eat them picnic-style. Barney lucked out, snarfing crumbs and bits of lunch meat tossed his way.

As the weather was warming up, it was apparent more boats were out on the lake, fishing, waterskiing, and tubing. Jet skis doubled in number throughout the season. There were those who disregarded the rules and the no-wake buoys, coming too close to the pier and kicking up spray on Nikki and Tommy. To Barney's annoyance, who had been resting quietly. Others, like the blue fifteen-foot runabout, cruised slowly further out, maintaining their distance and abiding by the restrictions.

Instead of lying back down after his dousing from the boat spray, Barney ambled out to the edge of the wooden pier and sat down, his gaze pointed in one direction.

Tommy took his napkin, sprinkled some water from his water bottle on it, and reached over to Nikki, swiping at a smear of green paint.

"I think you're turning into a Leprechaun, Lass," he said, mimicking an Irish brogue.

Nikki burst out in laughter.

The noise of the runabout went full throttle, catching their attention, and sped out to the center of the lake.

"Wonder what Heath is up to."

"What?"

"Heath Winters. That's his boat, Winters Remorse."

"Are you sure?"

"Oh, yeah. He and I worked on it a couple of times. I'd know it anywhere."

"Odd name."

"Maybe. Let's get back to it, Lass. We're burning daylight."

Nikki sensed a bit of evasiveness. What was it about Heath Winters that garnered such loyalty from people?

Nikki and Tommy worked until five o'clock, then spent the next half hour cleaning up the paint supplies and equipment for use the next day. They'd finished the backside facing east and the side facing south. Tomorrow they would tackle the lake side of the house facing west and the remaining side facing north.

She wanted to make him dinner, but he politely declined, saying he was meeting up with friends for game night. He needed to get home to shower, dress and head to the marina bar.

"Game night?"

"On Wednesdays, you check in at the bar at seven and sign up for a game controller. It's a first come, first served basis. I usually hang with three friends, and we play as a team."

"What kind of games?"

"Sometimes it's trivia, sometimes, scrabble or something else. You never know what the game is for the night until you get there. They use two of the big screens to show what's going on between the players."

"Sounds like fun."

"You should come tonight."

"I'll take a pass tonight. I need to clean up, and I have things to do around the house to get ready for my folks and Christopher. I'll try to come next week to see what it's all about."

"If you do, I'm grabbing you for my team."

"Thanks for your help... and expertise today, Tommy."

"Like I said... no problem. I'll see you at seven-thirty tomorrow morning."

"Coffee and breakfast will be ready."

Tommy surprised her by giving her a hug, then turned and walked up the hill to his jeep.

Nikki made a simple meal for herself and put together a bowl of kibble for Barney. She sat out on the deck, every bone in her body complaining. It was a tiring day but a productive one.

She picked up her phone and called her parent's number. It rang three times, then a little voice answered.

"Hi, Mommy! Grandma said it was you!"

"Yes, it's me! How was your day today?"

"I made a mess."

"You made a mess? How?"

"We fingerpainted at school. Then Joey put some paint on me, and I put some on him, and..."

"Oh, I see. I'm sure your teacher didn't appreciate what you boys did."

"I said I was sorry. Joey did, too. We had to promise not to do it again."

Nikki smiled as she remembered Tommy gently wiping the side of her cheek to remove the green paint.

Christopher went on to tell her about his plants growing in the backyard. Hearing him yawn, she said goodnight and wished him sweet dreams.

Sophia took the phone and told Nikki her dad was going to tuck Christopher in for the night.

"I heard you had help with the shutters. I can't wait to see them when we come up," Sophia whispered.

Word traveled fast... again.

"I couldn't have done it without Tommy. He's a godsend. I didn't know he was the one who installed them."

"Yes. He had fallen on really hard times. His mom, Addy, was diagnosed with breast cancer and was undergoing chemotherapy. The family depended on both parents' salaries, and with her not being able to work, it was tough. His dad couldn't take the pressure and started drinking heavily. One day, he just flat-out disappeared, leaving Addy and their three kids, the eldest being Tommy. He was twenty-three. He has two younger sisters. Tommy had been working at the lumber mill in the Kingston area, but there was a big layoff. Maggie and Hammy told us about it. We needed the old shutters replaced, and he was available. I guess we forgot to tell you. At the time, you were going through some rough spots and was pregnant with the mini-Picasso."

Nikki snickered as she had a vision of Christopher dressed in a painter's smock, a beret on his head, a brush in one hand, and a palette in the other.

"Not funny, Nikki," her mother joked. "He had paint in every nook and cranny when I picked him up at school. And his hair was a rainbow of colors."

Nikki couldn't hold it in and laughed so hard, she had tears in her eyes. Her mother joined in.

"I told your dad what you told me about your meeting with Mr. Westin yesterday. He's as flabbergasted as I am."

"I'm still trying to take it all in. I get now why I felt such animosity from the Foresters at the memorial service. It might also explain the mystery couple standing with them. The girlfriend's parents?"

"Nikki, if they were her parents, they'd be more upset with the Foresters than with you. Doesn't make sense."

"I suppose your right, but nothing about this makes sense. I'm hoping Trey can get it all sorted out with the estate and the insurance, and we can be done with it... once and for all. It can't happen soon enough for me."

The angst in Nikki's voice was obvious

"Think about Friday when you get to see your mini-Picasso." Her mom chuckled. "Seriously, Nikki, it was funny."

"I can imagine. Remind me to make sure all the paint I'm using is out of reach. Getting back to Tommy, have you heard anything more about his mom?"

"Maggie told me a few months ago Addy was doing well. She went back to work on a part-time basis, helping Frank out with the accounting at the marina. Her husband is still missing. Tommy's sisters are both married with kids. One lives in Spring Lake, and the other lives in Kingston."

"I'm glad to hear she is doing well. It's difficult to imagine how a man can walk out on his wife, especially when she's going through such an ordeal."

"It happens. They say you can tell the heart of a person by how much they give it to others."

Nikki knew what Sophia meant.

They talked more about Christopher and how surprised he would be on Friday. After hanging up, she headed upstairs to shower, then climbed into bed. No writing tonight. Barney looked tired, too.

Sleep came easily for both of them.

16

Clear skies and pleasant temperatures welcomed the day.
As promised, Tommy was there on time, and Nikki had coffee and breakfast ready for him out on the deck.

"We should be able to wrap this project up today from the looks of it. No bad weather to worry about." A gentle breeze blew a lock of his shaggy red hair across his forehead, and he pushed it back. Whipping out a red bandanna from his hip pocket, he tied it around his head. He smiled at her with a big grin and hazel eyes. He looked much younger than his twenty-eight years when he smiled. Yet, for his age, he had shouldered responsibilities few would have done.

"Tommy, I was thinking. After my folks leave on Sunday, I'd like to discuss repairing the wooden pier with you."

"Sure. I'd be glad to help you do it."

"This time, though, I'll pay you, and I won't take no for an answer. It's going to entail ripping out some of the decking, and I'm not sure if the pilings have any damage from the ice over the winter."

"Does payment include meals?" There was his heart-melting grin again.

"Of course, and the use of waders. I'm sure we're going to need them. The water temperature is still a bit too cold for me."

"Not a problem for me. I'm used to it."

With breakfast out of the way, they set about finishing up the shutter project. At noon, they sat out on the cement pier, having lunch. Tommy rose and walked out onto the wooden deck, knelt, and inspected what he could see without getting into the water.

"Your opinion, Dr. Caldwell? Is the patient salvageable? Or do we have to bury it?"

He laughed.

"It's quite salvageable. Pilings look good." Tommy pointed out the areas needing substructure work and made a few suggestions as to how to make the last section portable, making it easy to remove during the winter and store next to the boathouse.

"Geesh, Tommy. You really know your stuff."

"Yeah, from working at the mill, the marina, and jobs around the lake."

Nikki wanted to ask if he had done work for Heath but held back. Tommy might get the wrong idea. She also couldn't fathom why she was so obsessed with finding out more about Mr. Heath Winters.

After they hung the last group of shutters, they both surveyed what they had accomplished.

"Looking good, Nikki."

Nikki nodded and turned to see Tommy staring at her. He looked away quickly... too quickly.

"What's next on your list besides the pier?"

"The gutters. I went up on the ladder the other day to check them out. They need cleaning, and while up there, I noticed one section needs to be reinforced. The brackets were loose."

"You were on the ladder up there?"

"Yes, Tommy. I'm not some fragile flower, you know. I can manage things."

"But you should always have a spotter when up on a ladder. If you lose your footing or the ladder moves on soft ground, you could fall. If you're alone, who would know? You could lie on the ground for hours or days, and the animals would come at night and eat you for dinner." His grin betrayed him.

Nikki burst out laughing. "You have quite an imagination there, Tommy."

"Oh, Nikki," he said while shaking his head, "You have no idea what I can imagine."

There was silence between them... for less than a minute. Barney barked and ran down to the pier, hoping to scare off a speedboat coming too close to shore.

"Let's get this equipment cleaned up and put away."

"What about the paint sprayers? I need to get them back to Dan."

"Dan said for you to keep them for now. He figured you'd have other spraying to do while you're here."

"He's awesome. There are two gallons of paint we didn't use. I'm going to keep one for touch-up and return the other one. I need to go into town tomorrow to pick up some fresh produce and other groceries before my folks arrive, and I'll drop it off with Dan then."

They cleaned up around the area they used for the paint spraying and made sure the tools and supplies were put away. Tommy rolled up the tarp and put it in the back of his jeep.

"You turned down dinner last evening. How about tonight? I have a T-bone with your name on it."

It didn't take him but a nano-second to agree.

"I need to wash up. Okay, if I use the lower-level bathroom?"

"Yes! Of course."

Tommy made a trip out to his jeep and retrieved a duffle bag. While he was downstairs in the big addition her parents had attached to the lower level of the house, Nikki raced through the kitchen, seasoning the steaks and putting potatoes in the oven to bake, then laid out what she needed to make a salad. She'd make the salad after she cleaned up.

Barney watched the copper-headed whirlwind, his head swiveling as she moved about. She took the stairs two at a time, and seconds later, he could hear the shower running, while he sat just outside the bathroom door. A short while later, she was back in the kitchen, her long hair damp and exceedingly curly, pulled back with a ribbon.

Nikki was cutting tomatoes to add to the chopped lettuce when

Tommy entered the kitchen. He must have had a change of clothes in his bag... and a seductive aftershave. The scruff on his face was trimmed lightly. Nikki couldn't help wondering...

She quickly turned her attention to what she was doing before she cut herself.

"What can I help with? I know my way around the kitchen, thanks to my mom."

"You can pour us something to drink. What's your pleasure?"

No sooner were the words out of her mouth than she realized how they sounded.

Tommy must have recognized her dilemma and took the lead.

"Beer is fine with me. And you?"

Nikki was grateful Tommy was so tuned into her.

"Beer for me, too."

It was obvious Tommy had spent quite a bit of time here and knew exactly where the beers were kept in the back refrigerator.

"Glasses?" He called out.

"Nope, bottles."

Nikki placed the steaks on the grill she had lit earlier. They sizzled, sending up mouthwatering aromas. Tommy brought two bottles out to the deck and handed one to her.

"Cheers." They clinked their bottles together.

"Can you watch the steaks while I get the potatoes out of the oven?"

"Sure, but where're they going?"

"What?"

"The steaks... you want me to watch them. Are they trying to escape?"

His humor got to her. She laughed all the back to the kitchen.

Tommy checked the steaks, then walked to the edge of the deck and looked over the railing. "Hey, why don't we eat down on the patio?"

"I haven't eaten or even sat down there since... I don't remember when. Let's do it. I'll need help carrying plates and food down."

"Of course."

Fifteen minutes later, they were enjoying their dinner on the patio. Nikki took a moment to flip on the audio system, and "oldies but goodies" played softly.

"Sorry for the choice of music, but that's where my folks have it set."

"I actually like it. My mom plays it a lot."

"I was happy to hear your mom is doing well."

"Thank you. She's had good reports from the scans and is thrilled to be back at work, even if it is part-time. Working for Frank at the marina has its perks, too." Tommy cast Nikki a wink.

"Oh? You mean... Frank and your mom?"

"Yep. Frank's wife died over ten years ago from pancreatic cancer. He was by her side through it all. All cancer is bad, but some are worse than others. My mom and Frank grew up together in the same town and went through school together. They know each other's stories... their pasts. It helps when you know what someone has been through. It solidifies the relationship. If you can stand by someone who is going through hell, it gives strength to bond."

Nikki got quiet. Tommy instinctively knew she was thinking about her past and how it was impacting her today.

"What's your story, Nikki?"

"You mean my folks didn't share anything with you?"

"Not really. Heard bits and pieces. Figured you were in a marriage doomed from the beginning. Only met Peter once when he was up here. He certainly didn't make an effort to know anybody or anything here at Spring Lake. His mind appeared to be elsewhere."

"I realized that too late."

"Never too late. Nothing is ever too late. Changes can be made no matter when. It's up to you to follow the three Cs by Zig Ziglar."

She looked puzzled.

"You must make a choice to take a chance, or your life will never change."

"I certainly made a choice, a wrong one. Then I took a chance, and here I am now. My life has changed, admittedly for the better."

"If you hadn't made the first choice, you wouldn't have Christopher, right?"

Nikki smiled. "Right."

"You're a great mom, Nikki. You remind me of my mom... Oh, that came out all wrong. I certainly don't think of you like that... I better shut up before I dig myself a deeper hole. I apologize."

Nikki laughed as his face turned almost as red as his hair.

"It's fine, Tommy. I like being able to talk to you about my past and what's happening now. Us redheads need to stick together."

"What is happening now with you? Are you dating?"

"No. I've been asked out, but until recently, I hadn't been comfortable accepting. Of course, there are those determined to set me up with someone they know. So far, I've been able to steer clear of potential blind dates."

"I saw you dancing with Lance Winters and later with Heath."

"Lance asked me to dance to apologize for his previous behavior at the grocery store. Heath wanted to dance with me to badmouth his stepbrother. Believe me, there's nothing going on there... with either of them."

Nikki was surprised when Tommy said, "Heath is a good guy. His stepbrother... not so much. He's a player."

"Hm... Heath seems to have a fan club around Spring Lake."

Nikki waited for Tommy to comment, but he clammed up.

"Care to walk down to the pier? The sky is clear, and it's a three-quarter moon. Should be pretty out there."

Nikki could tell when conversation about Heath was being sidelined.

"Sure."

They stepped off the patio and walked toward the dock.

"Oh, wait... I left the lantern on the table."

"Leave it. Hang onto me. I have cat eyes. When we get closer to the boathouse, the lights will go on."

Nikki took his arm as Barney rushed past them to the dock.

When the boathouse lights clicked on, Nikki asked, "I suppose you installed those lights too?"

"Yes, Ma'am."

They reached the dock and sat down before the light on the boathouse switched off. The running lights and the hum of motors gave credence that there were quite a number of boats out on the lake.

The moon did indeed cast a brighter light. The temperature cooled, and Nikki shivered. Tommy pulled her close and put his arms around her. They sat huddled, not saying anything, and listened to the loons in a nearby marsh. As the minutes passed, the running lights on the boats appeared to perform a dance out on the water, and the lulling drone of boat motors made Nikki's eyelids tired. She rested her head against Tommy, who pulled her in tighter. Inhaling the sensual scent of his aftershave, fell into a peaceful slumber. They drifted off, both tired from the work they had done.

Her phone rang in her back pocket, rousing them. She wasn't sure how long they had been sitting there.

"Hello!"

"Hi, Honey. It's Mom. Christopher wanted to wish you sweet dreams."

"Sure, put him on."

Tommy motioned to Nikki he would move away so she could have a private conversation. Nikki shook her head and mouthed, "No." She held the phone out so Tommy could hear. He leaned in close to listen.

"Hi, Mommy."

"Hello, Sweetheart. What's happening there?"

"Grandma said there's no school tomorrow, and she's taking me shopping or something. I have to go to bed early."

"Oh, that's right. No school. Guess you'll have a fun day with Grandma and Grandpa then."

"Yeah. Grandma said we could stop for ice cream somewhere."

"Be good. I'll talk to you tomorrow. Sweet dreams, Christopher."

"Sweet dreams, Mommy."

Sophia took the phone and shooed Christopher off to bed. Grandpa Sean followed him up the stairs to his bedroom to read him a story.

"Okay. He's out of earshot. The little dickens caught me packing some of his clothes today. I told him I was checking to see the sizes because he was outgrowing everything, and we needed to go clothes shopping for him."

"Damn, you're good, Mom. Fast on your feet."

"You have to be with him. How'd the painting go today? Maggie said you and Tommy were almost finished."

Nikki wondered how or when Maggie saw them.

"Yes, all done. Tommy is going to give me a hand next week with the gutters. Several brackets need to be tightened or replaced."

"Well, I better go now. I have some packing of my own to do. Oh, give Tommy a hug for me and tell him thank you. Good night, Honey." Sophia hung up before Nikki could ask her how she knew Tommy was there.

When she looked over at him, he was trying to hold in his laughter.

"Nikki, moms are clairvoyant and every day increasingly so. You'll be the same way. Watch and see."

She smiled up at him. "It was wonderful having you help me the past couple of days and sharing your free time with me. Although I know you really would rather have been with your friends doing something fun."

"There's no place I'd rather be. God's honest truth."

There was no doubt in her mind he meant it.

"You have things to get ready for tomorrow. I'm going to head home after I help you clean up the patio." Tommy put his arm around her as they walked up the hill to the house. Barney trailed slightly behind them, checking out a few trees along the way. They picked up their dishes and carried everything up to the kitchen on trays. Tommy offered to help with the dishes, but Nikki insisted she'd do it.

"I'll see you soon. Remember, next week, we'll get started on those gutters."

Hoisting his duffel bag strap over his shoulder, he put his arms around Nikki and hugged her. Pulling back, he kissed her on the forehead.

"Sweet dreams, Lass," he mimicked in an Irish brogue. He strolled up the flagstone walk to his jeep. Halfway up the hill, he turned toward her, threw a kiss, and continued to his car.

Nikki watched as the jeep pulled onto the road. Barney stood beside her as she murmured out loud.

"This cannot be happening. I'm too old for him. I certainly don't want to lead him on or hurt him. I need to set the record straight the next time we're together... alone." She looked at Barney as if seeking affirmation, and he cocked his head to the side.

Going down to the patio to make sure she didn't leave anything out for animals to get into, she laughed to herself, remembering what Tommy had said earlier. After cleaning up in the kitchen and locking the doors, she headed up to bed.

Tomorrow she'd see her little Christopher. Just thinking about him gave her a warm fuzzy feeling.

And she did indeed have the sweetest of dreams.

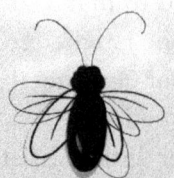

17

The sun rising behind the house cast its beams onto the lake. Nikki's bedroom grew brighter as the golden orb made its entrance to start the new day.

Nikki opened her eyes and smiled. Today would be special.

Within an hour, she had showered, dressed, and had a light breakfast. Barney sensed the excitement in her every move, particularly when she did a little cha-cha, listening to music while putting fresh linens on the bed in her parent's bedroom and on Christopher's bed in the bedroom nearest to hers.

She made sure there were fresh towels in the bathrooms, including the one in the downstairs addition. When she walked into the bathroom, she inhaled the scent of Tommy's aftershave, bringing back memories of the previous day... and evening. She knew she had to be careful with his feelings. Hers as well. She wasn't sure exactly what she felt. Was it an infatuation? A worried line creased her forehead. Her mind used their ages as an excuse—she was almost six years older than him. Both had a past filled with heartache and abandonment, so maybe she was drawn to him because he understood her history and vice versa.

And she had a child... a wonderful child.

While painting the shutters, they shared bits and pieces of their lives. Tommy spoke of his nieces and nephews and how much he enjoyed spending time with them. They ranged in age from six months to five years.

Would Christopher like Tommy? She was sure he would. Who wouldn't like Tommy?

Barney's bark let her know he needed to be let out to visit his trees.

"Oh! Sorry, Barney." She opened the slider of the lower-level living room area, and he took off, inspecting the first tree he found. "Come to the door upstairs when you're finished." Many times, she thought to herself how people must think she's nuts for conversing with her dog as if he understood.

Closing and locking the slider, she went to the laundry room and loaded the towels Tommy had used and the towels she had gathered from her bathroom into the washer, added detergent, and started the wash cycle.

Back in the kitchen, she made sure everything was ready and went over the list she had on the counter. She'd pick up fresh fruit and veggies at the grocery. A quick stop at the bait shop for mealworms, then onto the liquor store to get what she needed for her mom's favorite aperitif made with Aperol. She also needed to drop off the unused paint at the hardware store.

Nikki locked the back door and walked up the hill to her car.

Barney was still roaming about checking his trees.

"Come on, Barney. We're going to town." Hearing they were "going for a ride," his tail wagged double-time. Leaping into the co-pilot's seat, he barked, almost to say, "Let's go!"

In her mind, she was laying out where she would stop first. Tommy had put the unused paint can in the back of her car. Best to drop it off first at the hardware store, then on to the liquor store and the grocery. Last stop would be the bait and tackle.

She pulled in at the hardware store. "Okay, Barney, you can come with." After removing the paint can from the back of the car, she opened the car door for Barney. Instead of heading for the entrance to the hardware store, he headed for a man walking toward them—

Heath Winters. His head down, looking at a sheaf of papers on a clipboard, he looked up in surprise when Barney greeted him with a bark. Heath looked at Barney, then at Nikki. At first, he looked happy to see them, then a scowl appeared.

"Don't be knocking my dog down now, Mr. Winters. I know how good you are at doing that," she said in a joking manner.

His manner was far from cordial. "Wouldn't think of it, Miss McKay."

Whoa... cold. What bee got in his bonnet?

Nikki lugged the paint can to the door. Heath did show some courtesy and opened it for her. Barney followed closely with his head down. He was disappointed Heath hadn't made an effort to greet him.

Dan saw her walk in and ran around the corner to take the heavy can from her. After placing it on the counter, he gave Nikki a big bear hug.

"Got the shutters all done?"

"Yes, thank you. With Tommy's help, of course. I wanted to bring the paint sprayers back, but Tommy said you told him I should hang on to them for a bit since I might need them for more repairs and painting."

"Yep. I have no use for them now. If I need them, I know where I can get them. What's next on your list of repairs?"

"After my folks leave on Sunday, we'll start on the gutters."

"We?"

"Yes. Tommy insisted on helping me. I think he's scared I'll fall off the ladder and break my neck."

"Well, he does have a point. You should never climb a ladder by yourself. Always have someone there just as a precaution."

"I know. I'm positive Tommy will make sure I do."

"He's quite a guy, isn't he?"

"He sure is. I don't know how I would have completed the shutters so quickly without him."

Nikki turned to see Heath staring at her and not the kind of stare to make you feel good.

"Do you need anything for the work on the gutters next week?" Dan asked.

"Maybe a couple sets of brackets. Tommy said you would know what kind."

"Sure." Dan headed down an aisle.

Nikki avoided looking in Heath's direction, but she could still feel his icy stare.

"Here you go, Nikki. I'll put it on the charge card we have on file."

"Thanks, Dan."

She turned to leave, but Dan stopped her. "Hold up." He reached behind the counter and tossed Barney a biscuit.

Barney woofed it down.

"What do you say, Barney?"

He barked once and wagged his tail wildly.

Dan laughed. As she turned, she noticed Heath smiling, but he abruptly looked away when he saw her watching him.

What is it with Him? He's as unpredictable as the weather.

Nikki headed for the door with her purchases, with Barney following, totally missing Heath giving Barney a pat on the head.

She made a quick stop at the liquor store for the Aperol, then headed to the grocery. She was moving so fast, she almost did wheelies coming around the corners in the aisles.

"Are you trying out for the Indy 500 this coming weekend?"

Tommy stood in front of her cart.

"Oh... sorry. I've been rushing around to make sure I have everything."

His smile warmed her, especially after the cold reception from Heath.

Tommy looked in her cart. "Looks like you boosted the town's economy a bit."

"I know. I picked up Christopher's favorite things... goldfish crackers, cereal, ice cream. More than I should since they'll only be here until noon on Sunday."

"I'm sure it'll keep until he's back for the summer." He noticed packets of seeds. "Planting a garden?"

"Once he's back, but I'll have him start with some little peat pots I picked up in the produce section, then we'll transplant them in the ground later."

"We could build a little raised box garden for him. I can run an irrigation line to it."

She looked at him in amazement. "Really... you could?"

"Yep. It's an easy project."

"I don't want to impose... and I'll pay you for the supplies and your time... no refusal."

"We can start on it right after we get the gutters done."

"Thanks, Tommy." She hugged him. His arms went around her, and he pulled her tight against him.

"My pleasure."

Recognizing they were drawing the attention of shoppers and store clerks, they separated.

When Nikki was checking out, the cashier gave her the stink-eye. Nikki surmised she had a crush on Tommy. Shaking it off, she walked to her car and loaded her groceries.

Pulling into the bait and tackle shop, she was greeted by Suzie McConnell, who was out front sweeping the entryway.

"Hey, Nikki! What brings you to town, as if I didn't know? Your dad called and asked if we'd tell you to get some minnows when you stopped by."

Now how did dad know I'd be going to the bait shop? Must be "Dad" instinct.

Nikki let Barney out of the car and gave Suzie a hug when she reached her.

"Yep, and mealworms. I thought I'd take Christopher out to Seminary Bay. The water is so clear there. Even if we don't catch anything, he'd be able to see the fish."

"I guess I don't have to remind you to make sure he has his vest on."

"Of course! He'll be excited to see the new one you gave him."

As they entered the shop, Big Steve came around from behind the counter and gave her a bear hug.

"Be right back. I'll get your minnows for you."

"Mealworms, too," Suzie added.

A few minutes later, Big Steve returned with a minnow bucket and a carton of mealworms. Barney sniffed all around the bucket Steve set on the floor.

"On the card, Nikki?"

"Yes, please."

Big Steve handed her a receipt and pulled a dog biscuit out of a jar on the counter. He flipped it purposely in the air toward Barney, who went up on his hind legs and snatched it mid-air.

"Impressive, Barney," Suzie praised.

"See you later, I hope. We'll be around town this weekend."

"It'd be great seeing your folks and Christopher. Make sure to stop in."

Nikki nodded and picked up the minnow bucket and container of mealworms.

She and Barney had just reached her car when she saw Heath arrive with another cold look. Opening the side passenger door, she set the bucket on the floor to prevent it from spilling. Her irritation toward Heath was evident when she abruptly shifted the bucket and water sloshed out.

Why is he acting so cold?

As Barney hopped up into his co-pilot seat, Nikki turned angrily at Heath.

"What is your problem, Heath Winters?"

"Problem?" He was taken aback by her anger. "What problem?"

"You've been looking at me like you want to drown me or something. One day, you're nice and the next, you're nasty with your icy looks. What the hell did I do to provoke such animosity?"

Suzie stepped out on the sidewalk. "Tell her, Heath. Tell her what you 'think' she did."

"Suzie, stay out of this."

"The hell I will." Suzie looked over at Nikki. "He thinks you're shacking up with Tommy Caldwell."

"What!"

From the look on Heath's reddening face, what Suzie said was true. He believed she and Tommy were doing the horizontal tango.

She looked Heath square in the eye, her emerald eyes lit with fire.

"You can't possibly think that. Tommy is a friend, a good friend. I admit I have feelings for him, but in no way are we intimate. At this point in my life, and with the upheavals I've had recently, I'd be crazy to get involved with Tommy or anyone else, for that matter. Tommy has been helping me out at the house, trying to get it ready for summer when I can spend some quality time with my little boy and not have to work around the house. You and your Neanderthal thinking are so off-base, it's pathetic."

Suzie stood by the door, arms crossed, taking it all in and watching Heath for a reaction.

When he said nothing, Suzie did. She turned to Nikki.

"Tommy told me straight out he was there at your house to help you. He feels indebted to your parents for all they did for him and his family five years ago. And yes, Tommy has feelings for you, but he knows your history and is aware of what you want for your little boy. Neither of you is in a position to become more than what you are to each other... at least for now." Suzie turn to Heath. "Anyway, what gives you the right to be so judgmental? Don't judge her by what happened to you in the past. What Nikki does with her life is not your concern... unless..." She left the rest of her diatribe hanging out there for Heath and Nikki to figure out.

Barney sat in his seat, his eyes moving from Suzie to Nikki to Heath.

Silence. Suzie shook her head and walked back into the shop.

Nikki walked around to her driver's side and put her hand on the door handle to leave.

"Nikki... wait," Heath asked, no longer with the coldness in his voice or face. "I'm sorry I jumped to the wrong conclusion. It's just we had such a good time at your house after the incident at your neighbors, and I thought we could be... friends. Then I passed by while out on my boat the other day and saw you and Tommy on the dock, and you looked... involved."

"You should have asked me, Heath. I would have told you exactly what I said. I have a lot going on you don't know about and probably wouldn't understand. Tommy knows most and accepts me and our friendship as it is. I'd be lying if I said I didn't have strong feelings for him, but those feelings aren't at the stage of becoming more. They may never be. Besides, there's an age difference. I'd never want to be known as a cougar," she jested.

She saw a glimmer of a smile, but it in no way excused his behavior. His silence troubled her. It was evident from what Suzie had hinted at earlier that Heath had been burned badly in a relationship, and he was bitter. So bitter, in fact, he measured every relationship by the hash marks of the broken one.

When he came to check on her after the neighbor's break-in, his attitude had been different. He'd been open and friendly, although somewhat tentative. He warmed up as they talked, but his continued elusiveness was a stalling point. Now, he sat in judgment without knowing the facts. She wondered what the heck he was thinking in that thick skull of his.

She waited for him to say something... anything, but nothing. Opening the car door, she slid into the driver's seat.

"Heath, you'll never find truth or any peace by locking yourself up."

Nikki closed her door and pulled away.

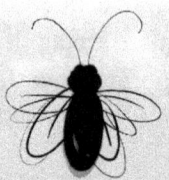

18

Nikki was determined not to let Heath Winters affect her frame of mind. Her parents and Christopher would be arriving soon, and she wanted to erase any negative feelings from her mind.

Returning home, she unloaded everything from her car, and stowed it away, then walked out onto the deck. The throaty rumble of a large, high-powered boat echoed from the lake, one of the boats the marina rented out. Nikki guessed the occupants weren't familiar with the lake and had drifted dangerously close to shore. There were large boulders under the water in some areas, and orange-and-white buoys marked their locations for boats to avoid them. One such buoy was a short distance from the other side of the boathouse, and it bumped along the side of the boat, and Nikki heard the boat's hull scraping. The boat reversed quickly, went into full throttle, and spun around, kicking up waves and wakes onto the shore.

"Idiots."

Agreeing, Barney barked twice.

Nikki paced about the house, going from room to room, upstairs, downstairs, out on the deck, and down to the patio. She was antsy. She looked at her watch at least a dozen times, calculating the time her parents left their home to when they should arrive... barring any delays on the road. It was Friday, after all. The upside was they left in the morning before the traffic got heavy.

She took binoculars and scanned the inlet road from the deck. Maybe she'd see their car on the road, and she could meet them on the driveway at the top of the hill.

As she peered through the lenses, she saw the big boat was now anchored near the bridge over the inlet. The guys fishing off the bridge didn't appreciate the boat anchored there. She couldn't hear what they were saying to the people on the boat, but from their expressions and the arm waving, they were upset.

Barney jumped up fast, bumping Nikki. She looked at him.

"What, Barney?"

He barked once, then ran down the steps off the deck and up the hill on the side of the house.

Nikki smiled. She knew.

Tossing the binoculars on the chair next to her, she ran through the house and sped up the flagstone walkway. Her parent's car crested the hill and came to a stop on the driveway.

"Mommy! Surprise!" Christopher shouted through the open window of the back seat.

Nikki's heart beat triple time.

Opening the car door, she unbuckled Christopher from his car seat, then lifted him out of the car and hugged him tight, twirling around with him in her arms. She didn't know she was crying until Christopher asked if she was sad.

"No, Honey. Mommy is happy." Nikki wiped away the tears. "Really, really happy." She smothered him with kisses and held him close.

"What about us," her dad teased.

They hugged tight. The kind where you knew you were deeply loved.

Her mom stood back and looked at the house. "Wow. Everything looks great. The shutters... the grounds... Nikki you worked your butt off. I can tell."

"I had help, as you know."

They unloaded the car and made their way to the house. Christopher was wearing his own backpack, and in his left hand, he carried a mini suitcase containing his precious Legos. Barney sidled up to him and walked protectively beside him all the way down the steep walkway, with Christopher's right hand holding on to his dog collar.

When they entered the house, her mom noticed the bouquet of fresh flowers on the table.

"Daffodils! I love them!"

"I remember." Nikki came up behind her mom and put her arms around her. "I saw them at the market and knew I had to get them for you."

Her mom turned around and hugged her. "You're one in a million, Kiddo!"

Once unloaded, unpacked, and able to relax, they all sat out on the deck.

"You know, every spring, when we opened up the house, we had to clean up around the property, and I wondered if there was ever an end to the repairs and upkeep." Her dad admired the work she'd done and applauded her efforts. "It's so nice to just sit and enjoy."

"When Tommy gave us a hand, it was a huge help," Sophia commented.

Nikki remembered how many times she had wanted to join them, but Peter always demanded she stayed home to attend corporate functions.

"I'm sorry I wasn't here more often to help."

"Honey, we understood your situation. And when you were pregnant with Christopher, we certainly didn't want you doing anything too strenuous or dangerous. Which reminds me... stay off ladders unless someone is with you."

"Sounds like someone spilled the beans."

Her mom shrugged.

Changing the subject, Nikki told them about the dinner reservations, adding Maggie and Hammy would be joining them.

Sophia was ecstatic. "I can't wait to catch up with Maggie."

"Seriously, Mom? I know you talk to her on the phone just about every day. At least since I've been up here."

Another shrug from her mom.

Christopher had been below, walking around picking up sticks that had fallen from the trees overnight and whatever else caught his eye. Barney followed him closely, and when he ventured too far down the hill toward the shoreline, he gently herded him back up the hill away from the water. Nikki smiled at the relationship between Christopher and Barney. It was as if Christopher knew Barney was his protector.

They decided to have a light lunch since they were eagerly looking forward to their dinner at Morton's. As they sat out on the deck eating sandwiches and potato salad Nikki had gotten in the deli department at the grocery, Sophia asked Christopher if he had something special to give to his mommy.

Christopher went back into the house, came out with a paper, and handed it to Nikki. It was a drawing of Nikki, Barney, and him in a boat fishing, all three with their red hair.

"I made this for you in school."

"Oh, Christopher! I'm going to put this where I can see it every day."

Getting up, Nikki walked into the kitchen, took a magnet out of a drawer, and placed the picture Christopher had drawn on the refrigerator.

"I got a gold star, too, Mommy." Right next to his name, Christopher Forester, on the top of the paper was indeed a shiny gold star.

Nikki knelt down to hug him.

"I love it, and I love you for making it for me."

When Nikki and Christopher walked back out onto the deck, Sophia asked, "What did you think?"

"I think we have a Picasso prodigy in the family."

Her dad asked, "Have you pulled the boats down yet?"

"Only to the water's edge while I cleaned the boathouse. I didn't launch them yet. I thought I'd give you the honor, Captain." She saluted him.

"Tommy winterized them in the fall, and in April, he worked on them to make sure they were ready to use."

"Oh! I didn't know. He never mentioned it."

"That's Tommy. He does things without bragging about it."

"Like the security lighting?"

"Uh-huh."

"We're working on the gutters next week. And, yes, I won't be up on the ladder. He will."

Sean nodded as he watched his grandson meandering around.

"I think I'll go stretch my legs and walk down to the dock. I'll take Christopher with me." Leaving Nikki and her mom on the deck, he jogged down the steps.

"You want to talk about it?" her mom asked

"Talk about what? Peter's estate issue?"

"No, I know about that. I'm talking about the Tommy and Heath matter."

No sense in asking where she got her information. Nikki took a deep breath and gave her mother the details of the encounters with Tommy and Heath.

"It seems you have strong feelings toward Tommy, but you're smart enough to know it probably won't go any further. He knows it as well. Not to say I wouldn't mind it if it developed into something more. Your father and I consider him a second son... family in a way."

Nikki nodded in understanding.

"Heath, on the other hand... well, it's obvious he has issues. The brooding and moodiness. He hasn't released himself from the past. As long as he hangs onto it, there's no future. But I see how he's affected you."

"Mom, he's a knuckle-dragging Neanderthal with a bad attitude. We seem to be at odds every time we're near each other."

Sophia laughed.

"What's so funny."

"Remembering when I met your father. I thought the same thing about him. That man could get my blood boiling. His boldness and insolence at times whipped up my anger... and his chauvinism."

"Dad... chauvinistic?"

"Oh, yes. With his 'women can't do that' manner, my animosity toward him grew to the point, I almost threw something at him. But I remembered what my mother would say.

"What's that?"

"Don't give anyone the power over you by responding in the same negative way. Stay quiet and make them wonder."

Nikki nodded.

"It drives your father crazy when I go quiet. It also makes him leery of what I'm thinking and gives him time to think about what brought on my silence."

Nikki had to laugh. "And yet you married him."

"Of course, but it was after he had mellowed a bit and learned to respect me for what I could do, not only as a woman but also as a partner in a relationship."

"I sincerely doubt mellowing would be impossible for Heath Winters."

"Oh, you'd be surprised. Once he comes to his senses and realizes the past is there to learn from, not to hang onto, he'll have a different attitude, a positive one. It will include how he looks at you." Sophia could still the doubt in Nikki's eyes. "Nikki, if you are at all interested in developing a friendship... or more with Heath, you need to be still. Go about like nothing he says or does matters. Show him your independence and not just as a woman."

"Even if he did, as you say 'mellow,' us being more than friends would be out of the question."

"Are you sure?"

"Quite sure." Nikki turned away to watch her father and Christopher out on the dock, signaling she didn't want to say anything further about Heath Winters.

Sophia looked at her skeptically.

Sean McKay walked up the hill from the dock, carrying a giggling Christopher on his shoulders. Barney ran around them, stopping at one or two trees along the way. When they got to the bottom of the stairs going up to the deck, Sean set Christopher down, and he and Christopher walked up the stairs.

"Whew! I don't know if it's the altitude or that Christopher has put on a little weight, but I'm out of breath."

"Maybe it's a little of both, plus the fact Grandpa Sean has put on a bit of winter weight," Sophia teased.

"You can blame your good cooking, Honey." Sean patted his belly.

Sophia laughed. "Such a charmer you are, Sean McKay."

Nikki loved hearing her parents' banter. Deep down, she hoped she'd have someone with who she could tease goodheartedly.

Her cell phone rang, and taking it out of her back pocket, she answered.

"Hello."

"Hi, Nikki. It's Trey Westin."

"Hi, Trey."

"I wanted to check in with you. Did your folks and little boy arrive yet?

"Yes, they did. They arrived around noon, and we've been catching up."

The roar of a speedboat sounded from the lake. Nikki was sure he heard it and guessed they were near water.

"I won't keep you. Let's connect after the weekend and set up a day and time to meet. I have some papers to go over with you and also update you on the Foresters."

"The Foresters?"

"Yes, they've been calling every day, asking for information on the estate. With you being the primary beneficiary, I really can't share anything with them other than the basics. They're becoming a real pain in the ass. Pardon the language."

Nikki laughed. "I can well imagine."

"We'll discuss more when we get together. I'll plan to spend overnight at a hotel near wherever you are, so we won't be rushed."

Trey was upfront with her, so she decided to be as forthright with him.

"I'm staying at my family's lakehouse on Spring Lake."

From his prolonged silence, she guessed Trey was surprised she told him where she was.

"Trey?"

"Yes. I'm looking over some notes and writing down where you are. I'll call you on Monday. I'm glad your parents are there." The tone of his voice had changed, as if he was troubled.

"Okay, we'll talk then."

After the phone disconnected, Nikki looked concerned.

"What's wrong, Nikki?"

"I don't know. Trey seemed fine. Then when I told him where I was, he sounded different. He said he would stay overnight in a hotel close by."

"Maybe he thinks there isn't any place in the area to stay that's up to his standards," her dad commented.

"No, Trey's not like that. I think he would be fine no matter where he stayed. Maybe it's just my imagination, but I think he's not telling me something."

Nikki noticed Christopher had fallen asleep in Sophia's arms.

"I'll take him upstairs and put him in his bed." She gently lifted him in her arms and carried him up to his room. Laying him on the bed, she pulled a coverlet over him and tiptoed out of the room. When she went back out to the deck, both her parents had fallen asleep in their lounge chairs.

Might as well catch a couple of winks myself.

Nikki went back up the stairs to her room and climbed onto her bed. Barney followed suit.

Her mind was troubled, but she didn't know why.

Unbeknownst to all, a storm was brewing.

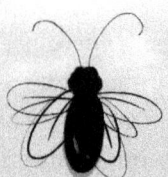

19

Nikki awoke to the rumbling of a motor down near their boat house and sounds coming from the kitchen downstairs. She jumped up and looked at the clock on the nightstand. Four-thirty. Barney had deserted her during her nap.

Racing down the stairs, she found her mom and Christopher sitting at the kitchen counter with his firefly jars lined up. Six of them. Sophia was threading fishing line through one of the holes on top.

Christopher saw her and said, "Look, Mommy. We have six of them to hang this summer."

"Oh, Christopher, they're beautiful!" she exclaimed, admiring the painting he had done on them. "I think there are unused shower hooks down in the tool room we can use to hang them."

Nikki heard the boat motor again.

"Is dad down at the boathouse?"

"Yes, and I told him not to get dirty, or he'll have to take a shower before we go to dinner this evening."

"I'll go check on him."

Sean had already winched the dinghy on its small trailer down the launch tracks and maneuvered it over to the other side of the dock.

"Motor starts fine, and there's plenty of gas. The little electric motor needs charging, though. We can charge it up tonight."

"Are you planning on launching the Bella Fortuna?"

"Sure... with your help, but we'll winch it back up before we go out tonight. We can leave the dinghy where it is. It's tied securely."

As her father released the lock on the winch, Nikki held tight to the lines as the boat trailer moved slowly down the tracks into the water. She was glad there was only a slight wind to struggle against. Once the boat was floating, she used the line to move it off the trailer and next to the farthest section of the pier. She tied it off, utilizing all the years of boat knot lessons her dad had given her and her brother.

"Good work, Nikki."

"Thanks, Dad. You taught me well."

Sean hopped down into the boat and pulled up the cowling covering the engine. Everything looked good. Leaving the cowling off, he went to the helm, inserted the key, and pressed the ignition. The engine started up and rumbled immediately. Sean smiled and looked up at Nikki standing on the pier.

"Tommy did good. You, too, from the looks of it."

"Dad, I can't take credit. I had planned to get it all cleaned up myself before you came, but I noticed it had already been done. Pretty sure it was Tommy."

Letting the boat idle for a while, he put the cowling back in place. He reached out for her hand and helped her jump into the boat. "Come sit." He patted the bench seat.

"What's up?"

"Your mother and I have been talking, and we're looking at slowing down and taking time for ourselves. Do some traveling and spend more time here. We've got enough qualified staff now to be able to do it."

"Dad, that sounds great. You and Mom deserve it."

"You sure?"

"Of course. To be quite honest, I've been thinking more and more about moving up here. Getting a place of my own. Going back to teaching... or writing. I'm sure Mom told you about what Trey said about Peter's estate. It would be easy for me to uproot and live here year-round, and at his age, I doubt it would even phase Christopher if we moved."

"Forget about getting your own place. Your place is here... unless, of course, you meet someone who knocks you totally off your feet, like your mom did to me and..."

Nikki rolled her eyes. "Dad, the thought is so ludicrous right now, I can't even imagine."

He laughed. "I can."

"Seriously?"

"Seriously. Now, let's get this boat back up in the boathouse, then we can get gussied up for dinner."

This time, Nikki handled the winch, lowering the trailer into the water under the boat and eyeballing the boat to make sure it was loaded straight. Her dad, using the ropes to guide it, moved the boat along through the water until it was as far atop the trailer as possible. As Nikki winched the trailer back up, the bow set itself firmly onto the keel roller, and nestled between the trailer bunks on the sides.

Nikki rushed over to the bow and hooked it to the winch line causing the trailer and boat to move in unison up the tracks. With the boat securely on the trailer in the boat house, Sean removed the drain plug to make sure there wasn't any water in the bilge, then set the plug on the captain's seat to remind him to put it back.

"Let's lock up here and get ready to go to town."

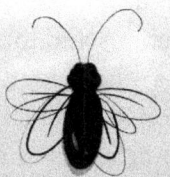

20

Up at the house, Christopher helped Sophia make up a dinner bowl for Barney, then put the bowl down on Barney's designated placemat.

"Sorry, Barney, you have to stay here tonight and guard the house."

Barney did his well-known head cock and proceeded to dive into his bowl.

Having washed up and applied minimal makeup, Nikki dug through her closet and drawers, choosing a dressy white t-shirt and a Bohemian style maxi skirt in sea foam green with a matching sweater. She slipped on her wedge sandals and did a quick check in the mirror.

"Not bad for a future soccer mom."

After letting Barney out for a tree inspection before they left for town, they made sure he had water in his bowl. Barney returned from his duties and sat by the door as his family left one by one. Nikki was the last one to leave the house and didn't hesitate to give him a gentle hug.

"You're in charge now, Barney. We won't be long."

She locked up and threw him a kiss through the window.

As she walked up the flagstone path, she heard the seemingly endless drone of boat engines. Traffic out on the lake had multiplied.

They drove her parent's car since Christopher's car seat was already in it, and Nikki made sure he was buckled in securely. Arriving at Morton's and finding a parking space was a test of patience. Hammy and Maggie were already outside the front door, and they waved and pointed to around the corner where the restaurant and bar staff parked.

Sean followed their directions and found an empty spot. Well, not totally empty. There was a chair with a big sign on it reading "Reserved for Christopher" on it. Sophia bust out laughing.

"It seems we have a celebrity in the car with us. Look, Christopher."

He angled upward, noticed the sign, and started laughing.

Hammy had hustled around to the parking area and removed the chair and sign.

"All yours!"

Pulling into the spot, Sean turned off the ignition and exited the car, throwing his arms around his buddy Hammy.

Maggie hugged Sophia as she left the car. "Now, where's the munchkin? I've got lots of hugs for him."

Nikki had unsnapped Christopher from his car seat and handed him over to Maggie, who covered him in hugs and kisses.

"My goodness, Christopher, you're getting so big!"

His giggles warmed Nikki's heart.

"Frank has a table all set for us, so let's head inside."

Frank Morton greeted them at the door. A beautiful woman with the most amazing hazel eyes and short red hair stood beside him. Frank hugged Sean and Sophia.

"So glad you could make it up here. I'd like you to meet Addy Caldwell. She's been a godsend to me here at the marina."

Addy smiled and shook hands, only to be engulfed in Sean's bear hug and then Sophia's.

"We're huggers, Addy," Sophia explained. "Hope you don't mind."

"Not at all. I'm a hugger, too."

Frank showed them to their table and made sure they had menus. One chair already had a booster seat for Christopher.

"What can I get you all to drink?"

The adults all ordered beer. Frank prompted Christopher, asking if he would like a cherry drink known as a Shirley Temple. He nodded after Nikki told him it was okay.

"Be right back with your drinks. Take your time looking over the menu. Sit. Relax."

Nikki watched as Maggie and Sophia talked, knowing full well there couldn't be much to catch up on since they spoke at least once a day, but far be it for her to comment. She admired that they communicated and shared their lives with one another as girlfriends do. Her girlfriends had dwindled down to nothing, thanks to Peter. His insistence she refrained from things such as 'girls' night out' or luncheons put a damper on her social life. Going shopping or out for an occasional lunch with her friends were in the category of not being acceptable for the up-and-coming young executive Peter had been at his company.

She fell for his ideology hook, line, and sinker, realizing too late, she no longer had friends to call and talk to.

If she moved to Spring Lake, she already had a list in her mind of who she would have in her friend's circle, people she knew who were genuine and caring. The more she thought about it, the more eager she became to set the wheels in motion for a move.

Addy Caldwell approached their table. "The waitstaff is bombarded this evening, so Frank asked if I would jump in and help. Have you decided on what you'd like?"

"Pretty sure we have," Sean responded. "Sophia, what would you like?"

"Definitely the fish special with the fries and coleslaw, please."

Sean told her he'd have the same. Hammy and Maggie added their fish specials to their order.

When it came to Nikki, she ordered the fried fish special as well and ordered Christopher his favorite fish sticks.

"Great! I'll put the order through to the kitchen. Can I get you anything else?"

Sean looked around the table. "No. I think we're all good. Thank you."

Smiling, Addy gathered the menus and headed to the kitchen.

Hammy looked over at Christopher. "So, what big plans do you have for tomorrow?"

"Mommy said she would take me out fishing if the weather is nice."

Hammy nodded. "I think I heard it was going to be fantastic weather tomorrow. I'll bet you'll catch some fish."

"We'll take the dinghy out and cruise the shoreline and maybe head over to Seminary Bay," Nikki added. "The water is crystal clear there."

"Good choice for a fishing spot."

Sophia looked concerned. "Are you sure you don't want to take out the big boat, Bella Fortuna?"

"No. The little one is fine for bobber fishing. And Christopher gets to try out his new rod and reel, and of course, his new boating vest."

"Well, just be careful. There's already been a lot of close calls out there on the lake this year. People just don't know how to handle their boats or follow regulations," Hammy said.

"Yeah. Did you see the big boat down near the inlet bridge? Surprised the fishermen didn't tar and feather him," Maggie commented.

"Had to be a newcomer. The boat is a rental from the marina."

Two servers brought out their plates of dinners. Addy stood near them.

"Remember, it's all you can eat tonight."

Maggie looked down at her plate and commented, "I don't know how I'll finish even this."

"Speak for yourself, Mags," Hammy teased.

Frank stopped by the table to ask how everything was. Between bites, they agreed the fish was great.

"Frank, did you rent out the big boat hanging around the inlet bridge?" Sean asked.

"No, not personally, but the owner has a berth he's leasing from us at the marina, and he rents it out to people. I've had complaints and sent him a message he had better inform his renters of the regulations or I'd have to cancel his dock privileges. Have you had problems, too?"

"The boat came close to shore, then full-throttled it out, sending up a large wake and multiple waves hitting the shoreline," Nikki answered. "Doused Tommy, me, and Barney while we were sitting on the dock. If we don't get a handle on these uneducated boaters, the erosion of the shoreline is going to increase."

"I'll send another message to the owner. If he doesn't respond, I'll contact the sheriff's water patrol. They'll stop the boat and insist they bring the boat into the marina. You can bet they won't like the fine they'll have to pay. I'll also make sure I give a lecture to the owner who rented his boat out. He's supposed to make sure anyone he rents to has a copy of the regulations before they go out on the water."

"Having a copy of the regulations doesn't mean they'll read them or abide by them," Hammy added.

Everyone at the table nodded in agreement.

Frank looked up and immediately had a broad smile on his face. "Hey, Heath! Surprised to see you here."

Nikki's head snapped around and made eye contact with Heath. Was there a slight upturn of his lips? Heath nodded hello to everyone, his gaze lingering on Nikki.

"Frank, do you have a couple of minutes? Need to discuss something with you."

"Sure." Frank bobbed his head toward the back area where he had his office.

After Frank and Heath left, Addy came by and passed around a special dessert menu.

"I hope you saved room for dessert. The chef came up with some really great ones for this evening."

As everyone was looking over the menu, Addy exclaimed, "Tommy!"

Tommy threw his arms around his mom. "Thought I'd surprise you. My buddies are hanging out in the bar."

"Tommy, please join us if you can. Have you eaten?" Sophia asked. "How about dessert?" Sophia rattled it off quickly as if he'd already said yes.

Nikki had to laugh.

"Careful, Tommy. My mom likes to fatten people up. She's always trying to do it to me."

"But it hasn't worked, has it?" her mom responded.

He smiled over at Nikki. "Don't mind if I do."

Whether it was planned, Sophia slid Christopher's chair closer to her and made room for Tommy to slide a chair between Nikki and Christopher.

Addy wrote down their dessert orders. Maggie and Hammy opted to share a blueberry pie à la mode, while Sean and Sophia chose to share a peach cobbler topped with vanilla ice cream. Nikki ordered a sundae for Christopher, then looked puzzled.

"I don't think I'll be able to eat a whole dessert. Tommy, will you share with me?"

"Sure."

"Your choice then. What looks good to you?"

Tommy knew everyone was waiting for his usual playful answer, but he decided to respond differently.

"I'm a chocolate lover, so how about the molten chocolate lava cake?"

Nikki was amazed. It was her favorite. She nodded to Addy, indicating it was her choice. Addy pocketed the pad with their orders, picked up the dessert menus, and left their table, turning slightly to give her son Tommy a wink.

Waiting for their desserts, conversation resumed about the seemingly unusual increase in boaters already out on the lake.

"It's still over two weeks until Memorial Day. People are hot to trot to get out on the lake either for fishing or skiing," Hammy exclaimed.

"Sophia and I were thinking about getting a jet ski to fill the empty space in the boathouse, but now I'm wondering just how safe it would be out on the lake with all those crazies out there," Sean shared.

"Why don't you use ours to see if you like it?" Maggie asked. "If you feel comfortable using it, maybe Tommy could put the word out for anyone thinking of selling theirs."

"Sure." Tommy nodded. "And I'll make sure it's in good working order."

Sophia and Sean looked at each other, then nodded. "Sounds like a good idea."

As their desserts arrived, Hammy noticed Sheriff Hansen and Deputy Parker walking through the restaurant and heading to the back office, followed closely by Dan Burke, owner of the hardware store and member of the town council.

Everyone at the table noticed as well, and everyone was wondering what was going on.

Tommy helped Christopher sit closer to the table, and he dove into his sundae with gusto.

As she moved the chocolate confection between her and Tommy, she said, "You first."

"Oh, no. Ladies first."

Nikki dug in with the same enthusiasm as Christopher did with his dessert. Melted chocolate oozed out after her spoon cut through the rich dark chocolate cake. Her taste buds screamed in ecstasy when the warmed chocolate hit them. She closed her eyes, savoring the experience.

Everyone at the table watched to see what her reaction was.

"Heaven," she said after enjoying the spoonful.

Addy had made sure there was an extra spoon, but as Tommy picked it up, Nikki had already put a heaping spoonful on her spoon and positioned it at Tommy's chin. He looked surprised at the amount.

"Your turn."

At the exact moment his mouth devoured the contents of the spoon held by Nikki, Heath walked by and did a doubletake. A dollop of chocolate had caught under Tommy's lower lip, and Nikki took her napkin to wipe it.

Christopher offered Tommy some of his sundae.

"Does the whole family think I need fattening up?" Those at the table laughed.

"No. Never. You're in great shape," Nikki responded.

21

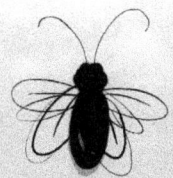

They finished their desserts and decided to move into the bar area to free up the table for those waiting in line for dinner.

Nikki held onto Christopher's hand, and when Tommy saw her maneuvering through a crush of people, he picked Christopher up on his shoulders. Christopher giggled.

"Okay, Christopher, you guide the way."

It warmed Nikki's heart to see Christopher and Tommy relate to each other. As they moved through the bar area, Tommy was greeted by several of his friends, particularly the females. Their group was shown to a large booth at the back of the bar area.

"Would you rather be with your friends?" Nikki asked Tommy.

"I'm just where I want to be."

As the band started playing, they ordered a round of drinks.

Sean nudged Sophia. "I'd love to dance the shoes off of my lovely wife this evening."

Sophia's smile lit up.

Nikki's parents and the Hardys got up to dance, leaving Nikki, Christopher, and Tommy at the table.

"Your parents are really special people."

"Yes, they are. They've been a huge help to me, supportive in every way possible."

"Isn't that the way it's supposed to be?"

"Some aren't as fortunate, and it affects their view of other people and the world." Thoughts of Heath came to mind.

"My mom has been my godsend throughout my life. When she became ill, I felt I was losing the best part of me. I did whatever it took to care for her and make sure she survived."

"And you did a marvelous job. She looks radiant. You could never tell she was so ill."

"I know she would have done the same for me. I think Frank can be credited with some of her sparkle."

"I have a hunch you're right."

"You're blessed, Nikki, great parents, friends, and a terrific little boy."

"Mommy, I need to go potty."

"Speaking of which, I need to take Christopher to the restroom."

"I can take him... if you don't mind."

Nikki hesitated. "Are you sure?"

"I take my nephews to the restroom when we're all out together. And diapered them all when they were babies. I can handle it."

Nikki nodded. "Christopher, Tommy is going to take you. Okay?"

His response was evident when he raised his arms up to Tommy.

"We'll be right back."

Tommy hoisted Christopher up to his side and carried him protectively through the crowd to the restrooms. Along the way, several of his friends teased him with comments meant as fun. Tommy merely smiled at them.

Nikki had just taken a sip of her Coffee Keoke when a voice asked behind her, "Since your suitor has left for the moment, can I have this dance?"

She looked up into Heath's face. He extended his hand.

"I feel the need to finish the dance we had last time. Only this time with my apology for screwing it up."

Nikki took his hand, rose from her seat, and followed him onto the dance floor. The band had switched to a romantic ballad. Her parents took notice, as well as the Hardy's. Nikki was sure they were wondering what was going on.

His arms enfolded her tenderly. "You look lovely this evening, Nikki."

"Thank you. You, too."

"I look lovely?" he teased.

"Oh, you know what I mean, Heath. And what's with this small talk? Unusual for you."

"You told me I needed to be friendly. So, here I am, being friendly. Getting out among the people instead of keeping my distance."

"Why the change?"

He paused. "Maybe circumstances changed. Maybe I made the choice to change. I unlocked myself... I sure hope I don't regret it."

"Why on earth would you regret being out there and making friends?"

"Friends can hurt you, especially those close to you."

"Friends can also be there for you when you need them."

"Like Tommy?"

"Are we going to go there now?"

"Just an observation."

"As I mentioned before, we're friends... close friends."

"How...?" Heath didn't say more.

Nikki looked up into his eyes. She knew what he was asking. She could also see he'd been hurt deeply in the past, definitely betrayed. She had no reason to say what she said next.

"Heath, I'm not in a physical relationship with Tommy or anyone else. Does it make you feel better to know?"

He stopped dancing and as if he looked into her soul, said softly, "Yes." His hand clenched a little more tightly on hers.

The song ended, and as the band started up with a fast number, Nikki noticed Tommy returning with Christopher.

Heath understood and released her. "Thank you for the dance, Nikki. Next time no talk, just dance." He smiled, a smile she felt deep within.

"Okay." She nodded in agreement. "Thank you, Heath."

Nikki went back to the table as Tommy was helping Christopher settle into his booster seat.

"Saw you out there with Heath."

Nikki wasn't sure how to respond. Tommy saved her, but it wasn't what she expected.

"Nikki, Heath is really a great guy. I know he comes off as detached, but he has a good heart and will always have your back. I've known him for quite a while now, and lately, it seems he's not as unapproachable as he once was. I think you have something to do with it."

Nikki was speechless. Tommy caught her surprised look.

"Once you get to know him, you'll understand." One of Tommy's female friends came by.

"Hey, T.C., are you up for some line dancing? The band is about to play a song perfect for it." The young lady looked over at Nikki. "Hope you don't mind if we steal him."

Nikki gave him a shove in the arm. "Not at all. Go for it, Tommy!"

Tommy looked at Nikki, who looked eager for him to join his friends and nodded to the young lady. "Okay... but don't laugh when I screw it up."

As Tommy got up to leave, Maggie and Hammy came back to the table.

The line dance began, and Nikki saw her mom and dad out there on the dance floor, trying to keep up with the younger generation. Soon, they returned to the booth laughing.

"Well, at least we tried." Sophia had tears in her eyes from laughing so hard.

Nikki watched Tommy out on the dance floor. He was having a great time with his friends, and she was happy for him.

On the other side of the dance floor, Heath sat at a table with Dan Burke. Although they appeared to be in a deep discussion, Heath raised his eyes more than a few times, looked directly at Nikki, and smiled.

It was obvious Christopher was getting sleepy. Nikki moved him onto her lap and cuddled him close.

"Mom and Dad, would you mind if I took Christopher home now? Maggie and Hammy could you bring you home later?"

"We can go now," Sophia piped up.

"No way!" Maggie responded. "Stay. We'll bring you home. I'll bet it's been too long since you and Sean have been out dancing."

"Thanks... and you are so right, Maggie," Nikki told them. "I'll get this little one in bed and myself as well. It's been a long day."

Sean tossed his car keys to Nikki, which she pocketed. Christopher had fallen asleep in her arms. She carefully got up from her chair at the end of the table and repositioned Christopher.

Heath came out of nowhere. "Can I carry him out to your car?" He must have guessed she would be leaving when he saw her dad give her the keys.

Before Nikki could answer, Heath had gently taken Christopher against his chest. Maggie and Sophia shared secret smiles while Hammy and Sean looked dumbfounded. This mountain of a man was cradling Christopher as gently as a kitten.

Nikki bid everyone goodnight, and Heath nodded, leading the way through the crowd to the doors. Once outside, they walked side by side. Nikki unlocked the car and opened the back passenger side where Christopher's car seat was located.

Heath placed Christopher tenderly into the car seat and snapped all the locks. Christopher didn't stir as Heath quietly closed the door.

Nikki registered more surprise. How did he know about children's car seats?

"Thank you, Heath," Nikki said softly.

"You're welcome," Heath whispered looking at Christopher. "He has your hair... like a bright copper penny."

Nikki was wondering if he wanted to ask her about her late husband, Peter.

"Christopher definitely takes after my side of the family. His father had almost black hair, as well as his family."

When she opened the driver's door and hopped up into the seat, Heath reached over and secured her seatbelt. His head was so close to hers, his scruff brushed against her chin, and she noticed a one-inch scar in his hairline.

"Be careful on the road going back to the house. Lots of maniacs out there, along with wildlife who like to cross roads at night."

"I will." Nikki hesitated. "Thank you for the dance this evening and for carrying Christopher out."

"No problem... and I hope we'll have another dance again soon."

"I'd like that." Nikki started the car and rolled down the window. "Goodnight, Heath."

He nodded and stepped away from the car.

Nikki backed out of her parking space and headed for the main road.

Heath had walked back to the door of the bar and reached for the door handle when he heard a car speeding through the parking lot. Probably someone who had too much to drink. He had a bad feeling.

He reversed his direction and headed for his pickup truck. Within a minute he was on the road.

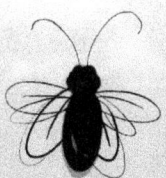

22

A bsorbed in her memories of the evening, Nikki passed by the shops in town and onto the inlet road. It was a single lane in both directions with no shoulder as it came to the inlet bridge.

A vehicle pulled up fast behind her with their bright lights on, blinding her in the rearview mirror. She raised her hand to shield her eyes. The vehicle was right up on her bumper, then it swerved into the oncoming lane. Nikki slowed to let the other vehicle pass safely, but the driver moved right, nearly sideswiping her car. As Nikki hit the brakes, she could see another vehicle behind her. The first vehicle floored it and took off down the road, straddling both lanes.

Her hands shaking as she gripped the steering wheel, she made her way to the turnoff to the lakehouse and breathed a sigh of relief.

"Crazy drivers."

The second car had followed her. As she came to the crest of the driveway, she noticed the vehicle looked familiar. Coming to a stop near the garage, she put the car in park but kept the doors locked. The driver of the other vehicle stopped, got out, and walked toward her.

Heath came up to her window. "Are you okay?"

She felt relief... and something more.

"Yes." Nikki turned off the car and opened her door. "Did you see the moron on the road? He almost pushed me off the road."

"Yeah. He came out of the marina parking lot immediately after you did. Are you sure you're alright?" His concern was genuine.

"Yes. A bit shaken up, but I'm okay."

Nikki went to open the passenger door to retrieve Christopher, but Heath stopped her.

"I'll get him. You go ahead and open up the house."

She nodded and walked down the flagstone walkway while Heath carefully unlatched the car seat and picked up Christopher, embracing him tightly to his chest.

Nikki held the door open for him and directed him up the stairs to Christopher's bedroom. Barney greeted them at the door with his tail wagging but didn't bark, as if he knew not to disturb Christopher. Entering Christopher's bedroom, she pulled back the sheets on his bed and watched as Heath laid Christopher down and removed his little light-up sneakers.

"He can sleep in his clothes tonight. I don't want to wake him," she whispered.

After tucking the covers in around him, Nikki leaned down and kissed Christopher on his forehead.

Heath stood in the doorway, taking it all in.

Nikki backed away and exited the room with Heath, and they returned downstairs to the kitchen.

"Would you like some coffee or anything?"

Nikki sensed Heath wanted something alright. What it was, he wasn't sure.

"I suppose a cup of coffee, if it's no trouble."

"No trouble at all." Nikki went over to the coffeemaker and turned it on, then took cups out of the cabinet. Barney was pacing near the slider, so she opened it to let him out.

"Sorry, Barney. Should have let you out sooner."

Once the coffee was finished brewing, she poured his cup. "Black, right?"

"You remembered."

"I remember a lot."

"Is that a good thing or a bad thing?"

"Depends."

"On?"

"Who, what, where, how, and when."

"Ah... always the English teacher."

Nikki laughed. Then looked solemnly into her coffee as she stirred in the brown sugar and creamer. "I miss it."

"Teaching?"

"Teaching, students, working with others who had the passion I did, encouraging others to grow and succeed."

"What about your writing?"

"Ah... so you have a good memory, too. Yes, writing. I had wanted to some writing while here, but it got sidelined, and ideas don't flow like they did before."

"Maybe you need something to inspire you. Like an artist who paints pictures or an architect who draws, they all have inspiration, a tiny flame that ignites an idea."

"Mr. Winters, I do declare, you have a poet within you."

"Oh, sure. Me, a poet? Now that's funny." His smile and laughter caused butterflies in her stomach.

"I'm serious. Have you ever written something to someone special, and your words came from your heart?" Nikki knew she might be treading on dangerous waters, and he might shut down their conversation. But he didn't.

"Maybe once... a long time ago."

"How did it make the person feel when they read it?"

He drew his brows together. "I don't know if it was ever read."

"Oh!"

"What kind of poetry did you write? The roses are red, violets are blue?"

"No, not hardly. I did some free verse, blank verse, sonnets... I've done Haiku, but it's not one of my favorites. Too restrictive."

"Does this mean there is a bit of a rebel in Miss Nikki McKay?"

His wit was admirable. She enjoyed these types of conversations...

especially with Heath. She'd forgotten how good it felt to talk about the things she liked.

"And what about Heath Winters... is there a wild side?"

He had to think long and hard before he answered.

"Once... a long time ago. Although I don't know if you'd call it wild. I was more out there, but things changed."

Nikki knew not to ask.

"I think we all go through changes during our lifetime. I know I'm not the same person I was ten years ago, let alone five years ago, but I'd like to think I'm better for what I learned in the process of changing. Whenever I have doubts about myself, I go off to a quiet place and think, or as my mother would say, meditate, and I leave the present and enter another world."

"Like when you sit out on the end of the pier with Barney?"

Nikki looked surprised.

"Yes, I've seen you out there. I like to cruise, do some casting, and drift. It's my form of what you call meditation."

An idea came to mind. "My baseball cap... it was you, wasn't it?"

He shrugged and smiled.

"It had to be you. Barney didn't bark. He must have known it was you."

Another shrug.

"Thank you for returning it to me. I couldn't figure out where I had lost it or put it, then Barney brought it to me."

He just grinned.

She gently knuckled his shoulder. He feigned injury, causing Barney to jump up.

"I'm not sure anymore who Barney will protect more since the two of you have become such good friends."

"Oh, I'm sure Barney is your prime protector and always will be."

"Speaking of Barney... where is he? He should be back by now."

No sooner were the words out of her mouth than Barney came back in. She closed the slider, and Barney sat on the mat near the door, looking out toward the lake. Nikki thought it odd when he didn't go upstairs to Christopher and settle in.

Nikki couldn't hold back a yawn.

"I best be going. Hope to have more of these enlightening conversations with you soon."

"Yes... me, too."

Nikki walked Heath to the door. At first, she thought he was going to kiss her, but instead, he hugged her tight, and the butterflies went into overdrive.

He let go of her and went out the door. "Nite, Nikki!"

She watched as he hiked up the hill to his truck. Why did she feel so disappointed he didn't kiss her?

She was headed up to her bedroom when the lights of a car crested the driveway. She could hear her folks talking with Maggie and Hammy, then heard the Hardys' car pull away. A minute later, her folks entered the house.

"Nikki, I thought you'd be fast asleep," Sophia exclaimed, surprised to see her in the kitchen area.

"I'm heading there now."

Sophia noticed the two empty cups of coffee on the counter.

"Company?"

"Oh... Heath. He noticed a lunatic pull out after I did and followed him. Thank God he did. Guy must have been drunk or something. Almost ran me off the inlet road near the bridge. Heath came up from behind and must have scared the guy, and he took off. Heath followed me home to make sure I was okay."

"Glad to hear you're all right. Did Christopher go down easy for you tonight?"

"He was conked out. Heath carried him in and put him in bed for me."

Nikki could well imagine her mother on the phone first thing in the morning, telling Maggie.

Nikki said good night to her parents and went up to her bedroom, Barney behind her all the way.

Sleep came quickly, with dreams of the most extraordinary kind.

23

Nikki awakened slowly. Without opening her eyes, she knew daylight was illuminating her bedroom. Bits and pieces of her dreams brought a smile to her lips.

As she rolled to her side, instead of coming up against Barney's wet nose, it was a finger. Not just any finger. It was Christopher's finger poking at her eyelid.

"Mommy, are you awake?"

"I am now," she answered, jerking back. "Good morning, Christopher."

"Barney and I are ready."

"Ready? For what?"

"Breakfast, then fishing. Hammy said fish get up early."

Thanks, Hammy.

"Is anyone else up?"

"Grandma and Grandpa are. I woke them up before I woke you up."

"Oh, I'll bet they were happy when you did."

He shrugged. *What is it with guys and shrugs? Do they take classes for it, or is it part of their genetic makeup?*

"Okay, um... Mommy needs to get dressed. Why don't you and Barney head down to the kitchen, and I'll be down in a few minutes."

Nikki waited until he was out of her room, then grabbed her robe off the chair beside the bed. After washing up, she slipped on her pink bunny slippers and went down to the kitchen. Sophia stood at the counter preparing coffee.

"Did you sleep okay, Nikki?

"Yes. Like a log. You?"

"Not really. Barney was pacing around the house all night. I took him out on the deck, thinking he needed to go water a tree, but he wouldn't budge from the deck. Just stood at the top of the stairs."

"Bear, maybe?"

"Or skunk. I'll never forget the time he got sprayed."

"He won't, either. Probably why he wouldn't leave the deck."

"He's out there now, sniffing around."

Sean joined them in the kitchen and sat at the kitchen island, watching Christopher put together one of his Lego kits. Sophia pushed a cup of coffee in front of him.

"Your father and I had a great time last evening. Didn't we, Sean?"

"Yep. Always have fun times with Maggie and Hammy, and I enjoyed getting out with my woman."

"I doubt I'll ever get the hang of line dancing. I kept turning the wrong way and bumping into people."

"Nikki, your mother and I are more into two steps or ballads... slow dancing... like what you and Heath were doing."

Nikki had wondered when Heath would come up in the conversation. She held her coffee cup close to her lips and didn't reply. She was sure they were looking for some kind of response, so she switched topics.

"I'll take Christopher out in the dinghy after breakfast while there aren't as many boaters on the lake. More will hit the water around noon."

"Are you sure you want to take the dinghy instead of the big boat?"

"Yes. Not to worry. I'll stay close to shore and away from the boat traffic."

After breakfast, Nikki helped her mom clean up the dishes while her dad took Christopher down to the boathouse to get the bait and tackle.

By the time Nikki had changed into her cutoffs, t-shirt, red hoodie, and sneakers and got down to the boathouse, Christopher stood on the dock in full regalia. Wearing child-sized cargo pants, a long sleeve knit shirt, a floppy fishing hat, and sunglasses, he carried his new fishing rod and a small tackle box. His bright orange life vest made him look twice his size.

"His line is ready except to snap on the leader with the hook. I suggest you wait until you get where you want to fish."

Nikki nodded. She knew all too well about hooks. Her brother Brian had a scar on his shoulder from one. After almost twenty years, there's still the debate about who caused it.

Barney hovered around the pier. When he saw Sean lifting Christopher into the dinghy, he started barking and jumping around.

"No, Barney. You have to stay here. We don't want any rocking and rolling. We won't be gone long."

"How long, Nikki?" Sean asked.

"An hour... maybe an hour and a half. No more. I have my phone."

Nikki had Christopher sit in the middle while she sat at the stern. The little gas engine started right up. Once they found a spot to fish, she'd turn it off and flipped on the small electric motor. Sean had told her he had tested the electric motor earlier, and it was all charged and ready to go. He released the stern line, gave it to Nikki, then took hold of the bowline. Holding it until Nikki had backed the dinghy out just past the dock, he tossed the bowline into the boat.

"Have a great time, you two! Bring home dinner!"

"Bye, Grandpa!" Christopher waved to Sean.

Barney was relentless, barking and running back and forth on the pier.

"Don't worry, Barney. You can go next time."

Sean watched as the dinghy moved slowly close to shore but lost sight as soon as they rounded the bend at Hobbs Bluff.

"Come on, Barney," Sean called to Barney, but he wouldn't move.

He sat down at the end of the pier, looking at the water. "Okay, suit yourself."

"What was Barney barking at down there?" Sophia asked, when Sean walked into the kitchen.

"I think he wanted to go with them. Couldn't get him to come back with me. He's sitting at the end of the pier, pouting."

Sophia looked concerned. "Barney doesn't pout." She walked out onto the deck and saw him sitting at the end of the pier.

Nikki arrived at Seminary Bay after cruising close to shore for twenty minutes. She cut the engine, lowered the shaft of the little electric motor, flipped it on and setting it at its lowest speed to maintain its direction.

"Okay, Christopher, this is a good spot." His smile melted her heart. She picked up his fishing rod and attached the leader with the hook. "Remember what grandpa and I told you about how careful you have to be. You can't swing the rod around with the hook on it."

Christopher nodded emphatically.

Nikki reached into the tackle box, opened a small container, attached a mealworm to the hook, and adjusted the location of the red and white bobber. She moved closer to Christopher and showed him where to grip the rod, then held on to his hand and helped him release the spool.

"See. Now you have enough line to flip it out a little. Then you push this little button to lock it. The bobber will float, and when a fish nibbles on the worm, the bobber will bounce up and down."

His eyes were as big as saucers.

Nikki helped him toss the line out and lock it.

"What now?"

"Now, we wait for a hungry fish."

Christopher looked so intense watching the bobber. A few boats trolled by further out, causing some waves, and Christopher got excited when the bobber moved. "Mommy?"

"No, just a wave. You'll know when you get a bite. Just hang onto the rod as best you can. I'll help you."

Watching him, Nikki's heart was full. He was so eager to learn about everything. She looked around at the lush foliage at the edge of the shoreline. The wildflowers grew right up to the edge of the water. She thought she spied a raccoon camouflaged in the dense thicket. She felt fortunate to have a place here at Spring Lake to share these moments with him.

They drifted along in the bay peacefully until Christopher's bobber bounced deep and sprang back up twice. Nikki saw it.

"Mommy!"

Nikki moved closer to Christopher and held the rod for him, snapping it to set the hook.

"Okay, now turn the crank slowly and smoothly." Nikki straddled the seat with Christopher between her legs. She kept her arms around him and held onto the rod while he reeled the line in.

"Keep going, Honey. You got it!"

When the line came next to the boat, Nikki reached over, grabbed it, and pulled it over into the boat.

Christopher was bug-eyed, watching the fish flapping around on the floor of the dinghy.

"Wow! You caught a bluegill!" Nikki grasped the fish and gently removed the hook from its lip.

Christopher looked concerned. "Did it hurt him?"

"I don't think so. He's a little guy, though. Do you think we should let him go to grow up more?"

Christopher nodded as he stroked a finger along the side of the fish.

"I'm with you, Christopher."

Leaning over the edge of the boat, Nikki put the fish back in the water. It sent up a splash when she released it, making Christopher laugh. Nikki put a fresh mealworm on his hook and watched as he cast his line out.

"You're a quick learner, Christopher," she praised as she helped lock the reel.

She looked at her watch. "Ten more minutes, then we'll head back to the house."

"Can we do this again, Mommy?"

"Of course!"

Christopher was all smiles.

Nikki noticed more boat traffic in the area, some who weren't adhering to the no-wake buoys. The little dinghy was rocked by the waves.

"I think we should bring your line up, Honey. Mommy will take the hook off."

After Christopher reeled in his line, he handed the rod to Nikki. She unsnapped the leader line, took the worm off the hook, and tossed it into the water, then latched the tackle box and stowed it in a compartment under the seat.

Nikki turned off the electric motor, brought up the shaft, and secured it. Starting the engine, it chugged for about ten seconds, then died. She tried again, and it ran for only five seconds, then quit.

"That's odd."

"What's wrong, Mommy?"

"Not sure."

Nikki checked the choke. She hadn't flooded the engine. Leaning over the back of the boat, she checked if the fuel line was pinched. Looking closely, she noticed the fuel line was almost torn all the way through. She was puzzled about what it could have caught on to make such a puncture.

"Well, I guess we'll have to use the electric motor to go back. It will take a little longer. I better call Grandma, or she'll worry." Nikki took out her cell phone and punched in her mom's number.

"Nikki, are you on your way back?"

"Yes, but it's going to take longer. Got a problem with the engine, so we'll have to use the electric motor to come back."

"Why don't we come get you, and we'll tow the dinghy? It won't take long for us to get Bella Fortuna launched and on the way."

Nikki was concerned about the number of boats in the area and the constant rocking of the dinghy. It would be harder to control the direction of the boat with the little motor.

"Okay. We're in Seminary Bay. I'll stay close to shore and move in your direction."

"We're on our way, Nikki."

"Mommy, are we okay?"

"Yes, Honey. Grandma and Grandpa are coming to get us. I'll keep us going until they come."

Nikki lowered the shaft of the electric motor back in the water, locked it in place, and flipped the switch. The hum of the motor was music to her ears. She turned the rudder to keep as close as possible to the shoreline and out of the way of the large boats and their wakes.

Twenty-five minutes passed, and by now, she thought she would have sighted Bella Fortuna speeding from the direction of their lakehouse.

She spotted a large boat headed her way but knew from the colors it wasn't the Bella Fortuna. It was the rental from the marina. They were coming in fast, totally ignoring the no-wake zone and dangerously approaching the rocky shoreline. Nikki knew of several reefs jutting out like fingers from the shore, which would pose a hazard for such a large boat.

She hoped they would slow down, but when they didn't, she took off her red jacket and waved it at them. She knew they must have seen her. The boat sliced through the water at full throttle, pounding the water and sending up enormous sprays of lake water.

Nikki threw her arms around Christopher and held him tight, bracing them both.

The sound of metal, fiberglass, and rock simultaneously coming together reverberated throughout the bay.

Holding firm to Christopher, Nikki looked up to see the big boat turn sharply, sending up a wall of water onto the dinghy. Nikki covered Christopher with her body, taking the brunt of the force. There were over eight inches of water in the dinghy. Nikki realized the best thing to do was head for the shore. She knew of a shallow spot and maneuvered the rudder in its direction. The electric motor was dying out.

She heard the sounds of a large boat approaching. Hoping it was her parents, she looked up. It was the wrong color. The boat cut its engines and glided slowly to where the dinghy was.

"Nikki!" Heath's voice rang clear.

"Heath. Thank God!"

He maneuvered his boat next to the dinghy and reached over.

"Give me Christopher."

Nikki had a difficult time standing with the floor of the boat filled with water. Wrapping her arms around Christopher, who was scared and shivering, she lifted him, and Heath took him onto his boat, covered him in a large towel, and set him down.

"Come on." Heath held out a hand to Nikki. "Let's get you out now."

Standing on the middle seat, balancing herself and trying not to slip on the wet surface, she took hold of his hand. She got one foot up on the gunwale, and Heath hoisted her onto his boat, then put a towel around her and had her sit near Christopher.

"Are you hurt?"

"No." Her teeth were chattering. "Just wet and cold. How did you...."

He cut her off. "Later. Let's get you and Christopher home."

As Heath went to start the engines, the Sheriff's water patrol boat arrived.

"You got them, Heath?" Sheriff Doug Hansen asked.

"Yeah. I'm bringing them home."

"We'll take care of the dinghy."

Nikki was still shivering and tried to say thank you. Heath did it for her.

"Thanks, Doug. I'll get with you later."

Heath started the engines, and as they pulled away and headed to the lakehouse, Nikki noticed the Sheriff and his crew tending to her little dinghy.

She enfolded Christopher in her arms and silently said a prayer of thanks. Heath took notice of what she was doing. She looked up at him, and his expression surprised her.

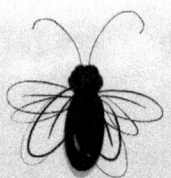

24

As Heath came around the bend at Hobbs Bluff going full speed with his boat, Winter's Remorse, he could see a group of people on the McKay's dock.

Barney was barking up a storm and alerting everyone.

Heath reduced throttle as he approached and expertly guided his boat to the dock and shut down the engines. Sophia and Sean rushed close to get to Nikki and Christopher, while Tommy Caldwell, with Maggie and Hammy Hardy, secured the boat lines. Deputies Lou Parker and Cindy Carter, aka CeeCee, stood nearby.

Heath took Christopher from Nikki, handing him to Sophia. She passed him to Sean, who clutched him all the way to the house. It was obvious Sophia had been crying. Hopefully, they were tears of joy at having Nikki and Christopher found safe and sound.

Heath hopped onto the dock and reached to help Nikki off the boat. Her feet never touched the ground. He hoisted her into his arms and set off for the house.

"S-S-Seriously, Heath, I c-c-can walk," she stuttered.

"I know you can, but not now. I can still feel you shivering."

Nikki did feel quivery inside and out. She wondered if was from being cold and wet or from something else.

She was deeply concerned about Christopher. Not so much by being doused with cold spring lake water but by the incident. Anger rose within her. What the hell would cause the idiot boater to act so irresponsibly? He would have been blind not to have seen her waving from the dinghy.

They'd been having such a great time before it happened. Christopher had asked her questions about the fish in the lake—what they liked to eat, how long it took for them to grow. She hoped his enthusiasm wouldn't diminish because of what happened.

Entering the house, Sean brought Christopher upstairs to the bathroom. Sophia ran very warm water in the tub while Sean removed Christopher's vest and wet clothes.

Meanwhile, Heath set Nikki down on a kitchen chair and removed her sodden shoes. Her feet were ice cold.

"We need to get you out of these clothes."

"Why, Mr. Winters, aren't you rushing things a bit?" Nikki responded, trying to make light of the situation. All the while, her teeth were chattering, and she was shaking.

He broke out in laughter at the ridiculousness of the situation. It was comical. She looked like a drowned rat and was sitting there trembling. Laughing, she abruptly stopped as the gravity of circumstances hit her full force. Shock setting in, her face crumpled, and tears flowed as she wept. Holding her tight against his chest, her body quaked from the sobs. He rubbed her back, increasing the warmth in her body. When she calmed a little, he removed the towel around her and gingerly walked her into the downstairs bathroom. He turned on the shower and looked at her.

"I'm better now. I can take it from here."

It looked like he was going to say something, but then he backed out of the bathroom and closed the door.

Nikki peeled off her clothing and entered the shower. She wanted to hurry and see Christopher, although she knew he was in the best hands possible with her parents. Standing under the showerhead, she allowed the hot water to run down her body. The trembling subsided as she lathered up, head to toe, then rinsed and turned off the shower. Stepping onto the bathmat and wrapping a towel around her, she noticed a stack of her clean clothes sitting on the nearby hamper. Her mother must have brought them in while she was showering.

Dressing in the white fleece sweatpants, heavy sweatshirt, and thick wool socks, she found her pink bunny slippers on the floor next to the hamper. She wiped the fogged mirror and grimaced. After she toweled dried her thick red hair the best she could, she ran her fingers through it and failed miserably at trying to manage it.

She gathered the wet clothes on the floor and hung them over the shower door. When she opened the bathroom door, Heath leaning against the door frame. Obviously, he had been listening at the door.

"You okay?" he asked, straightening.

"Uh-huh. I need to get to Christopher."

He moved out of her way as she hurried up the stairs. The ears on her bunny slippers flopped back and forth at high speed.

Christopher was in his room with her parents and Barney. Barney had burrowed in next to him on the bed.

Heath lingered in the doorway as Nikki sat at Christopher's side and kissed his cheek. He didn't look scared or upset. He looked sad.

"What's up, Buttercup?" She used his favorite line.

"Does what happened mean we won't go fishing again?"

"No! Of course, we'll go fishing again. Lots of times."

"In the dinghy?" She was about to say they'd probably use the big boat, but Christopher added, "I like the little boat. Will it be okay?"

"It's fine, Christopher," Heath interrupted. "The water patrol brought it back here and drained all the water. They're putting it up on the rails now. Your fishing rod and tackle box are down in the boathouse, ready for you to use again."

Nikki's head was buzzing with so many questions, but they'd have to wait. All she wanted to do was hug her child and keep him safe. She was glad Christopher seemed to be more concerned about not being able to fish again and seemed unruffled by the incident.

"I think a nap would be good right now. When you wake up, we'll have something special to eat. Okay?" Christopher smiled, nodded, and scooted down under the covers. Barney shimmied closer to him.

After kissing Christopher on the forehead, Nikki told Barney, "Good boy, Barney. You nap with Christopher."

"Mommy?"

"Yes, Christopher?"

"I love you."

"I love you more."

"I love you mostest." He giggled.

She tousled his red locks.

Turning, she found her parents had left the room. Heath followed her down to the kitchen. Her parents sat at the kitchen island with Maggie, Hammy, and Tommy, all wearing scowls.

Something was up, yet another question of the many she had.

When there was a knock at the door, Tommy opened it to let in Sheriff Doug Hansen and Deputy Carter. Nikki couldn't help but notice the smiles exchanged between Tommy and CeeCee.

The Sheriff turned to Nikki and asked, "Nikki, if you're up to it, could you tell us what happened out there?"

Nodding, she told them about how they were fishing in the bay just offshore. Boat traffic around them had picked up, and several weren't complying with the no-wake zones. She had decided to head back home, but when she went to start the gas engine after switching off the electric motor and pulling up the shaft, the engine kicked on briefly, then shut off. She made another attempt, but the same thing happened. When she checked the choke, the connections, and the fuel line, she noticed the fuel line had a rip in it. She called her mom to tell her they'd be using the little electric motor to head back.

"I told Nikki we'd head in her direction with Bella Fortuna to pick up her and Christopher and tow the dinghy back," Sophia interjected,

"I was already down at the pier, getting ready to launch Bella Fortuna when Sophia told me what happened," Sean added. "When I went to get the boat's drain plug off the seat in the boat to reinsert it, it was missing. I knew I had put it there, but it was gone. We looked around but couldn't find it."

"I called Maggie to fill her in and see if they had their boat out, but theirs was being worked on by Tommy over at their boathouse," Sophia continued.

"I told Tommy what was happening, and he called Heath," Maggie piped up.

Nikki's head was bouncing from one to another as they spoke. She realized then why her parents hadn't come with the Bella Fortuna and how Heath rescued them.

"What about the boater who almost rammed you," the Sheriff asked,

Nikki leaned against the counter and shivered as she remembered in vivid detail what had happened.

Heath instinctively put his arm around her, to no one's surprise, except Nikki. She felt the warmth from his body and relaxed.

"He kept coming closer... heading for us at full throttle. I waved my red jacket to get his attention, but he didn't slow down a bit. I know he saw me. I shielded Christopher as best I could. I knew if we were knocked out of the boat, I could get us to shore, as long as we weren't injured. So many things flashed in my mind.

"His boat, as big as it was and drafted deep, hit one of the reefs. More than likely, at his speed, it tore through the hull. Once he hit the reef, he swerved quickly to escape further damage, causing the swell to rise and surge over the dinghy with Christopher and me in it." Nikki took a deep breath. "We took on a lot of water. Too much. I tried to use the electric motor to get closer to the shore, but it was also failing. Probably from the wires getting so wet."

"The other boat?" the Sheriff asked.

"Just took off. I was too concerned about Christopher to notice where it went."

The Sheriff looked angry. "We brought in two patrol boats from other areas to look for the boat. Hitting the reef might have caused substantial damage, so it won't get far. Frank Morton gave us all the information on the boat from his records, and we're trying to reach the owner. We need to check out the dinghy."

Check out the dinghy?

The Sheriff looked over at Sean. "And your boathouse and the Bella Fortuna."

Sean nodded in understanding.

Sheriff Hansen and Deputy Carter left. Again, Tommy and CeeCee exchanged looks and smiled when she turned to leave.

Heath excused himself, saying he'd be right back. He walked down the hill with the Sheriff and the Deputy.

Sophia looked at Nikki. "Honey, why don't you go lie down?"

She wanted to talk to Heath and thank him for what he did, but her system seemed to be shutting down, and she wanted to close her eyes for a little while.

"I'll sit on the chaise on the deck. If I fall asleep, let me know if Christopher wakes up."

Sophia nodded. "Take a throw from the sofa with you. You need to keep warm for a while."

Nikki snatched one of the throws from the living room and wandered out to the deck. The afternoon sun shed its heat, and she looked up to feel it on her face. Her hair had dried into a mass of untamable curls. Sitting on the chaise, she leaned back and spread the throw around her and swiftly drifted off.

Her dreams were unpleasant. The rumblings of a boat engine startled her awake. Taking a deep breath, she got up and walked to the deck railing. With the presence of the sheriff's patrol boat at the dock, the boat traffic in the area had minimized quite a bit. Any boats nearby stayed outside the no-wake zone and cruised at lower speeds.

Another patrol boat pulled up to the dock, and one of the deputies hopped out and spoke to the Sheriff. Tommy took off down to the dock to see what they found out.

Sean and Hammy came out on the deck when they heard the other patrol boat pull in. Soon, Maggie and Sophia joined them on the deck. Heath was still down there and heard what was reported. Hastening up the hill, he saw Nikki at the rail. She smiled down at him and she wondered if he was thinking about Shakespeare's balcony scene from Romeo and Juliet like she was envisioning. His smile said it all. She hoped their story wouldn't be a tragic one, and she knew in her heart he'd make sure it wouldn't be Heath took the stairs two at a time up to the deck and stood near Nikki.

"They found the boat. Whoever was manning the helm tried to

run it through Bear River. It got stuck a short distance from where the river flows into Spring Lake. Its hull is damaged pretty bad, and it took on water below deck. Surprised it got as far as it did. With the excess weight of the water, it ran aground."

"Did they catch the guy?"

"No. No one was aboard. A small inflatable life raft was missing, though. On top of that, the owner finally returned Frank Morton's call and told him the person who rented it was bogus—fake name, contact, and credit card information. The transaction was done online. All the owner did was leave an envelope with the keys and boat information at the marina for the renter to pick up. Frank's canceled the owner from ever renting a berth there."

"Any description of the guy who picked up the keys?" Hammy asked,

"No, and no security camera video, either. Frank's in the process of getting them installed. He feels bad about what happened."

"It's certainly not his doing," Sophia said.

"Of course not. I'll make a point of letting Frank know we don't blame him in the least," Sean added.

Nikki was numb... mentally and physically.

Sean motioned to Sophia that he wanted to talk privately with her, and they went back into the house. A short time later, they returned.

"Nikki, your father and I have decided to stay longer. Maybe a day or two. Maybe you'd rather head back home."

Home? This was home now.

She saw that Heath was waiting for her response.

"No, I don't want to go back. I'm staying. There's really no need for you to stay. I can handle things here. Besides, Christopher has his school. If he missed even a day, it would make him anxious."

Sophia could see her point. "Then we'll stay one extra day and head home on Monday. There will be less traffic then, anyway."

"In that case, we should all chill this evening, and tomorrow, we'll have a cookout at our place," Maggie offered. "We need to get things back to normal."

"Sounds like a great plan, Maggie. Let's you and I put our heads together for the menu." Maggie and Sophia headed into the house, arm in arm.

Sean noticed the Sheriff waving from the dock, motioning for him to come down. Heath opted to stay with Nikki on the deck.

Tommy was hip-high in the water at the rear of the dinghy when Sean and Hammy got there. Anger was written all over his face.

"What'd you find?" Sean asked.

Tommy was eager to tell them. "I put new wires and lines on both the gas engine and the electric motor two weeks ago. The fuel line leak wasn't because it was pinched or worn. It was cut." Tommy held up the line, and sure enough, it was a clean cut through three-quarters of the line. Ample enough to allow the fuel to pass through for a while before it split farther open. "And the wire caps were loosened on the electric motor. You wouldn't notice unless you looked from the correct angle."

Tommy looked at CeeCee, who reached into her pocket and pulled out a small plastic bag used for evidence collection. Inside was the drainplug for the big boat

"Where'd you find it? I looked all over the boat for it," Sean asked CeeCee.

"In the bushes on the other side of the boathouse. Someone didn't want you taking out your boat."

"This is crazy." Sean rubbed at his forehead and closed his eyes. "Why would anyone sabotage both our boats? The kids who've been breaking into the boathouses around the lake?"

"No." The Sheriff shook his head. "I don't think it was them. This is different, with too many coincidences. The guy with the big boat and the tampering with your boats... something else is at play here."

"We'll need to keep this as evidence." CeeCee added as she raised up the plastic bag with the plug. "Maybe get some fingerprints."

"I've got a spare plug you can have if you want to go out on your boat," Hammy told Sean.

Sean looked downcast. "Not sure if I want to go out on the Bella Fortuna anytime soon."

"Sean, don't think that way. As Maggie said, we have to get back to normal. You don't want the little guy feeling antsy about what happened."

"You're right, Hammy. Just need to find out what normal is now."

Hammy and Sean made their way back to the house. Sean wasn't sure what or how he was going to tell Sophia and Nikki what they found out when he got there.

The second patrol boat had pulled away from the dock to resume checking around the cabins and houses in the Bear River area.

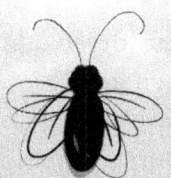

25

Tommy stayed down at the dock and made sure the dinghy was safely stored in the boathouse. CeeCee helped him guide the boat up the rails as it was winched up. She certainly knew her way around boats. The water remaining inside on the bottom had drained out as the bow angled upwards on the track.

Tommy had known CeeCee for eons. They grew up together and went to the same school, but he never thought of her as a girl he'd date. He remembered her as a gawky teenager, always on the quiet side. She didn't hang out like the other girls did. CeeCee worked behind the counter at the grocery store during high school, then at Annie's Antiques for a bit while going to the community college in the next town. He'd never seen her at any school functions or sports events. As far as he could tell, she wore little or no makeup and was very low-key. He really didn't know much about her family other than her dad worked at a factory. He was unaware of any siblings.

"When do you get off duty, CeeCee?"

"I've been off for the past couple of hours, though a law enforcement officer is truly never off duty. When I found out what happened, I wanted to help." She was curious. "Why'd you ask?"

"Simply wondering if you'd like to grab a bite with me."

She blinked in surprise. "Really?"

He nodded.

"Just a minute." CeeCee walked over to the Sheriff and had a brief conversation. The Sheriff looked over at Tommy, who felt like a bug under a microscope. When the Sheriff nodded and smiled, CeeCee handed him the bag with the boat plug and returned to Tommy.

"I'm now officially off duty, and yes, I would like to get something to eat with you."

"I need to get into some dry clothes. Would you mind if we stopped at my place so I can change?"

"No problem. We can leave as soon as I help the Sheriff shove off the patrol boat."

Tommy and CeeCee worked in unison to get the Sheriff on his way. He was heading to the marina to gather whatever information he could about who rented the big boat and if any other residents had problems with their boat equipment. The burglaries were one thing. Putting people in jeopardy was a whole different thing.

Tommy and CeeCee stopped up at the house before leaving.

"We're heading out now. The Sheriff took off for the marina to check on some things, and your boats are all tucked in and locked up."

Christopher had awakened from his nap, and came down the stairs into the kitchen, followed closely by Barney, who didn't seem to want to leave his side.

"Hey, Christopher! I heard you caught a fish this morning. Let me know when you go again. I'd love to go with you," Tommy said enthusiastically.

Everyone went silent, waiting on how Christopher was going to respond.

"Really? You want to go fishing with me?"

"I sure do. I need someone like you to show me how to catch fish."

"Yeah!"

Nikki uttered a sigh of relief, not realizing she had been holding her breath. The last thing she wanted was for Christopher to be afraid of going on the boat or being in the lake.

"Barney's going to come, too. He told me." The four-year-old who had a special relationship with his furry friend.

Sophia made a point of addressing Tommy and CeeCee. "Are you two off to do something special?"

Tommy looked over at CeeCee. "Grabbing something to eat after I change out of these clothes."

CeeCee nodded.

Nikki definitely felt a vibe between the two of them.

After Tommy and CeeCee left, Maggie did a little happy dance.

"What's with the dance?" Sean asked.

"Can't you tell, Sean?" Hammy responded.

"What?"

"Our wives like to play matchmaker whenever they can."

Sean looked at Maggie, then at Sophia. Both had grins on their faces.

"I'll never understand women." He put his head down and shook it side to side.

"Takes a lot more years of practice. Trust me," Hammy replied. "And even I don't understand everything."

"And you never will, Honey." Maggie teased. Leaning over, she kissed his cheek.

"So, you two are in the matchmaking business?" Nikki asked, looking at her mom and Maggie.

"Only if we think it'll be a good match," Maggie answered. "We all know Tommy so well. He's got a big heart. Unfortunately, it's been broken a few times. But for the better. It's taught him to be choosy. Oh, there are a lot of females who would love to corner him and tie him down, but he's managed to avoid those. He was raised by a wonderful woman, and I think he's looking for someone with the same attributes... quiet, thoughtful, caring, unpretentious. Not like some from around here who are high-maintenance types."

"So, you think CeeCee is a good fit?"

"Yes... and then some. Her mama took sick at an early age, much the same as Tommy's, but she didn't survive. CeeCee is an only child, so it's just been her and her dad. She became the lady of the household when she was in grade school, cooking, cleaning, taking care of her dad. Her father is a hardworking gentle man and always provided for them. Nothing fancy.

"Little by little, her father paid off her mother's hospital bills. At times, he worked a double shift at the factory. I think she was worried if he worked too hard, he'd get sick, and then what? CeeCee insisted on helping out financially and worked after school and on weekends. She was incredibly smart in school. Graduated with honors and went on to the community college. She took criminology and law courses."

"At one time, she thought about joining the military, but she didn't want to leave her dad alone," Hammy added. "That's when Sheriff Hansen stepped in. He had given a seminar at the college and was so impressed by CeeCee, he persuaded her to try out for the police academy. She did, and the rest is history."

"Her father pinned her badge on her at her graduation from the academy," Maggie shared.

Nikki turned to Heath, who had been standing quietly off to the side. "Did you know any of this?"

"Some. I had the pleasure of getting to know CeeCee during the meetings to build a satellite county sheriff's office here in Spring Lake."

Everyone looked surprised.

Hammy was the first to ask. "What satellite office? Where?"

"The one I'm building. You know the old abandoned mercantile building around the corner from Morton's Marina?"

They all nodded.

Heath

"Well, it's going to be gutted and restructured to make sure it's sound, then it will house a substation for the Sheriff's office. Seemed like a perfect solution for the needs of the population growth, and the location is great for the stationing of patrol boats at the marina. Paperwork and investigations will take less time."

"Well, I'll be damned." Hammy grinned. "Hadn't heard any scuttlebutt about it."

"We had to keep it on the down low until the council signed off on it. Fortunately, all the members were in favor, especially with what's been going on lately with the thefts. And Frank Morton was eager to get the property off his hands."

"So, the meeting last night at the restaurant..."

"The final documents were approved and signed. It'll be in the local paper next week."

While the adults were talking, Christopher sat at the kitchen island, coloring pictures. Barney was lying on the floor next to the stool, listening and watching. His eyes moved to whoever was talking, and his brows would waggle.

Nikki walked over to the counter. "Christopher, that's beautiful!"

Christopher had drawn a tree, a redhaired woman, and a redhaired boy sitting under the tree with a red dog. A rainbow covered the top of the paper.

"Next, I'll draw us fishing."

"Perfect."

When Maggie and Hammy headed back to their house, Sean insisted Sophia take a walk with him, leaving Christopher, Nikki, and Heath at the house. Nikki made Christopher a peanut butter and jelly sandwich, one of his favorites, while he worked diligently on a special drawing.

Heath went onto the deck and leaned on the railing, looking out at the lake. He was pensive as she came up beside him.

"Hard to believe all that's happened today." Heath nodded. "Heath, can I ask you a question?"

"Oh... are we doing tit for tat questions again?"

She laughed, a sound he was growing more and more fond of.

"No. I'm curious. When you said you were building the new sheriff's facility, you must have a construction background... right?"

He nodded.

"Are you the mysterious benefactor who helped Frank Morton out with the marina restaurant and bar?"

He straightened and turned to Nikki. "What if I was?"

"That's not an answer."

He sighed heavily. "Then, yes, I am."

"Why so secretive?"

"I like to keep my private life private. Once you open up, more people try to insert themselves into your life, and chances are someone will get hurt. Particularly me."

"Do you honestly believe what you just said?"

He nodded again.

"How can you form a bond with someone then?"

"Simple. You don't."

His line of thinking was foreign to Nikki. Something dreadful must have happened to Heath for him to think the way he did.

"I've got news for you then. You have a bond with Frank, the Sheriff, and several people around town."

"It's a different kind of bond. It's business."

"You mean to tell me you don't have any kind of feelings for these people other than business."

"Sure, I do. My feelings are those of respect. They're honest, hardworking people with ethics."

"What about affection? Like when you put your arm around me earlier and when you carried me up the hill... was that just business?"

He looked exasperated. "No, definitely not business. It was concern... for your wellbeing." Agitatedly, he ran his fingers through his shaggy blonde hair.

"I know what you're asking. If I have feelings for you—the kind of feelings that could lead to so much more." His past closed in on him. He closed his eyes. Thoughts of Laura and all he had professed to her, and then her betrayal. Opening his eyes, he looked at Nikki.

"I can't do this, Nikki."

She looked puzzled. "Do what."

"This... you and me. One of us is going to get hurt. We'll end up hurting each other, then we'll hate each other."

"Wow! Somebody really did a number on you. I feel sorry for you, Heath. Without feelings, without caring deeply for someone, you've lost your humanity. You go through the motions like a robot, but there's no substance. You've become nothing more than a cold machine. Can you honestly tell me you've shut off all your emotions? If you can, I call bullshit! I've seen how you react to people, even when you found Christopher and me in the dinghy. I saw raw emotion. It wasn't 'just business,' as you say."

He was listening to her every word, watching her go through her own set of emotions—empathy, concern, anger, frustration, confusion, sadness—all directed at him?

"It's so very hard for me to comprehend you not having feelings. Even though we've been at odds too many times since we met, I realized today I have feelings for you... the depth of which, to my own disbelief, I'm having a difficult time grasping." She looked troubled by her own revelation.

"I'm not the kind to turn off my feelings. Long ago, I learned by doing so, I only hurt myself. In order for me to salvage whatever self-respect I have left after confessing I have feelings for you, it would be best if you left."

Heath felt as though he'd been hit with a brick. He certainly wasn't expecting that.

"Nikki, you don't understand. I can't..."

"Save it, Heath. And it's *won't*, not can't. When somebody says they can't do something, it's because they lack the skill to do it. When somebody says they *won't* do something, it's because they lack the will to do it. In your case, you won't allow yourself to feel." Nikki turned and walked back into the kitchen.

Who was he kidding? Heath knew she was right, and deep down, he knew he had feelings for her—strong ones. The kind you hope turned into something more—something forever. He needed to tell her.

A few minutes later Heath found her in the kitchen with Christopher.

"Heath, my drawing is all finished. Mommy is printing my name at the top."

Heath smiled at Christopher and looked at the picture where Nikki was printing Christopher's name. C H R I S T O P H E R F O R E S T E R in big, bold letters.

Heath blinked, and the blood in his veins turned icy cold.

Looking at Nikki, he asked, "Forester?"

"Yes, my husband, Peter's last name."

Feeling as if he was going to be sick, he hurried down to the dock and jumped into his boat. A few moments later, Nikki heard his engines start up, then he pulled away and headed toward the far end of the lake.

"Mommy, where did Heath go?"

"I don't know, Sweetheart. Maybe he had an appointment."

Sean and Sophia returned from their walk fifteen minutes later.

"Oh, it's gorgeous out there, Nikki! You and... where's Heath?" Sophia stopped and looked around.

"I don't know. He left a bit ago. Christopher was showing him the picture he drew, and all of a sudden, he left."

"He didn't say anything?"

"Just asked about the Forester name."

"How strange." Sean looked at Sophia.

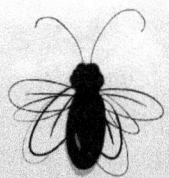

26

As the day wore on, Heath's actions troubled Nikki. He kept running hot and cold. To leave so abruptly was puzzling.

Sophia and Nikki were in the kitchen showing Christopher how to make pizza dough when her mom asked, "I wonder what made Heath take off like he did?"

Nikki shrugged. "Who knows? Just when I think I understand him, he does a complete turnaround. I know he's been hurt in the past. Must have been very bad for him to cut himself off from life."

"What about you and your feelings toward him?"

Nikki shook her head dejectedly. "I care much more than I should, but I know a one-sided relationship doesn't work. Investing in a relationship with Heath Winters is a losing proposition."

Sophia knew Nikki didn't believe her own words.

"Christopher, you want to play checkers with me?" Sean called from the deck.

"Yes!" He hopped down from the stool at the counter

Sophia knew it was a diversionary tactic to get Christopher out of earshot. Sophia needed to tell Nikki what Sean had shared with her on their walk. By the time Sophia finished telling her about the cut fuel line, the wires that were tampered with, and the drain plug, Nikki was dumbfounded.

"Now, are you sure you still want to stay here?"

Nikki's expression turned to anger and disgust. "Yes! What kind of sick mind does such awful things? I'm not giving whoever it is the satisfaction of me leaving."

"Promise me you'll be extra careful while here."

"I will."

"Hammy told Maggie as well, and they'll be looking in on you."

Later as they ate pizza out on the deck, Nikki was quiet. Too quiet. It appeared everything was weighing heavily on her mind. She knew her parents were concerned about her decision to stay, but she was not about to run scared. She'd be careful and wouldn't take any chances. Besides, she had Maggie and Hammy nearby.

"I think we all should go out on the big boat tomorrow," Sean suggested as he reached over for another slice of pizza. "I want to make sure it runs properly in case you need it while you're up here."

Nikki understood what he meant.

When Nikki tucked Christopher into bed later, he asked if they could fish from the big boat.

"Sure, Honey!" Nikki was pleased he hadn't been showing any signs of anxiety about going out on the water again.

———————

THE NEXT MORNING, Nikki's dreams were more nightmares than anything else. She was sure it came from everything happening the day before. The boating incident, finding out about someone tampering with their boats, and Heath's actions were all troubling. As much as she tried to brush the negative thoughts away from her mind, they were still there in the background.

After showering and dressing, she peeked into Christopher's room. Barney, snuggled up with him, raised his head slightly. Seeing Christopher was still asleep, she put her index finger up to her lips as if Barney would understand. Nikki closed the door and went down to the kitchen.

It was evident her parents were already up. Her mom had started the coffee maker and set out some bowls of fresh fruit.

After pouring herself a cup of coffee, she walked through the living room to the deck, where her mom sat in one of the lounge chairs.

"Morning, Mom." Nikki sat on the adjoining chaise.

"Morning, Nikki. Your dad is down at the boathouse."

"Checking things out to make sure we didn't have any visitors during the night?"

"More than likely."

"You know, Mom, the more I think about it, whoever messed with our boats probably did it when we were out to dinner Friday night. I think if they did it in the middle of the night, the lights would have been triggered on the boathouse, and I'm sure I would have noticed it from my bedroom. When I let Barney out after we put Christopher to bed, he took a long time to come back in. I wonder if he might have sensed something."

"Seems plausible. Barney was really upset when you pulled away in the dinghy. He wouldn't leave the dock."

Sean came up the hill to the house and climbed the stairs to the deck.

"Everything looks good. Hammy walked over earlier and gave me the extra drain plug he had, and I installed it. Let's figure on going out around nine, spend an hour out on the lake, then head in. I know your mom and Maggie have the BBQ menu to work on."

"I'll help with that. Where do you want to eat, the patio down below or up here on the deck?"

"I think up on the deck would be best since the grill is up here."

"Christopher and I can get it all set up."

Nikki's phone rang. "Hello."

"Hi, Nikki! It's Trey Westin."

"Hi, Trey! What's up?"

"I know you may still have company, and I hate to bother you, but can we meet up this coming week? It's important."

"Sure. I'm open all week."

"Great. Is Tuesday okay around ten in the morning?"

"Okay. Can you meet me here at the house? It's about twenty minutes farther than Kingston. I can message you with directions."

"Perfect. Looking forward to seeing you."

After switching off the call, Nikki told her parents about Trey coming.

"He said it was important."

Christopher, clad in his pajamas and dinosaur slippers, walked out on the deck with Barney, who went down the stairs to check on his trees.

Christopher climbed up into Nikki's lap.

"Are we going out on the big boat today?"

"Yes. Grandpa Sean said it's all ready, and we're going to have fun. We're going to leave about nine o'clock, so we need to have breakfast and get ready."

"Can Barney come?"

"Yes, Barney is going to come with us."

After breakfast, Nikki took Christopher upstairs and laid out his clothes for him to put on. He was already so good at dressing himself, except for the occasional slipup of putting his shirt on backward. His shoes from the day before had dried out, so after donning socks, he slipped them on and closed the Velcro strap. Nikki wore her jeans, a sweatshirt, an old pair of sneakers, and her baseball cap.

Thirty minutes later, Sean had already launched the boat from the boathouse and had it next to the pier. He had stowed the fishing tackle box and rods in a side compartment. The Styrofoam container with the mealworms from the day before had survived being washed out of the dinghy and was placed near the rods. Sean lifted the cooler Sophia had packed with water bottles and snacks onto the boat, then helped her step down into it.

When Nikki, Christopher, and Barney arrived, Sean picked up Christopher and set him down in the seat next to Sophia. He had on his bright orange vest, sunglasses, a fishing hat, and a look of fierce determination. Barney hopped aboard and settled in on the floor.

Sean started up the engines, and Nikki released the stern line, tossing it into the boat, then moved to the bowline, untied it, and held it as her dad eased the boat back. Hopping into the boat, she coiled up the line and tucked it away. Once they were out about ten feet from the pier, her dad turned the boat and shifted the gear to move forward. They went slowly until outside the no-wake zone, then Sean sped up.

Christopher sat between Nikki and Sophia, and both were pleased he was looking so happy.

"Christopher, you want to sit on my lap and help me steer?" Sean asked.

Nodding, he scrambled over to Sean, who picked him up. He gave him directions on how to hold the wheel, and from Christopher's smile, you could see he suffered no apprehension from yesterday's ordeal.

"Where should we go look for fish?" Sean asked Nikki.

Hesitant to go near Seminary Bay, she pointed to the far end of the lake. She wondered why she picked Hawks Bay. She knew Heath had his place there.

Her dad raised his brow, and she nodded.

It took twenty minutes to get there. They followed the shoreline, passing the Bear River outlet flowing into the lake, then onto Hawks Bay. The water was calmer here than in other parts of the lake, so most of the weekend boat traffic didn't venture here. So long as Sean kept it idling, the boat only drifted a short distance, which was perfect for the type of fishing they were going to do.

Sean handed Christopher to Nikki. She set him down on the bench seat, and Barney sat next to him. Taking the rods and tackle out of the side box, Nikki proceeded to set up Christopher's reel, then sat with him as they cast out his line.

"Now, remember, Christopher. Keep your eyes on the bobber."

Sean leaned back in the captain's chair and fiddled with his new fish finder equipment while Sophia pulled a book out of her tote bag and stretched out on the seat. She was in her zone.

Nikki couldn't help from looking up at the homes nestled just beyond the shoreline. Heath lived in one of them. She thought she'd be able to tell which one if she saw his boat, Winter's Remorse, out by a pier, but none of the docks along the bay had their boats out, and all the boathouses were closed up.

She was disappointed. She couldn't fathom why he left like he did and wanted to know why.

As Christopher was eyeballing his bobber, she reached into one of the side compartments and pulled out binoculars. She scanned each boathouse closely, then peered upward toward where she thought homes would be located. One or two were quite visible, but the rest were difficult to see because of the trees.

"Mommy! I got one!"

Nikki tossed the binoculars on the seat and held the rod as Christopher cranked.

"Oh, wow, Christopher. This is a big one."

"I'll say." Sean jumped up and snatched a net attached to the inside of the boat. "It's a keeper for sure."

Sophia put her book down and looked over the edge of the boat.

Nikki wasn't sure if Christopher's little rod was going to hold up to the weight of the fish, but it did. Christopher kept reeling it in and laughed when he saw the fish jump out of the water. When they got it next to the boat, Sean reached over with the net and scooped it up, bringing it to the floor of the boat. It was flopping around and spraying water on everyone.

Christopher giggled while Barney watched the fish and wondered what all the excitement was about.

They were so busy, no one noticed the large boat approaching them at a very slow speed, its engines running quietly. Nikki helped Christopher release the drag on the reel, so they could get the fish out of the net and remove the hook. Sophia turned and was the first to notice the big boat. She nudged Sean, who looked surprised.

Nikki picked up the fish by its gills and held it up for Christopher.

"It's a good-sized white bass. Awesome, Christopher."

Christopher looked at her, then over her shoulder.

"Hi, Heath! Look what I caught."

Nikki almost dropped the fish. Her father took it and stowed it in the live box filled with lake water.

Standing at the helm, Heath took his sunglasses off but didn't look at Nikki, directing his comments to Christopher.

"You've become a great fisherman. One yesterday and one today, so far. Are you going to try for more?"

Christopher nodded excitedly.

"You're in a good spot. I fish here often and always catch fish."

"Heath, we're having a BBQ later at the house. Can you join us?" Sophia asked.

"No. Sorry. I have plans, but thanks anyway."

Nikki guessed he didn't really have plans, it was simply his way of keeping people at a distance. Yet, here he was, coming over to talk to Christopher.

Heath waved goodbye and put on his sunglasses on, as if to hide that he may have looked at her. He reversed his engines and moved away slowly from the Bella Fortuna with nary a wake. Once far enough away, he headed forward and a short while later, pulled into one of the docks along the bay. Nikki watched as he tied up his boat and walked up a hill, losing sight of him in the trees. As far as she could tell, he never looked back.

She felt such an ache in the pit of her stomach. Their push-me pull-me relationship was draining. She promised herself she'd never come down to this end of the lake again.

———

Heath

As HEATH WALKED up the hill to his house, he felt like he had a load of bricks on his shoulders. He waited until he was on the path through the thickest of trees before he turned toward the Bella Fortuna. Nikki stood watching for him, but he knew it was impossible for her to see him unless she had x-ray vision. He could tell by the slump of her shoulders, she was dejected.

Christopher said something to her, and her demeanor changed. He couldn't hear her response, but her subsequent laughter— laughter he loved to hear—echoed over the lake. Earlier, he'd wanted to jump from the Winter's Remorse to the Bella Fortuna, grab her, hold her tight, and explain why he reacted as he did but hadn't been sure how she would respond. Did she know the pertinent facts of her estranged husband's death and the death of the woman who was with him?

Then there was this niggling thought that the events of her husband's death and the awful trouble out the lake the day before were somehow connected. He still found it incomprehensible that he and Nikki had been destined to meet. What power brought them together? What was the plan?

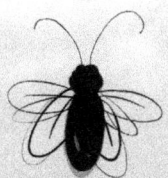

27

Christopher ended up catching three fish that morning, two white bass and one smallmouth bass. He was beyond happy.

Maggie and Hammy were there to greet them when they returned to the dock. Christopher couldn't wait to show them the fish he caught. Sophia and Maggie immediately headed up the hill to the house to put together everything for the BBQ.

Nikki overheard Sean mention to Hammy that they had seen Heath out on the lake and invited him to the BBQ, but he declined, saying he had other plans.

She helped Christopher out of the boat and set the live box on the dock.

"Look what I caught!"

Hammy looked inside the box. "Holy Cow! Those are some big ones. Are we eating them tonight?"

"Grandpa said they were keepers and since they've been in the live box a long time, and we should eat them."

"Then I guess you need to clean them since you caught them."

"Clean them?" Christopher looked dazed.

"Not to worry, Honey." Nikki laughed. "Mommy will do it, and you can watch if you want to."

He still acted unsure about it.

Nikki took the fish out one by one, put them on a stringer, and carried them up the hill to the lower-level patio. After rinsing them off, she headed into the utility room and put them in the sink. Christopher was watching her intently, with Barney following closely. She set Christopher up on the counter and showed him what she was doing. Once the fish was cleaned, she wrapped them in paper towels and brought them up to the kitchen.

"Look at those beauties!" Maggie exclaimed. "How are you going to cook them?"

"Season and wrap them individually in foil, then onto the grill. Won't take long."

"Mommy, are you going to leave their faces on?"

Maggie and Sophia almost lost it.

"I had planned to, Christopher. Is it okay with you? They're your fish."

He thought about it for a few seconds, looking closely at the fish, then nodded.

"Leave their faces on. They look like they're smiling."

Sophia, Maggie, and Nikki all looked carefully at the fish. Then one another. Smiling fish? Far be it for them to disagree with a four-year-old fisherman, who just happened to be the only one who caught any fish that day.

"Faces on it is then," Nikki said.

The rest of the day went smoothly. They enjoyed a meal of fish, brats and ribeye steaks cooked to perfection on the grill, potato salad, and Maggie's jarred green beans, she had preserved last fall. Sophia had made her famous Panettone bread pudding for dessert, served with ice cream.

They were all sitting out on the deck at dusk when Christopher jumped up and ran to the railing.

"I see one!" he exclaimed.

"See what?"

"A firefly!"

"It's too early in the season for... Oh, my gosh. He's right! Look!

The fireflies are here!" Sean shouted, just as excited as Christopher. Sean took off into the house and returned carrying a cardboard box filled with the colorful jars Christopher had painted. Inside the corner of the box were the perforated lids already hooked to wires.

Everyone was handed a jar and a lid, then they all went down the steps to catch fireflies. Nikki stayed next to Christopher and watched as he snatched two glowing flyers and slipped them into the jar, giggling all the while. Barney was equally enthused as he ran and jumped about.

Nikki heard her mom and dad laughing as they caught theirs. Maggie and Hammy had a side contest going as to how many they'd catch.

Sean started collecting the jars after the lids were screwed, then he and Hammy hung them from the lower branches of the trees. Christopher stood beneath them and twirled about until he was dizzy.

Nikki was sure the nighttime boaters out on the lake must have thought they were all crazy for celebrating the return of the fireflies. Of those boaters out on the lake, one, in particular, was happy watching them and regretted not being with them.

Heath

WINTER'S REMORSE drifted along the shoreline outside of the no-wake zone. Heath knew Nikki's parents would be returning home with Christopher the next day, and she'd be all alone at the lakehouse. Besides wanting to talk to her to explain what happened, he also wanted to let her know he was there for her. As time went on, the thoughts of something dark and evil grew stronger. In all his life, he loved only two women. One was dead, and he'd be damned if he'd let anything happen to Nikki.

Realizing how he felt, he knew he had to share his feeling with her, something he'd found hard to do over the past five years. He hoped she would welcome his effort and his honesty.

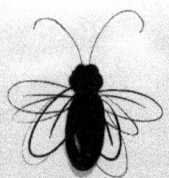

28

Nikki awoke with Christopher snuggled in tight on one side of her and Barney on the other.

Christopher had insisted on sleeping with her, knowing he would be going home with Grandpa Sean and Grandma Sophia the next day. Nikki was happy he wanted to be with her. His warm breath on her cheek filled her with joyfulness.

Staring up at the ceiling, she wondered how she could be any happier than she was right now. Heath's face came into her mind. She shook her head to clear the thoughts.

Lost cause.

Nikki turned her head toward Christopher and found him watching her.

"Mommy, will you look after the fireflies while I'm gone?"

"Of course. The ones we caught last night will fly away, and we'll catch them again when you come back." She didn't have the heart to tell him she would empty the jars in the bird feeder. The proverbial circle of life.

Nikki laid out Christopher's clothes while he showered and when he was finished, she showered. After Nikki was dressed, she and

Christopher headed down to the kitchen, where Sophia was busy making breakfast.

"Hmm... something smells good."

"Pancakes, scrambled eggs, and sausages. A big breakfast for a long drive home. We'll probably stop halfway to stretch and get something fast to eat, though." Sophia gave Nikki a look.

"No, Mom, I'm staying."

Sophia conceded with a nod.

"Maggie and Hammy will look in on you."

"Oh, I'm sure they will."

"Let us know how your meeting goes tomorrow with Trey Westin."

"I will."

"You will what?" Sean asked as he entered the kitchen.

"Give you a rundown on my meeting with Trey Westin tomorrow."

"Wonder what he has to tell you that's so important."

"Don't know. Guess I'll find out soon enough."

After eating breakfast and cleaning up the kitchen, Sophia went upstairs to pack up, although she said there was little to pack since they'd be back in a couple of weeks.

Nikki agreed and asked her to leave any dirty clothes here, and she would wash them and put them away.

Within an hour, Nikki was waving goodbye at the top of the hill near the garage. She couldn't help but get misty-eyed. Barney whimpered at her side.

"It's okay, Barney. They'll be back in no time, and we get to spend the whole summer doing fun stuff."

Nikki had just finished washing the sheets and putting them in the dryer when she heard a truck pull up at the garage. It didn't sound like Hammy's or Tommy's. Then she remembered. Trying not to look foolish, she walked briskly to the back door. Heath was still sitting in his truck. She wondered if he was just going to sit there, leave, or come down to the house.

After a few minutes of watching, he got out of his truck and

approached the house. His face was a myriad of expressions—
confusion, fear, anxiety, and something she couldn't define.

As soon as he came to the door, she opened it and moved to the
side, allowing him to enter.

"What brings the reclusive Heath Winters to my door?" She was
being snarky and immediately regretted her words and tone. She
could tell he was battling within himself.

He took her hand firmly and walked her into the living room,
gently urging her to sit down. Barney followed them, his tail wagging
slowly. Heath's silence was driving her mad, but she waited patiently,
knowing he wouldn't be here if he didn't have something important
to say.

"Nikki, what I am about to tell you might be disturbing."

Her first thought was of her parents and Christopher driving
home... but they'd only left an hour before Heath arrived.

"My parents and Christopher?" she asked alarmingly.

"No. Oh, no. I'm sure they're fine heading home."

"Then what's so disturbing?"

He still wasn't sure how he was going to tell her and decided to
blurt it out.

"My ex-fiancé was Laura Statler."

Nikki looked confused. "So?"

"She was in the car with your husband Peter Forester... when they
crashed, and both were killed, as well as the baby she was carrying...
Peter's child."

Nikki went numb. When she could finally speak, it was in one-
word questions.

"How? Why? Who?"

"You wondered why I had shut myself off from the world and only
allowed myself to become friends with a few people."

She nodded, still in disbelief.

"Laura and I were engaged to be married. She wanted to start a
family right away, but I wasn't ready. I was doing extremely well with
my own architect and engineering firm, but it was a drain on my time.
I knew I couldn't be a good father being away from home working all
the time. I was raised in a family like that and know all too well how

it deteriorates families. My mom passed away when I was eight years old. My fondest memory is spending a couple weeks one summer here at Spring Lake before she died. My father remarried a widow who had a son, and he adopted him. Lance Winters, my stepbrother. My father worked his ass off, giving my stepmother everything she wanted. I was pushed aside and rarely saw him."

Nikki listened intently as Heath bared his past and his soul to her.

"Since I really didn't have any kind of family life, I made my own life. Worked my way through college, got my degree, and started working for an architectural firm. I was fortunate to be taken under the wing by one of the lead architects, who pushed me to start up my own firm. With his help, I was able to do so."

"Your father and stepmother?"

"Estranged... unless they need something. Occasionally, they ask me to help Lance out. It's why he was here in Spring Lake. He was trying to get me to invest in one of his crazy schemes, but I refused."

"Getting back to Laura..."

"Several years ago, when I told her I was ready to marry but not start a family, she left me. I had a feeling there was more to it than what she let on, that she was interested in someone else who could give her what she wanted. I'd heard she had been seeing some wealthy guy, and she had moved into his condo. Later I heard rumors the guy was married. That's when I moved here to get away from everything reminding me of her and her deceit. I set up my house so I could work from home in architecture and engineering and was rare for me to venture out. Everything was done online.

"I had to return to the city not long ago to sign some documentation on a project and ran into her at a restaurant. She was sitting at the bar, drinking heavily and alone. I sat down next to her. She looked sad and very surprised to see me. She confessed she'd made a mistake, telling me the guy she hooked up with was married and dragging his feet about getting a divorce. She'd just found out she was pregnant and was afraid to tell him. I didn't know what to say. Her phone rang, and I saw the name on her caller ID. It was Peter Forester.

"She told me it was Peter, her master, and she was being

summoned. She was slurring her words and could barely walk. I asked if she had a ride, and she told me she'd take an Uber. She shared with me that Peter told her he didn't want to buy her a car because it would be a red flag if his wife found out.

"She could barely dial her phone, so I called for an Uber, and when it arrived, I made sure she got in and gave the driver an extra tip to make sure she got there safely. It was the last time I saw her and shortly before she died.

"I blamed myself for the breakup for over five years, but I was a fool for doing so. I only recently realized our feelings for each other were quite different."

Nikki was trying to absorb everything he was telling her, but it was a lot to take in.

"I need to tell you something else."

"Good Lord, Heath. What else could there possibly be? I found out Peter was having affairs. It's one of the reasons I filed for a separation and moved to my parent's home with Christopher. He was far from a good father. He was an absentee husband and father. We were only a convenient track up the corporate ladder."

"Nikki, I asked Sheriff Hansen to look into Laura's death with his connections in law enforcement. The way she seemed so afraid of Peter bothered me."

"Interesting. I was recently told there was an investigation into the accident. What did the Sheriff find out?"

"The investigation is ongoing, and there's evidence it may not have been accidental."

A chill ran up her spine, and she shivered.

Heath took a throw off the back of the sofa and wrapped it around her, keeping his arm resting on her shoulders. She felt comforted knowing he was here, but she still had so many questions rambling around in her head.

"I still can't get my head around the fact how we're connected in all this. Here we are, over one hundred eighty miles from where it happened, and we ended up in the same town."

"And add in all the coincidences... bumping into each other in town the way we did, the boating ordeal, and what about the guy who almost ran you off the road?"

"You think it's all related?"

"I don't know." He drew her closer. "What I do know is I'm glad I'm here with you now, and I'm happy I opened up and shared my past with you. Tommy was right."

Nikki turned her head and looked at him. "Right about what?"

"That I could trust you. Trust is a big thing to me."

"Oh, I so understand what you mean. Will you let me know if the Sheriff finds out anything further?"

"Yes. And you...If you hear anything else."

"Of course. We can shake on it." She held out her hand.

He wrapped his big bear claw around her tiny hand, brought it to his lips, and placed a tender kiss on her palm.

Nikki shuddered.

"Cold?"

"No... just the opposite."

She unintentionally licked her lips, sending the emotions he held in check for the past five years into overdrive. There was no way they could be buried anymore. Leaning in, with her warm breath on his skin, he ever so gently placed a brief kiss on her lips. Nikki wanted more.

So, she took what she wanted without asking, and Heath responded, quenching his own need.

She pulled away slightly and looked into his eyes. Yes, she could see into his soul and loved what she saw. Stroking the side of his face with her index finger, she played with the scruff on his chin, and he smiled.

"Keep doing that, and you're going to get more than you asked for, Miss McKay."

"And exactly what do you think I'm asking for, Mr. Winters?"

"I can't begin to tell you."

"There you go again with the can't thing. I already told you the difference between can't and won't."

"Okay then. I won't tell you. I'll show you."

The urgency of his kiss amazed her as his pent-up emotions overflowed into hers. Never had she felt such heart-pounding passion. She was on fire from within and grasped the fact only Heath could create such a fire, and she had no desire for him to extinguish it.

Pressing her back onto the sofa, his hand ran along her side and down her hip, stirring responses in her body she had felt lost forever.

He ravaged her mouth until they were both breathless. Breaking away, he looked down at her. Her flaming red hair had come undone from her ponytail and fanned out around her head. Her fire showed in her green eyes. She was part vixen, part fairy, and part imp, each with its own characteristics. A sexy spirit who was magical and mischievous, but she was also all woman. She had reached into his soul and held it in her hands. He wasn't sure if he ever knew what love was, but she made him believe in it.

Nikki's phone rang. Her parents were on the road with Christopher, and with everything that had happened, it was important for her to answer. Heath moved off to the side, and she sprang up, grabbing her phone.

She was breathless when she answered. "Hello."

"Hi, Honey. Were you running or something? You sound out of breath."

"Um... yeah, I was out on the deck when I heard the phone."

"Oh, were you entertaining anyone?"

Obviously, Maggie had messaged her mother after seeing Heath's truck near the garage. No sense in not telling the truth.

"As a matter of fact, yes. Heath is here."

He looked at her quizzically, so she put the call on speaker.

"Oh, good. We stopped for a bite to eat. We're still an hour away from home. I'll call you when we get there... unless you think you might be busy. If you are, you can call when you're free."

For some reason, the song *Matchmaker, Matchmaker* came to mind.

"Okay, Mom. Be safe. Give the munchkin a kiss for me."

"Love you, Nikki!"

"Love you more, Mom." In the background, Nikki heard Christopher call out, "Love you mostest, Mommy!"

When Nikki switched off the call, she noticed Heath smiling at her.

"Your mom knew I was here?"

"Mom and Maggie have a line of communication open twenty-four seven, three-hundred sixty-five days a year... three-hundred sixty-six days during leap year."

He laughed out loud. "It's nice."

"What is?"

"Having those kinds of relationships."

"Well, don't look now, Mister Winters, but you've already got some."

"So, you think there's hope for me, Miss McKay? I'm not a lost cause?"

She remembered thinking he was a lost cause, but now... no way.

She shook her head and smiled.

"Can I ask you for help doing something, which requires someone who's not vertically challenged like I am?" she asked, remembering a chore she hadn't done yet.

"Sure."

"Come on." She gathered up the cardboard box sitting out on the deck and headed down the stairs. He followed her to the trees with the fireflies in them, mostly dead ones. She pointed up at the branches where the firefly jars were hung and indicated he should take them down and put them in the box she held. One by one, he removed them, handing them to her. When they were all done, she went over to the patio, opened the birdfeeder, and emptied the little corpses into the feeder.

She noticed he kept smiling.

"What?"

"You."

"Me what?"

"You continue to amaze me. You know I saw you and your family out here last night putting the jars up after you caught the fireflies."

"You did?"

"I was out there on the lake. Watching. I saw you and Christopher prancing about under the trees."

"We weren't prancing. We were dancing, I'll have you know. We were doing the Dance of the Fireflies." She twirled around to show him. "See... it's quite different from prancing."

"Okay. You win. I was wrong. You were definitely dancing."

It was blatantly obvious he loved being with her.

He carried the box with the empty jars up to the deck, then stood at the railing and watched as she sat on the double chaise lounge, screwing the lids back on the jars.

She realized she was doing what was called busy work to calm the physical reactions her body was experiencing. She was nervous, knowing it was only a matter of time before they became intimate. At least, she hoped so.

If her phone hadn't rung when it did earlier, she was sure they would have been doing more than talking right now.

She was sure he recognized her apprehension and possibly was hesitant to move things along quicker. Her marriage to Peter left her with some insecurity when it came to intimacy, and she knew he sensed it having some knowledge of her past. It was evident he wanted so much to hold her and show her he wasn't like Peter.

She finished with the jars, set the box down on the deck beside the chair, and leaned back. Sitting next to her on the chaise, reclining beside her, he reached down and clasped her hand in his.

It was comfortable sitting together, listening as the drone of boat engines diminished with the weekenders having left. They drifted off to sleep under the warm afternoon sun.

Barney had been sleeping on the deck. When he got up, he stretched and shook. The clinking of his dog tags woke Nikki and Heath.

She turned to her side as he turned to her. He smiled and traced his finger from her upper cheek across the bridge of her nose to the other side. "Hello, Freckles."

She raised an eyebrow. "That's almost as bad as calling me Red like your stepbrother did." She grabbed his pesky finger and gently bit it.

"Ouch!" Heath cried out as he feigned injury.

She giggled.

She abruptly sat up. "Are you hungry? I am."

Barney's head turned sharply, and his eyes opened wide.

"I think Barney and I are both hungry, but not necessarily for the same thing." Before he could reach over and grab her, she rolled to the other side and hurried into the kitchen.

When he joined her, she'd already taken food out of the refrigerator.

"Welcome to Sophia and Maggie's Ristorante. I hope you don't mind leftovers. We have plenty to choose from."

He looked at everything on the counter. Brats, ribeye steaks, potato salad, green beans.

"Holy cow! These are leftovers? Did you have the Fifth Regiment over?"

"Maggie and my mom always cook enough for an army, so be prepared in the future."

She wasn't the only one surprised by what she said, and she hoped she wasn't assuming too much regarding their relationship.

He smiled as he replied, "Duly noted."

After heating up their choices, they sat out on the deck and ate. Barney was quite happy with his new friend, who was kind enough to share some of what he had on his plate.

"You realize, of course, you have made Barney a friend for life."

"Wouldn't have it any other way." Heath flipped him a small piece of steak and watched as Barney caught it mid-air. Heath laughed. "Is there an entertainment surcharge?"

"You'll have to ask his agent."

"Who's his agent?"

"Christopher, of course."

"How did I not know that?" He rolled his eyes.

"How about dessert?"

"You're kidding?"

"My mom's Panettone bread pudding with vanilla ice cream on top." Nikki waggled her brows in enticement.

"Okay, you sold me."

After indulging in dessert, they sat on the deck, side by side.

Fireflies twinkled among the trees, and a full moon cast its spell across the water.

Nikki stared up at the sky, watching the stars.

"Heath, do you believe in Godwinks?"

"Since I don't know what a Godwink is, I don't know. What is it?"

"It's supposed to be a sign someone experiences. A coincidence so astounding, people believe it's an intervention by a divine being. My mom believes in Godwinks. I'm starting to wonder if us meeting the way we did was one."

Heath was quiet for a moment.

"I'm not a religious person. I can't remember the last time I was in a church unless it was for a funeral or wedding. When I was very little, my mom would take me to church. After she died, there wasn't anyone who wanted to take me. Do I believe in a higher power? Probably."

Nikki stifled a yawn.

Heath looked at his watch. "I'd better get going. I have an early meeting with the construction crew in the morning. Now that we got the approval from the city, we can start on the work at the old mercantile building."

"And I have an appointment as well. The gentleman who is handling Peter's estate and the insurance is coming to fill me in on what's happening. This time, I won't have to drive to Kingston to meet up with him."

"Oh, so that's who…"

Nikki looked puzzled.

"I was at the courthouse in Kingston on the same day and saw you and some guy walking Barney in the park," he explained.

"Do I detect a bit of jealousy?"

"Nikki, you know my past. It's made me very skeptical at times."

"I get it. I really do. When you told me about Laura, I wondered how many times Peter was with her when he was supposed to be with Christopher and me. He always had an excuse for not being around for us. When I found out about the condo, I could just imagine him with someone else when he missed Christopher's birthday celebration."

"Trust has been an issue with me since I found out she'd been with your husband."

"Trey is a nice guy who is helping me find my way through all the legalities of the estate. In all honesty, I wish I knew someone I could introduce him to. Most of my friends are married now, and what single friends I had when I married Peter are gone. One of his goals was to alienate me from my friends."

"Guess we both have to rebuild our faith in humankind."

They walked into the kitchen, and he offered to help her clean up.

"No. I'll put on some music and do the Dance of the Fireflies while doing the dishes."

"I'd like to see you do it sometime."

Barney trailed behind as she walked him to the back door.

"Barney, go check your trees." He took off and made several stops before he finally settled on one particular tree.

Heath chuckled and put his hands on her shoulders.

"Sleep well tonight, Freckles."

She pretended to slug his shoulder, but he took her fist and kissed it. Pulling her into his arms, his lips descended to hers, and she responded fervently. The kiss ended up a culmination of kisses, leaving them both winded.

"Tomorrow night?"

She smiled and went up on her toes to give him one more quick kiss.

"Be careful driving."

"Will do, Freckles."

After his truck pulled away, Nikki did indeed dance through the kitchen while she worked.

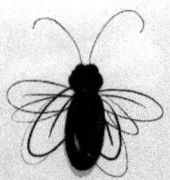

29

Nikki rose early, showered, and tossed on her robe. Barney followed her downstairs to the kitchen. She hummed as she turned the coffee maker on and emptied the dishwasher, putting the clean dishes away. After pouring herself a cup of coffee and polluting it with brown sugar and cream, she cleaned Barney's water dish and ran fresh water into it.

It was eight-thirty, and Trey would be there at ten. She had time to mix up a quick breakfast muffin recipe and pop them in the oven to bake while she dressed. Gathering the ingredients for the apple, cinnamon, and oat muffins, within ten minutes, they were baking in the oven.

Hurrying upstairs, she put on her nice jeans, a pink t-shirt, and a white Tommy Bahama button-down shirt left unbuttoned. Slipping sockless into her sneakers, she sat at the vanity in the bathroom and applied mascara, blush, and a bit of lip gloss. She brushed through her untamable red locks and pushed them back with a headband, leaving a few wisps at the sides of her face. Leaning back, she looked into the mirror. "It is what it is."

The buzzer on the oven sounded as she reached the bottom step. She checked to see if the muffins were cooked through, then took the muffin tin out of the oven with an oven mitt in the shape of a green frog. Christopher's choice at the home goods store while they were out shopping one day—a memory near and dear.

Nikki went out on the deck to make sure the table was clean and set out placemats. It was just as beautiful out there in the morning as it was at night.

Her mobile phone rang. It was Heath.

"Good Morning!"

"Good Morning, Freckles."

She was laughing inwardly at his teasing.

"I thought you were in a meeting this morning?"

"I am. We're taking a break, and I thought I'd give you a call. Did you sleep well?"

"Yes, I did."

"Did you have sweet dreams?"

Nikki was surprised. That was something she would ask Christopher.

"Yes, about some big Neanderthal."

"Then it must have been a nightmare, not a dream. Neanderthals are big and mean."

"Not this one."

"Did he have a name?"

"Yes... Heath."

"Heath the Neanderthal. Sounds like an evil character in a children's book." Heath made a sound like he was growling.

Even though Nikki didn't have her phone on speaker, Barney heard the growl and barked.

"Uh-oh. You're in trouble now. Barney didn't like your growl." She started laughing, and Heath joined in.

"Tell Barney I was only kidding." Nikki heard voices in the background. "Gotta go. The guys are waiting for me. Talk later."

"Okay. Bye, Heath the Neanderthal."

A few minutes after Heath's call, Nicki heard a car pull up the drive and recognized Trey's vehicle. She went out the back door to greet him as he walked down the path.

"Welcome to my little corner of the world."

He looked around in wonder. "I like your little corner, Nikki." He reached out and gave her hand a warm squeeze. He was dressed casually, much different from when she met him in Kingston. Instead of carrying his briefcase, he carried a thin courier's folder.

"Come on in. How about some coffee? You take it black, right?"

"Yes, thank you."

Barney walked over to him like an old friend.

"Hey, Barney. Remember me?"

The tail wagging increased.

Nikki walked over to the counter and told him they could sit out on the deck and nodded in the direction. "I'll bring your coffee out there."

Nikki poured his coffee and hers, adding her cream and brown sugar. She placed the cups on a tray with a basket filled with freshly baked muffins and carried it out to the deck.

"Those look delicious. I could smell them as soon as I got out of my car."

"Thank you. Help yourself."

He plucked a muffin from the basket and broke it open. After popping a piece in his mouth, he smiled. "Delicious."

He didn't open the folder. Instead, he asked how she was doing.

"Fine, except for some strange things happening here."

He leaned forward. "Such as?"

She told him about someone tampering with the boats and the near collision out on the lake.

"The Sheriff's investigating. The guy took off after running the rented boat aground in the river channel."

"Anything else occur that seemed off?"

"Some idiot was driving recklessly on the outlet road and almost ran me off the road, but I'm sure he was drunk. I found out later he had left Morton's Restaurant and Bar right after me. Maybe he thought I was driving too slowly. I don't know."

"Any strangers approach you?"

"Strangers? Everybody knows everybody here. Heath is the only person new to me, but he's been here for several years."

"Heath Winters?"

"Yes. You know him?"

"No, not personally, but his name came up in the insurance investigation. At one time, he was engaged to the woman who died in the car with Peter."

"Yes, I know."

"You know?"

"Heath told me. He actually was the one who told me the name of the woman, Laura Statler."

"Her parents are trying to lay claim to Peter's estate because she was carrying his child when she died. They don't have a leg to stand on, but they are very bitter. When I tried to reach them, I was told they were at their summer home... at Little Spring Lake. Maybe it's just a coincidence."

"That's only twenty miles from here. That's why you asked me if I had been approached by any strangers, isn't it?"

"Yes. People do weird things, especially if money is involved. Of course, there's also the Foresters."

"Pamela is gallivanting in Europe, according to what Peter's parents said at the memorial service. I can't imagine Clare or Charles Forester becoming involved in pursuing Peter's estate. They have plenty of money and assets of their own."

"Maybe, maybe not. There are rumors they made some bad business deals, and it hit them hard."

"Is there anything else I should know?"

"Yes." Trey rubbed at his forehead. "The accident was definitely no accident. Peter's car was tampered with. That's why I am asking you to please be careful. Promise me."

Nikki felt a chill and shuddered.

"I will."

She asked Trey if he would like to take a walk down to the pier, and he smiled.

"Sure."

As they followed the worn path down the hill, Trey was looking around and commented on the landscape.

"We all pitch in, even Christopher. We started a little garden for him on the side of the house. My mom helped him plant seeds and seedlings, but I imagine until we get some chicken wire around it, it will be a garden buffet for the animals."

Standing on the dock, Nikki pointed out all the points of interest and the best spots for fishing.

"Do you fish, Trey?"

"Not for many years. I did with my dad when I was little." He inhaled deeply. "It sure is relaxing here."

"On the weekends, this place is crazy. You came at the right time."

"I'm staying at the Bayside Inn this evening."

"It's at the other end of town. Nice place, and the owners keep it up very well."

"Places to eat?"

"The best place is Morton's Restaurant and Bar over at the marina."

"Would you like to join me for lunch or dinner?"

Nikki knew she wanted to save her evening for Heath. "Lunch would be fine." She looked at her watch. "It's almost noon. You could follow me there, then you can check in at the Inn."

"Okay."

Twenty minutes later, Nikki pulled into the restaurant parking lot with Trey behind her. When they walked into the restaurant, Frank greeted her warmly.

"How's our Nikki?"

"All good, Frank. I'd like you to meet Trey Westin." The men exchanged greetings and shook hands.

"Just the two of you today?"

"Yes," Trey replied.

No sooner had they been seated than Heath, Dan Burke, Sheriff Hansen, and Steve McConnell walked in.

Coincidence? Not hardly.

Heath winked at her.

Of course, they were led right next to their table. Was Frank in cahoots with Heath? She saw the two of them nod at one another. The Sheriff said hello to Nikki, and she felt obliged to introduce Trey.

"Trey, I'd like you to meet, Doug Hansen, our awesome Sheriff, Dan Burke, one of our town's esteemed councilmen and owner of the best hardware store around, Steve McConnell, our bait and tackle guru, and last, but not least, Heath Winters our resident architect, engineer, and Neanderthal."

Everyone burst out laughing, including Heath.

Trey watched the looks between Heath and Nikki and was pleased by what he saw.

How it all happened, Nikki wasn't sure, but soon they were all talking and deciding to push the tables together. At first, talk centered around the new Sheriff's office being built in town. A few legal questions arose, and once the group found out Trey was not only an estate manager but also an attorney with a land development and zoning background, he was asked his opinion.

The subject of what happened to Nikki on the lake was brought up. The Sheriff mentioned the investigation, and Trey asked if he could have a couple of minutes with him after lunch. The Sheriff agreed.

Dan Burke and Steve McConnell left, while Heath, Sheriff Hansen, Nikki, and Trey remained.

When Heath got up to leave, Trey asked him to stay. It was mid-afternoon, and they were the only ones there in the restaurant. An hour later, the four of them were still at the table. Frank had brought them several rounds of coffees.

After hearing Trey's information, the Sheriff shared more of what he knew and suspected, and Heath added more information.

Nikki was stunned.

"So, someone in the Foresters' circle of family and friends is suspected of trying to harm me and my son?"

"No doubt," Trey responded.

"With the additional information I have now, I can do more investigating and work with the investigator in your office, Trey," the Sheriff added. "Thank you."

"The most important thing here is that we keep Nikki and Christopher safe," Trey answered. "I understand Christopher is back at Nikki's parent's house or at her brother's home, but Nikki is alone at the lakehouse." Trey looked at Nikki. "Would you rather return to the big city, Nikki?"

"No! I'm not running scared back to my parents. This whole thing is so bizarre." Her anger was evident.

"She won't be alone at the lakehouse," Heath spoke up. "I'll make sure of it."

When they all left the restaurant, Trey took Heath aside.

"You're a lucky guy, Heath. Take care of her. I'll be in touch soon." He walked over to Nikki, who was talking to the Sheriff. "It was nice meeting you, Sheriff. I'm staying at the Bayside Inn this evening if you need to reach me. Here's my card."

The Sheriff took the card and nodded. "Hope we can get this cleared up soon. Thanks, Trey." He bid goodbye to both Nikki and Trey as Heath walked up to them.

Trey turned to face her. "Nikki, you're in good hands. Please take care. I'll be in touch soon." Trey got into his car and headed down the road to the Bayside Inn.

"Just you and me, kid. Not a bad deal," Heath teased.

Nikki knew full well he was trying to lift the pall that had settled around them.

Heath put his arm around her and walked her to her car.

"How about dinner at my place tonight?"

"Sure, but I need to let Barney out or bring him with me."

"Bring him. We'll stop by your house, pick him up, and I'll drive you both to my house."

Nikki was eager to see Heath's house and even more so to spend time with him. Stopping by her house, she let Barney out to check on his trees, then loaded him into Heath's car.

"Are you sure you don't mind dog hair?"

"Not at all."

They followed the road leading to the far end of the lake. With more forest than where Nikki's lakehouse was, at times, it was so dense, hardly any sunlight filtered through. No wonder she couldn't see the house from the lake.

They approached an elaborate iron gate about eight feet high. Heath clicked a remote, and it swung open in the middle, allowing any large vehicle to pass through.

Heath was watching for her reaction.

"Impressive. It looks like it weighs a ton."

"Pretty much. I had a difficult time working with it."

"What?"

"It was originally from an old mansion that was going to be razed. I bought it as scrap and reconfigured and welded it to my specifications."

"So, you weld, too?"

"A little."

She saw his smirk and knew there was probably much more he did.

They followed a crushed stone drive up to a bricked drive. A sharp bend on the drive brought them to the garage on the side of the house.

Again, he waited for her response.

"A little cabin in the woods?"

"Everyone has a dream. This was mine."

Cabin was an understatement.

Heath left his truck parked on the drive and ran around to the passenger side to open Nikki's door, then let Barney out.

Barney ran from tree to tree, claiming each one as his.

Heath opened the front door and turned off the security.

"Since this is your first time here, is there a protocol or something? Like, do I carry you over the threshold?"

"That's only for newlyweds, not dinner guests."

"Maybe we should start a new trend." He swooped her up into his arms and carried her into the foyer.

She squealed. "Have you lost your mind?"

He set her down and lifted her chin with his fingers.

"Yes."

He kissed her gently, and the scruff on his chin ignited her. She hungered for more than his gentle kiss. It was in her eyes. He hoisted her up until she wrapped her legs around him, and he held her as he walked to a hallway. One way went to the great room and the other to his bedroom. He stopped.

She answered his silent question with a nod, and he strode to his bedroom. Moving to the side of the massive carved timber bed, he gently released her arms from around his neck and eased her back onto the bed as she uncurled her legs.

He laid down beside her. "You sure?"

"Yes. Are you?"

"Most definitely."

When Heath got up to remove his boots and Nikki's shoes, he noticed Barney had found a cushy spot on a rug near the bedroom fireplace. His eyes were closed, but Heath knew he was listening and watching.

After removing his boots, Heath removed Nikki's sneakers and walked around the bed, pulling down the blankets to the foot of the bed. Picking Nikki up again, he set her in the middle.

He stood there watching her as he started to remove his shirt.

"Stop. Let me." Getting to her knees, she scooted over to him on the bed. She slowly undid every button as she looked into his eyes. When there were no more buttons, she leaned in and brushed her lips on the fine golden curly hairs on his chest.

Heath shuddered.

Her tongue traced along his collarbone, tasting his salty scent. When she pulled back to unbutton the top snap of his jeans, he moaned.

"Nikki..."

"What, Heath?"

"You need to stop, or I won't be able to."

"Is this another one of your 'can't or won't' situations?" she teased.

He gently pushed her away to finish removing his shirt, then undid his jeans. The protrusion in his jeans was evident. Before taking his jeans off, he bent over her, unzipped her jeans, and slid them down her hips, revealing white lace bikini bottoms. Drawing her up by her hands, he removed her white shirt, then her pink t-shirt, revealing a simple white lace bra matching the bikini panties.

"You're beautiful."

After living with her husband's belittling comments, she'd never thought she was beautiful, especially after giving birth to Christopher, her eight-pound bundle of joy.

When she looked look away, he noticed.

"You are beautiful, Nikki. Don't let anyone tell you otherwise. And don't be ashamed of your body. Too many women have things done to their bodies, thinking they need to be perfect. Instead, they become imperfect because they are no longer natural."

Heath pulled off his jeans. His erection bounced at its release, but what drew Nikki's attention was an ugly scar running down the length of his hip to his thigh.

"I'm not perfect,"—he pointed to the scar—"thanks to my stepbrother. He messed with my motorcycle as a joke, and I crashed down a ravine. Yet another reason he and I don't gel."

"Nikki, true beauty isn't on the outside. It's inside... here." He touched the skin over her heart, then his finger trailed between her breasts. Lying beside her, he leaned on his arm and kissed her with a passion they both felt. She gave him all of her, and he gave himself to her completely.

An hour later, they were still in each other's arms, totally naked and listening to each other's heartbeats. She looked at the clock he had on the nightstand.

"I really should call my parents, especially Christopher. I don't want them to worry."

"And I should get up and make you the dinner I promised."

Heath walked over to a bureau, and Nikki admired the view. Pulling a sweatshirt out of the dresser, he tossed it to her. It was so big, when she put it on, it went down to her knees. He put on a pair of sweatpants, which did nothing to hide his package underneath.

Nikki retrieved her phone from her purse and dialed her parents.

"Hi, Mom!"

"Hey, Honey. How did the meeting go with Trey?"

She didn't want to alarm them with everything she'd learned.

"Very well. There is still an investigation into the accident. How's Christopher?" Nikki changed the conversation, hoping her mom wouldn't ask any more questions.

"He's fine. He told his classmates about his adventures up at the lakehouse and how many fish he caught. He's with your father right now in the yard, tossing a ball around. Is Heath with you by any chance?"

Nikki cringed. "As a matter of fact, Barney and I are at his house. He's making us dinner."

"How wonderful! Your father and Christopher just walked in. Hold on."

"Hi, Mommy!"

"Hey, Christopher. Grandma told me you had a good time at school today."

"Yeah, I colored a picture of the fireflies."

"Did you save it for me?"

"Yes. I'll bring it when we all come."

"Okay, Honey. Have sweet dreams tonight."

"You, too, Mommy."

"I love you!"

"I love you more."

"I love you mostest!"

Hanging up the phone, Nikki wished she could hold Christopher.

She went down the hallway and found the kitchen easily enough. Heath was busy sauteing mushrooms, steamed vegetables were already in the warming oven, and the smell of steaks on the grill permeated the air.

"Is there anything you can't do?"

He thought a second. "Bowl. My fingers are too big to fit in the holes of the bowling ball. I end up just picking it up and rolling it. Usually straight into the gutter."

Nikki chuckled, envisioning him bowling.

"Not funny, Nikki!"

"I think your fingers are just fine," she said, trying to appease him. She waggled her eyebrows, and he snapped the dishtowel at her bottom.

Finishing up with the mushrooms, he checked on the steaks.

"Wine?"

"Sure."

"Pick one." He pointed to a wine fridge in the corner of the kitchen.

She pulled out a bottle of Cabernet. "This one?"

"Good choice. My girl knows her wine."

Hearing him say "my girl" gave her a warm-all-over feeling.

Sitting on thick cushions on the floor, they ate by candlelight at a beautifully carved wooden table in front of a blazing fireplace, which dispelled the night's chill. Heath was the dutiful host, making sure Barney had enough to eat. So much so, Barney was sacked out on the hearth rug.

Heath raised his glass. "Here's to many nights like this."

They clinked glasses and sipped their wine.

"I'm planning on keeping you here tonight."

"Well, that suits me fine since I have no intention of leaving."

"I'll bring you and Barney home in the morning. I have another meeting in town, and we can get together later. Okay?"

"Perfect. I still have things to do around the house. Tommy is coming by to work on the gutters this week. I've been forbidden to go up on the ladder."

Heath looked at her sternly. "Stay off the ladder."

"Yes, Sir. Any other orders?"

"Oh, yes... several."

30

Early Wednesday morning Heath got up quietly and entered the shower. He turned abruptly, hearing a sound. Water streamed down Nikki's body as she moved toward him.

"I wanted to surprise you and make you breakfast before you woke up." He wrapped his arms around her.

"I think breakfast can wait... just a little while, don't you?" She went up on her toes and kissed him.

He lifted her up onto the bench seat and nuzzled his mouth at her breasts.

"It can wait."

An hour later, Heath dropped Nikki off at her lakehouse, giving her one of his signature kisses, then headed to town for his meeting.

Barney took off to check his trees.

At nine o'clock, Tommy came by, and Nikki had a cup of coffee waiting for him.

"How's it going with you and CeeCee?"

"All good." Tommy smiled broadly. "She's something else, isn't she?"

"You two seem to be a perfect match."

"Have Maggie and your mom enlisted you into their group?"

"No, not hardly. I've been on their radar, too, you know, but recently...."

"You and Heath, right?"

It was Nikki's turn to smile.

Tommy set up a ladder on one side of the house, hung some of the brackets on his toolbelt, and started up the ladder.

"I'll let you know if I need you. For now, I can handle this."

"You sure?"

"Yep."

Nikki went back into the house and down to the laundry room. The linens she washed and folded the other day sat on the dryer.

"Might as well put them back on the beds," she told Barney as he followed her around.

"Mom, Dad, and Christopher will be back up here in a little over a week, and their beds will be all ready for them. Brian is coming up with his family, so I need to freshen up the spare rooms. Lots to do, Barney." She was feeling unbelievably happy. Nothing could ruin her day.

At noon, there was a knock at the door.

"Nikki?" It was Maggie.

"Hi, Maggie!"

"I baked some brownies. I thought you and Heath could enjoy them."

Nikki held back a laugh. "I'm sure we will. He'll be back later."

"I gave two to Tommy. He's going to give one to CeeCee."

As if on cue, Tommy came to the door.

"All done, Nikki."

"Seriously?"

"Yep. I gotta go now. I have some chores at home, then I need to get cleaned up for game night. CeeCee is going with me."

"Have fun."

"You and Heath should come."

"I'll check with him. I'm not sure if he's made other plans."

"Okay."

"Bye, Maggie. Thanks for the brownies. Bye, Tommy."

"I'm heading back to the house before Hammy eats the rest of the brownies."

"Thanks for the brownies, Maggie. I'm sure Heath will love them."

She smiled at Nikki. "Not as much as he loves you, Nikki."

Again, the song *Matchmaker, Matchmaker* played in her head.

Heath arrived around one o'clock. "Sorry, I got tied up. I thought I'd be here sooner." He seemed frazzled.

"Everything okay?"

"Yeah, I had to go over some things with the Sheriff."

"About the new station?"

He hesitated. "Yes." He stared out at the lake.

"Feel like going fishing?"

"Sure! Bella Fortuna or the dinghy?"

"The dinghy."

"I'll pack some drinks and some of the brownies Maggie made."

"Just don't spoil your dinner. I'd like to take you to Morton's later, okay?"

"Sure. Tommy was here today. He did the repair on the gutters. He mentioned there's some kind of game night on Wednesdays at Morton's?"

"I've heard about it, and everybody says it's fun for all ages."

Nikki and Heath launched the dinghy, then retrieved a couple of rods and a small tackle box. She slid her dad's old pocketknife into her pocket. She invited Barney to join them. He sat up front, enjoying the wind in his face, his ears flapping as they moved through the water.

Stopping a couple of times, they tried their luck and although they didn't catch anything, they were happy. Heath asked her about her life as a teacher. She asked him about architecture and what he liked to design the most. The more they talked, the more they learned about each other.

When they returned to the lakehouse, they decided to leave the dinghy tied to the dock. Maybe a moonlit cruise would be on the agenda. Gathering the rods and tackle box, she stowed them in the boathouse.

"Thanks for this afternoon." Heath put his arms around her. "I needed to relax, and being with you made it all the better." He kissed the tip of her nose.

She loved this gentle, loving side of him.

Heath and Nikki were fortunate to find a table at Morton's. Tommy and CeeCee sat at a table next to them. Tonight was "Word Game," and the big screens indicated there were four screens with two teams for each screen. Tommy and CeeCee hunched over their controller, forming words with tiles with different values. Moving the buttons on the controller moved the tiles on the screen.

A server came by, and Heath and Nikki ordered beers and burgers.

Nikki looked over at Tommy and CeeCee's controller and whispered something to CeeCee. She smiled and moved the tiles into place, scoring the highest point value.

"Is that cheating?" Heath asked.

"Nope," Tommy replied. "You can play as teams with up to four people."

Soon Heath and Nikki were part of the team, and they outscored the other teams.

"It pays to have two intelligent and beautiful women on our team!" Tommy announced.

Heath agreed.

Nikki looked at her watch. "I really should get back to the house. Barney needs to be let out and fed."

Heath picked up the tab for all four of them, then took Nikki's hand as they worked their way through the bar out to his truck.

When they got to the house, Nikki opened up the slider to let Barney out, and he took off like a bat out of hell. "Guess he had to go bad."

Picking up his bowl, Nikki took the bag of kibble and poured it into his dish. She placed it on the floor, then picked up his water dish, cleaning it and refilling it.

She stood at the slider, waiting for him. "Barney, come and get it. Dinner's on."

Heath came beside her. They both heard a strange sound, a mixture of howling and whimpering.

"Barney!"

They rushed down the stairs. Clouds had covered the moonlight, so they followed the sounds of whimpering. They didn't go very far. Barney was laying down at the edge of the patio. There was white foam coming out of his mouth.

"Oh my God! Barney!

"It looks like he ate something poisonous. We have to get him to the vet."

Heath picked up Barney and carried him to his car. He laid him on the back seat and Nikki climbed in next to him. On the way to the vet, Heath called Dr. Walker on the car phone and told him what happened. Dr. Walker would be waiting for them at the animal hospital. Next, he called Hammy and Maggie, told them about Barney and asked if they would lock up the lakehouse.

When they arrived at the animal hospital, Heath carried Barney in as Dr. Walker opened the door. Dr. Walker's assistant led Heath to an exam room, where he laid Barney on an exam table. Nikki was trembling uncontrollably, and Heath went to her, putting his arm around her.

"I had let him out while I put together his dinner. He took off, and when he didn't return as he normally did... then we heard him crying."

"It's obvious he ate something poisonous. We have several varieties of poisonous mushrooms here, plus there's a toad that secretes a toxin harmful to dogs." After the doctor swabbed Barney's mouth, he handed the swab to his assistant for testing. The doctor flushed Barney's mouth to remove any poisonous residue. The assistant came back from running the swab through an analyzer and handed the doctor the printout.

"Insecticide. We need to put in an IV and use some activated charcoal to absorb the toxin."

"We don't have anything like that lying around the house. We store anything dangerous up high in the garage. Is he going to be alright?" Nikki asked, her voice cracking.

"He's very healthy, and it looks like he didn't ingest much. Let's put him on the IV for a while."

It wasn't much of an answer.

Dr. Walker and his assistant shaved part of Barney's left leg and inserted the IV needle. The solution hung on a metal pole, and Nikki watched it as it dripped.

"Nikki, do you want to sit down?" Heath asked.

"I'm not leaving him." She remained standing next to the table, lightly touching Barney's leg.

The assistant reached around the corner from the exam room and brought a chair in for her.

Maggie and Hammy arrived and joined them.

"Can you stay with her a few minutes?" Heath whispered to Maggie. "I need to make a couple of calls." When Maggie nodded, Heath motioned to Hammy.

In the hallway, he told Hammy the Sheriff was investigating the strange series of events. He needed to alert the Sheriff about Barney's being poisoned. Tomorrow, they would look around the property for whatever the beloved dog had ingested.

Heath dialed the Sheriff and relayed what happened. He told Heath he was going to call Trey Westin to give him an update and see if he had anything new to report. Next, Heath called Sean and Sophia. Needless to say, they were upset. He hated telling them, but it was important they were aware, so they could report anything unusual.

31

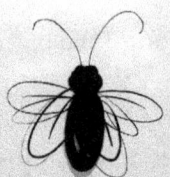

Two hours later, Nikki sat on the floor at the lakehouse next to Barney, who was lying on a soft blanket. His right foreleg was still taped where the vet had inserted the IV line, and the area around his mouth was inflamed. The poison had cleared his system, but he was so weak, Heath had to carry him down to the house from the car when they returned from the animal hospital.

Heath got onto the floor beside her. "He's going to be okay, Nikki. The doctor is sure of it. We got him there in plenty of time."

"I know... but to see him like this... so frail and barely moving. It's not Barney. My sweet, lovable crazy Barney." She stroked his red coat. His eyes opened slightly, then closed. "I couldn't bear to lose him, Heath."

"You aren't going to lose him. He just needs to rest up. Dr. Walker was sure he'd be as good as new soon."

"I don't understand what's going on. The boat incidents and now this?"

Heath was quiet... too quiet.

Nikki guessed he was just as puzzled as she was and didn't have any answers.

"I need to get back to my house to pick up a few things. I plan on staying here tonight. Are you going to be okay for a little while? I won't be long, maybe forty-five minutes, and hour at the most."

"Yes, I'll be fine. Go ahead, but hurry back." She smiled at him, melting his heart.

He kissed her lips softly. The tenderness turned to something more, and it was difficult for them to break apart. Nikki's heart pounded, and she felt warmth coming from within. From the look on Heath's face, he felt the same.

Standing, he took his keys out of his pocket.

"One hour or less."

A few minutes after his truck pulled away, Nikki saw the lights on the boathouse flicked on and quickly turned off. Must have been a raccoon or something. She couldn't remember if she locked up the boathouse when they returned from their outing on the lake. She needed to check to make sure the dinghy was secure, as well as the boathouse.

"I'll be right back, Barney."

Nikki stopped in the kitchen to grab a flashlight out of the junk drawer, then walked in the dark down to the boathouse. Fireflies surrounded her.

She smiled, remembering how excited Christopher was that they had hatched earlier than normal as he caught them in his colorfully painted jars. Her father had hung the jars from the lower branches of the trees, and Christopher was thrilled to walk under them and watch the twinkling of the lights.

As she came close to the boathouse, the security light didn't turn on.

"Damn. Don't tell me a packrat got in again and chewed the wires." She slowly walked toward the boathouse, the flashlight guiding her way. When she came to the side door, she saw it was open. "Shit. I didn't close it." She slowly walked through the door and flashed the light on the switch. She flipped it up and down. Nothing.

She thought she heard scraping near the dock and worried one of the lines securing the dinghy had pulled loose from the pier. Making her way down to the dock, the lines were all secure. As she turned to go back to the boathouse, she was hit in the back of head by a heavy object.

Nikki awoke, lying on the dock, her hands and feet bound with zip ties. She felt something warm and wet on the back of her head. As she rolled to her side, she noticed a puddle of blood on the dock.

"You just won't die, will you? No matter what I do, you're still alive."

Nikki recognized the voice and cringed as the woman spewed words filled with vitriol and hatred. Dressed in camouflage clothing, she was disheveled. It was obvious she'd been in hiding for some time.

"What have I ever done to make you hate me so much?"

"Don't play innocent with me. You latched onto Peter for his money and all the things he could give you."

Nikki was scared, but her anger rallied.

"That's ludicrous. Peter pursued me and insisted we marry. Little did I know it was for the wrong reasons. He needed me to create a picture of a happily wedded couple to advance his career. Our marriage was totally one-sided. As for his money, I didn't know about the inheritance and trust fund he had from his grandparents, and he never told me about the insurance policy."

"Like I'd believe you," she scoffed at her. "You've already taken up with some guy... make that plural guys. You're nothing but a money-grubbing bitch."

"What are you talking about? Peter and I had been living apart for several years. He was the one with extramarital affairs. As a matter of fact, the woman who died in the car accident with him was pregnant with his child."

The woman looked surprised, then smiled.

"All the better, then. Three birds with one stone."

It was Nikki's turn to look stunned.

"You... you caused the accident?"

The woman's smile turned into a sneer.

"Damn, you are so naïve. Of course, I did. Just like the one you're going to have soon."

Nikki's head ached from where the woman had hit her.

"Then I'll take care of that child of yours, whether it be at your funeral or afterward. No one is going to stand in the way of me getting what I deserve."

She walked along the shoreline to where a willow tree hung over the water. Pulling a small life raft out from under the branches, she tied the dinghy to it. Kicking Nikki in the head, she used her foot to shove Nikki's prone body off the dock into the dinghy. Immediately she threw a tarp over Nikki. Nikki was dazed but instantly noticed the strong smell of fuel.

Nikki was sure she'd have to do something soon to save herself. Fortunately, her hands were zip-tied in front of her, not behind her. She wriggled around, trying not to rock the dinghy to alert the woman that she was conscious. Nikki felt for the pocketknife in her side pocket, twisting her arm around her body to the point it was painful. Her fingers were able to move the knife up and out of her pocket. The slapping of the water against the dinghy and the pier covered the sound of the knife landing on the floor of the dinghy. Nikki waited a few seconds, then picked up the pocketknife and carefully snapped it open. Turning her hand in an awkward position, she had to make several tries, sawing at the plastic, but it finally broke.

She was becoming dizzy and nauseated by the fumes from the gasoline. Bringing her knees up, she touched where the zip tie had secured her feet. Angling the knife downward, she started slicing the zip tie. Hearing the woman on the dock, Nikki couldn't tell what she was doing but knew she had to hurry. The zip tie finally broke, freeing her legs.

Nikki lifted a corner of the tarp to see where the woman was. She was dragging some old cinderblocks stored on the side of the boathouse over to the dock. When she placed them on the dock and turned to go back for more, Nikki threw the tarp off and jumped up on the dock. Her head was spinning, and her vision was blurred. With the pocketknife in her hand, she launched herself at the woman. She knew it was a kill-or-be-killed moment. As they struggled on the dock, Nikki was becoming dizzier, and the wound on her head was bleeding profusely from the woman's kick. When she tripped backward over one of the cinderblocks, the woman smiled and pushed her over the edge of the dock into the water. Nikki tried to grab onto the dock, but the woman stepped on her hands.

The woman reached down and picked up one of the cinderblocks and held it up over her head, smiling demonically down at Nikki in the water. Before she could drop it onto Nikki's head, a snarling sound came from the behind the woman. Barney slammed his body full force into her, catapulting her sideways off the end of the dock while still holding the cinderblock. Ribbons of blood spread through the water.

All Nikki heard before she lost consciousness was Barney whimpering, and she prayed he was alright.

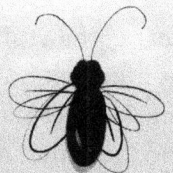

32

Heath

Heath called as he was leaving his house to let Nikki know he was on his way and immediately knew something was wrong when she didn't answer her cellphone. After several attempts to reach her, he called the Sheriff and told him he suspected something had happened to Nikki. Sheriff Hansen was at the marina and took off across the lake on the patrol boat, with Deputies CeeCee Carter and Lou Parker.

When Heath arrived at the house, the first thing he noticed was Barney wasn't lying on his blanket. Sounds from down by the boathouse echoed up the hill to the house. He took off down the hill and found Barney lying on the dock. Then he saw Nikki face down in the water.

"Oh God, no!"

Jumping into the water, he flipped Nikki over, pulling her to the shore. The Sheriff arrived at the dock to see Barney lying motionless on the dock. CeeCee immediately grabbed the emergency pack and went to Nikki.

Deputy Parker saw a body floating halfway under the dock and pulled it onto the shore. He checked for any signs of life, then looked at the Sheriff and shook his head. He radioed into dispatch to send an ambulance and the coroner's van.

Knowing that Barney had been poisoned, the Sheriff went to him and found him in bad shape. He radioed Dr. Walker, and they spoke for a minute, then the Sheriff returned to Barney, whose breathing was shallow.

"Easy, Barney. Help is on the way. Hang in there, Boy."

The Sheriff looked over to where CeeCee was working feverishly on Nikki. Heath had the most god-awful look on his face. Knowing about Heath's past, he felt for him. Just how much can one man take?

It was at least twenty minutes before the ambulance arrived. The paramedics raced down the hill and administered aid to Nikki. CeeCee was able to get a pulse, but it was weak, and there was no telling how long she had been faced down in the water. They loaded her on a stretcher, but due to the rough terrain on the hill, they had to carry it up the hill instead of rolling it.

Heath followed closely, insisting he ride with them. The Sheriff nodded.

As they were shutting the doors on the ambulance, Heath saw another of the Sheriff's patrol boats arrive at the dock. Hammy and Maggie, seeing something going on and hearing the sirens, came over in their golf cart, looked terrified.

Heath sat still, watching the paramedics do what they could for Nikki.

If ever there was a time for prayer, this was it. Closing his eyes, all he could see was her face when she smiled. He didn't know the words to pray, but he knew what he felt and hoped it was good enough to be heard.

It took thirty minutes to get to the hospital in Kingston. It was late at night, and he was sure there were deer and other animals crossing the road at this hour.

Please get us there safely, so Nikki can get the help she needs.

As they pulled up to the emergency entrance, a team of emergency personnel descended on the ambulance. Nikki was whisked through the automatic doors and down a hallway.

Heath paced in the waiting room, wringing his hands. Sheriff Hansen arrived and realizing Heath was blaming himself, he walked over to him.

"Any word on how she's doing."

"No... but I'm not sure they'll tell me anything since I'm not family."

"I'll take care of that. What about her parents? Have they been contacted?

"Yes, I called them. They're on their way."

"What route are they taking?" Heath told him, and the Sheriff stepped away for a couple of minutes to place a call. When he returned, Heath asked him about Barney.

"Not good. From what I could gather, Barney intervened and attacked the woman who was trying to kill Nikki."

"Who was she?"

The Sheriff took out his phone and showed Heath a photo of a driver's license—Pamela Forester.

Heath felt sick to his stomach.

"But we ruled her out. She was in Europe."

"Somehow, she snuck back into the country, probably by way of Mexico, with the clear intent of stopping Nikki and Christopher from inheriting Peter Forester's trust fund and the insurance."

It had been two hours since Nikki had been brought to the hospital and still no word from the doctors.

Maggie and Hammy showed up and hugged Heath.

"We've been praying all the way here. God is good, Heath. Remember that."

"I hope you're right, Maggie, because I couldn't bear to lose her."

Sheriff Hansen had walked over to the nurses' station to talk to the nurse on duty. She got up and went through a door adjacent to the station. A short while later, she returned to her desk, and a doctor came out into the waiting room, still in his scrubs.

"Is Nikki McKay's aunt or brother here."

The Sheriff nudged Heath and nodded at Maggie. They got the message.

"Yes," they both answered.

"We had to do a medically-induced coma. There's a slight swelling of the brain, and I felt it was necessary to alleviate any pain. We will monitor her closely. Shortly, we'll be moving her to intensive care. Once she is there, you'll be able to see her, but only for a short time and only one of you at a time."

"She's going to be okay, right?" Maggie asked.

Hammy put his arm around Maggie when he noticed her trembling.

"We're doing the best we can under the circumstances," the doctor replied. "I need to get back in there now. The nurses will advise you when Miss McKay will be settled in ICU. It could be another hour or so."

Heath was deflated. He had hoped for a more positive report from the doctor.

Flashing lights appeared, coming from down the hallway outside the emergency entrance, then three people rushed in. When they saw Maggie, Hammy, and Heath, they ran to them.

"How is she?" Sophia immediately asked. "How's our Nikki?"

Maggie relayed the information the doctor had told them.

Sean moved his wife over to the sofa in the waiting room and insisted she sit down. Sean sat next to her, and the man who came with them sat on her other side.

Maggie and Hammy sat in chairs across from them while Heath remained standing. His clothes were still stained with Nikki's blood and damp from the lake water.

Sean took notice. "Heath, thank you for what you did. If you hadn't been there…"

Heath nodded, not sure what to say.

Sophia realized she hadn't introduced the man who had come with them. "Heath, this is our son, Brian, Nikki's brother."

Heath reached out his hand, which Brian took immediately.

He thought of Christopher and asked where he was.

"He's at Brian's house with our other grandchildren," Sean answered. "Probably being completely spoiled by our daughter-in-law, Julie."

"You got that right." Brian agreed. "If it were up to her, we'd have a dozen more rugrats. She loves being a mom. I love being a dad, but I'm so outnumbered by the females in the house."

Heath felt more at ease as they talked about their family. Maggie and Hammy chimed in with tidbits about their kids and grandkids. He was sure the conversation was not just for his benefit but for theirs as well.

Sean asked about Barney. Nikki had contacted them when Barney had been poisoned, and she and Heath had rushed him to the vet. Everyone looked over at Heath. He wasn't sure how to tell them. The Sheriff answered for him.

"Barney was injured trying to protect Nikki."

A communal gasp arose from them, and Sophia moaned, "Oh no."

"I had the other patrol boat rush the vet across the lake to tend to him. I wasn't sure if Barney could be moved safely in his condition. He was in bad shape. They brought him back to the animal hospital on the boat. I haven't heard anything from Dr. Walker on his condition."

The nurse came out and asked to speak with Nikki's aunt and brother. Sophia and Sean looked confused, even more so when Heath spoke up.

"Nikki's parents are here now."

"Oh! Then you should know Nikki has been moved to ICU, and you can see her, but one at a time and for only a few minutes."

Sean told Sophia to go first, and the nurse escorted her down the hallway to a set of large doors.

Sophia entered the room the nurse directed her to. It was dimly lit. Multiple pieces of equipment with blinking lights and Nikki's vitals moved across the screen on a monitor. Sophia swallowed back a sob as she saw her daughter lying motionless with her head bandaged. She went to her bedside.

The nurse followed her into the room and whispered to her, "You can talk softly to her."

"Can I touch her hand?"

The nurse nodded.

Sophia took Nikki's hand and noticed how cold it was. She hoped the warmth from her hand would warm up Nikki's.

"Hi, Honey. It's Mom. You sure know how to shake things up, don't you?" Sophia took a deep breath. "Christopher is having a sleepover at your brother's house. Surrounded by girls and being spoiled for sure." Sophia was looking to see a response... any response—a twitch of the eyelids, a hand movement—but nothing. She let go of Nikki's hand after kissing it.

"I'll be by later on, Honey. Daddy's coming to see you in a few minutes."

When Sophia walked back into the waiting room, she nodded to Sean, and the lump in her throat became unbearable. When he approached her, she broke down, and he held her tight and rubbed her back.

Heath watched the interaction between them. Part of him wished he had Nikki's kind of parents when he was growing up. Her family was everything his wasn't.

Sean settled Sophia on the sofa next to Brian and followed the nurse to Nikki's room in ICU. He was taken aback when he saw how fragile she looked with her head wrapped in bandages and hooked up to all the blinking equipment.

The nurse told him about talking to her, and he nodded. She explained although she was in a medically-induced coma, hearing familiar voices had a healing effect on the brain.

From what he knew about water accidents, the longer victims were in the water, the more the possibility of brain damage from of oxygen deprivation. He not only was grateful for Heath getting her out of the water but hoped she hadn't been faced down for long.

He was beside himself with worry. What about Christopher? He didn't know how he would tell him if....

He had to stop thinking negatively.

Sitting in a chair the nurse had moved next to the bed, he touched Nikki's arm.

"You know the darndest thing happened on the way here. We were on our way, and every time we crossed into a county, sheriff's patrol cars surrounded us. Brian was driving our car, and the first time it happened, I thought it was because he was speeding. God knows he was. I would have if I'd been driving. Instead of pulling us over, they motioned for us to keep going. One patrol car pulled in front of us with lights and sirens going with another one was behind us doing the same thing. Then every time we crossed into another county, that county took over. It happened all the way here. When we came to a state route crossing, patrol cars were there and had held up traffic so we could continue through. They must have known there was a very important person waiting for us."

Sean was rattling on. He stopped talking and stroked her hand. So tiny and frail. He remembered how she held the fishing rod for Christopher and helped him reel in the fish. A tear traveled down his cheek. Would he ever see her fishing with Christopher again? He prayed he would.

When Sean returned to the waiting room, he joined Brian and Sophia on the sofa. He saw the inquiring look on Heath's anguished face. Sean said something to Brian, and he nodded. Sean went to Heath.

"I think Nikki's brother Heath needs to see her." Heath wasn't sure if he heard right.

Sophia nodded. "Go see your sister, Heath."

The Sheriff, who was sitting with Maggie and Hammy, stood and motioned to the nurse. "Could you please take Nikki's brother to see her, please?"

The nurse smiled, guessing what was going on, and led Heath to Nikki's room.

Standing in the doorway, he was overwhelmed by the equipment and seeing Nikki's body so lifeless. The atmosphere was as sterile as the machines.

The nurse told him what she had told Sean and Sophia, motioned to the chair beside the hospital bed, and silently left.

Heath

HE WASN'T sure what to say to her. His thoughts were all jumbled as he searched for the clarity to tell her what he felt. Taking a deep breath, he began to speak.

"Nikki, I'm so sorry I got there late. I could have prevented this from happening. I want you to know I would trade places with you if I could. I remember the day we met so vividly. You were so ornery and so damn cute. I think you thought the same of me, except for the cute part."

Heath wanted so much for her to open her eyes and see him—see his hurt, his anxiety. He wanted to show her how much he cared.

"I'll always be here for you, Nikki... and for Christopher." He rose from the chair and placed a kiss on her nose. "See you later, Freckles."

He walked down the hallway toward the waiting room but stopped halfway to compose himself. His eyes had filled with unshed tears, and he wiped them away. Entering the waiting room, it was obvious by his red eyes, he was deeply affected by seeing Nikki.

Thirty minutes later, the doctor came out to talk with them. "I know you all want an update. She's doing much better than we expected. Whoever found her, pulled her out of the water and performed resuscitation saved her life."

Everyone turned to Heath.

"I only did a little. The deputy on the sheriff's boat really administered aid to Nikki. She got a pulse."

"She's stable, and there are signs the swelling has diminished but not entirely. We're going to wean her from the drugs inducing the coma. It will be wait-and-see for now. I suggest you go home to get some rest. We have your numbers and will update you. The next twenty-four hours are critical."

Maggie looked at Hammy. "I don't want to leave."

"Me neither, Mags, but we should get some rest and come back tomorrow morning."

"Maggie, go home rest up." Sophia wrapped her arms around her friend. "We'll see you tomorrow."

Maggie nodded. After Maggie and Hammy left, Sophia told Sean she wasn't leaving. If necessary, she'd sleep on the sofa.

Sean looked at Heath. "Now you know where Nikki gets her stubbornness."

"Oh, you got that right," Brian added. "Don't forget the feistiness. Remember when we were at the park and some kids were bullying me? It didn't matter that she was a shrimp. She snarled and chased them down the street."

For the next forty-eight hours, they took turns doing vigils at Nikki's bedside. During that time, a lot transpired away from the hospital.

Maggie and Hammy had gone back to the lakehouse and found evidence of Barney's poisoning. They brought a large plastic bag with what they found, a metal pie tin with remnants of raw meat. Small insecticide pellets had been stuffed inside the meat, then the meat balled up. Dried saliva, probably Barney's, was crusted around the dried-up meat. Barney must have nibbled on the meat and tried to spit it out. The items were taken to the county lab for fingerprint identification.

Pamela Forester's body was held at the morgue, waiting for her parents to claim it. Other evidence was found, implicating her in the deaths of her brother Peter Forester and Laura Statler, who was with child.

Laura Statler's parents dropped the claim against Peter's estate, finally realizing they had no claim whatsoever.

Sean and Sophia decided to take Christopher out of school earlier than planned and brought him up to the lakehouse. They had told him Nikki had an accident and hurt her head, but he would see her soon. They wanted him to be near when Nikki came out of a coma. Even though they didn't know when, they prayed it would be soon.

Trey Westin made the trip up to the hospital and sat with Nikki's parents. He explained everything about the inheritance and insurance. He knew it was important for them to know if Nikki needed medical care, there were funds available to make sure she received the best care possible. He had been working with the Sheriff in putting the puzzle pieces together and traced how Pamela Forester was able to get back into the country unnoticed and pull off such fiendish acts.

Heath was on vigil duty. Holding Nikki's hand, he watched her face. The bandages had been removed from her head and were replaced with a smaller two-inch square bandage. The bruising on her arms and legs was fading, as well as the one on her forehead. She still had a blackeye, which had changed to her favorite shade of purple.

Heath spoke to her—sometimes teasing, something serious, always lovingly. Occasionally, he would touch the freckles on her cheeks and smile, remembering how feisty she got when he called her "Freckles."

That time, when he did, her hand twitched. The nurse explained it could be a nerve reaction, but Heath refused to believe it. It was Nikki. He insisted on staying longer and but there wasn't any more movement. Sophia showed up to take over, and Heath went out to the waiting room.

Something caught his eye down the hallway outside of the ICU section of the hospital.

"Sean, I need to pick something up. Actually, two things. Call me if anything happens."

"Sure, Heath."

Heath drove to the lakehouse where Maggie and Hammy were sitting with Christopher. When he got there, he explained to them what he wanted to do.

"Are you sure, Heath? It may not be allowed."

"I'll take my chances." Forty minutes later, Heath arrived back at the hospital.

"Sean, I need your help."

Ten minutes later, Heath and Sean walked into the hospital, each carrying a rather large duffel bag. Maggie and Hammy rolled their eyes and sat in the waiting room while Heath and Sean headed for ICU.

The nurse at the desk was familiar with the family's vigil and their comings and goings and switching places. She looked up and then back down at her paperwork, thinking nothing of them walking by.

Once inside Nikki's room, Sophia stood up and wondered what was going on.

Heath and Sean put their index fingers to her lips.

Sean unzipped the duffel bag he carried, and Christopher came out. He held his finger up to his lips.

"We have to be really quiet," he whispered to Sophia.

Heath unzipped his bag, and a furry red head popped up. Intuitively, Barney remained calm and quiet.

Sophia picked Christopher up onto her lap. "Talk in a whisper to Mommy."

Christopher nodded.

"Hi, Mommy. Grandma said you were sleeping a lot. I miss you and want you to come home soon. We have to catch more fireflies. I love you, Mommy." He looked sad when there was no response.

"She's sleeping, but she can hear you talking," Sophia whispered.

Christopher got really close to Sophia's ear. "Are you sure she heard me?"

"Yes. Very sure."

Sophia helped Christopher down, then rose from the chair and moved to let Heath sit. He held Barney's leash.

Heath lifted the beloved pet onto his lap. Barney was still a bit weak and wobbly, but when he saw Nikki, his tail wagged triple time. He cocked his head one way, then the other way as if trying to figure out why Nikki was so still. He nosed her hand and licked it, then kept nosing her hand as though he was trying to wake her up. Still no response.

Sophia placed her hand on Heath's shoulder. "At least you tried. The doctor is still hopeful. It just takes time."

Sean told them he would stay while Sophia and Heath walked Christopher and Barney back to the waiting room.

As they left, the nurse did a doubletake and smiled.

They got to the waiting room, and Heath sat down while Barney sat down next to his chair. Heath scratched behind the dog's ears.

"We tried, Barney."

Christopher snuggled on Sophia's lap.

"I saw a service dog down the hallway earlier and thought maybe, just maybe, it would work."

"You never know, Heath," Maggie said. "Seeing the service dog in the hallway made you bring Barney and Christopher here for a reason. It's one of those coincidences called Godwinks. Christopher was able to see his mommy, and Barney was able to see the woman he saved. Yes, she's asleep, but she's alive, thanks to him and to you."

Seeing Nikki's doctor running down the hallway, they all wondered what had happened. Was he going to Nikki's room or someone else's?

Barney tugged on his leash, wanting to go back to Nikki.

"No, Barney. Stay. You can't go back there now."

He whimpered.

"Do you think something's wrong?" Sophia whispered to Heath so Christopher couldn't hear.

"I don't know."

A few minutes later, Sean and the doctor walked into the waiting room. Sean had been crying, but they weren't tears of sadness. They were tears of joy.

"Nikki's awake. She's asking for Christopher and Barney."

The doctor walked over to them. "Sometimes, the best medicine in the world is love."

Heath found his own tears falling and swiped at them.

The doctor turned to Heath. "And sometimes rules are meant to be broken." He nodded at Barney and Christopher, then at the door to the ICU.

Sophia carried Christopher, and Heath led Barney—actually, Barney led Heath—to Nikki's room.

The doctor followed them into the room and stood off to the side with two of the ICU nurses, both with watery eyes.

Nikki was still pretty groggy, but her eyes lit up when she saw Christopher and Barney. Her smile melted Heath's heart.

She reached for Christopher and hugged him. "I love you, Christopher."

"I love you more, Mommy."

In unison, Christopher and Nikki said, "I love you mostest!"

Sean and Sophia took Christopher from Nikki. "Honey, you don't know how happy we are right now. We'll talk later. Rest up."

"I think it's what I've been doing, Mom."

Sean and Sophia left with Christopher, who waved to Nikki over Sean's shoulder.

Barney stood up on his back legs and licked Nikki's hand.

"You saved me, Barney. I saw you. You saved me. You're my guardian angel."

He barked once, then nosed her hand and licked it again. Nikki stroked Barney's head and scratched behind his ears. He sat down and placed a paw on Heath as if to say, "your turn."

Heath looked at her and said, "I can't believe it."

"There you go again with can't and won't mixed up, Mr. Winters."

He laughed.

"But I do believe... I love you, Nikki McKay... so very much."

"You better, Heath Winters, because I love you to the moon and back."

Other than his love, his kiss was all she wanted from him.

EPILOGUE

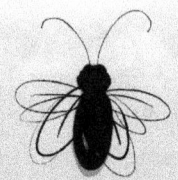

A little over a month later.

Nikki sat out on the dock with her parents, Maggie and Hammy, Christopher and Barney, waiting for the regatta of boats to pass by for the annual event held to celebrate the 4th of July. Heath called and said he'd join them after he took care of some last-minute business.

Nikki had physical therapy for the few two weeks after regaining consciousness, but her overall condition was back to normal.

Heath's construction project for the Sheriff's office in town had been completed, and a ceremony would take place the following week for its official opening.

Sheriff Hansen assigned CeeCee Carter to head up the office. She and Tommy Caldwell were madly in love, and Maggie and Sophia were congratulating themselves on a well-planned match.

Trey Westin was able to close out the Forester account and moved the inheritance funds and insurance payout into an account for

Nikki. He told Nikki and her family that the Foresters picked up the tab for her medical expenses. Trey wondered if it was out of guilt or the fact they wanted to change people's opinion about their family. Either way, it was a huge help to Nikki.

Addy Caldwell and Frank Morton disappeared for a weekend and came back married to the joy of Tommy and the rest of their family.

The regatta began, and the first boat to pass by was the Sheriff's patrol boat. Sheriff Hansen waved to Nikki and her family. CeeCee and Lou Parker were aboard and waved as well. Next came the members of the Spring Lake Town Council on a party pontoon boat. Dan Burke, Steve McConnell, and their wives waved and shouted hello. More boats from business owners and residents waved as they passed by.

Barney started barking.

Christopher jumped up and down. Nikki smiled as she saw Heath and Tommy on Winter's Remorse. All the boats came to a stop when Heath stopped in front of their pier. He hopped up on the dock and walked over to Nikki while Tommy took over the boat.

"Heath what are you doing?" When he got down on one knee, she knew. Her hand went to her mouth. He held up a ring.

"Nikki McKay, I *can't* imagine my life without you. I *can't* believe how we met or how we were at such odds in the beginning. I *can't* see any future without you, Christopher, and Barney. And I *can't* believe how much I love you. I *can't* wait to make you mine forever. Please say you'll marry me."

Nikki's eyes blurring with tears, she nodded.

"Is that a yes?"

"Yes, Heath Winters, I will marry you."

The boaters all hooted and hollered.

Her family and friends cheered as Heath placed a ring on her finger and kissed her.

"I *can't* believe you said yes, Freckles," he whispered in her ear.

She whispered back, "Don't call me Freckles."

Fireworks were set off from a floating barge, arranged by the Sheriff.

"So that makes three of them." Sophia and Maggie had their heads together. "Who's next on the list."

THE END

Destiny is no matter of chance. It is a matter of choice. It is not a thing to be waited for, it is a thing to be achieved.

— WILLIAM JENNINGS BRYAN

SPECIAL NOTE FROM AUTHOR PENELOPE BELL

I actually wrote this story over forty years ago on a typewriter with pages of handwritten notes for the outline. It kept haunting me, so I finally gave in and dusted off the cobwebs and transcribed it to my computer.

Once I started, I couldn't stop. It's a romantic mystery filled with a roller coaster of emotions and "who-dunnit" clues throughout.

Take a journey through the pages, I promise it will have you wondering, hoping, and believing.

Author Penelope Bell

THANK YOU READERS!

If you enjoyed MOONLIGHT & FIREFLIES, I'd be so very grateful if you wrote a review. Just a few lines would be great.

Reviews are the best gift an author can receive. They encourage us when they are good, help us improve our writing when they are not, and help other readers make a more informed choice when purchasing a book. Reviews keep Amazon algorithms humming and are the most helpful aid in selling books!

To post a review on Amazon or for Kindle:

1. Go to the product detail page for MOONLIGHT & FIREFLIES on Amazon.com
2. Click "Write a customer review" in the Customer Reviews section.
3. Post a rating and write your review, then click Submit.

If you have read any of my previous books and haven't written a review, I would appreciate it if you would.

With sincerest thanks,
Penelope Bell

MY SPECIAL THANKS...

To my dear family and friends for your love and support. Without you there is no way I would be able to write what I love. Paul, Kim, Merrick, Jason and Richard... I LOVE YOU!

To the local businesses who are always in my life, especially the Herndon family at Handlebar J's, Scott Bohall at Treasures, MacDonald's Ranch, the Open Beta Musical Group, and Jo at the English Rose Tea Room... all have contributed greatly in my writing.

To those awesome people who continue to make me feel special and give me so much encouragement... Tonia Miller, Jeanine Coleman, Lynnette Cool, Lisa Bishop, Lynn Rouyer, Lorraine Sanders, Peggy Hagar, Grace Bartosik, Ariana at Hand & Stone, and Samantha Kirk and Tiffanie Van Eimeren at MD Skin Lounge and "Twitch."

To my connections in the legal profession who I have worked with for many years, your incredible insight, details and information were invaluable.

To my readers who continue to give me the impetus to be the best writer I can be.

And last, but not least, to my incredibly talented team at Dragonfly Ink Publishing, Editor Sandy Ebel, Graphics Artist Antonette Santillo, Publisher Dakota Willink, and Publishing Assistant Cheryl Maddox. You all rock!

Penelope Bell

ABOUT PENELOPE BELL

Penelope Bell was born and raised in the suburbs of Chicago. Her love of reading and writing took hold at a very young age—you would always see her with a book or a pen and paper in her hands. She loved mysteries and stories about horses or dogs or tales of knights in shining armor. As she grew older, romance stories intrigued her, especially if they were historical and took place in foreign countries.

When she was 20 years old, she went on a three-week road trip with her parents, traveling through the Rocky Mountain states, down the west coast, then throughout the southwest. The memories were long-lasting and impressionable, and over the following years, she made several trips to the southwest, savoring the atmosphere, varied terrain, and climate. The snow-capped mountains of northern Arizona, the Ponderosa pine forests, the Grand Canyon, and the high and low desert regions beckoned her. Her parents had retired and moved to Arizona, and when an opportunity presented itself to her, as a divorced mother of two, she relocated to the greater Phoenix area, traveling cross-country with her teenaged children, two affectionate cats, and a silly but protective Irish Setter.

Caring for her children and her aging parents and working a full time job didn't allow for much reading or writing time, but somehow, she managed to squeeze some of it in to her life. It brought her happiness and serenity.

Writing is her passion with photography coming in as a close second.

Penelope self-published several "coffee table" photography books, one of which included her poetry and short stories. Her family has always been supportive of her writing and encouraged her to publish her novels.

Penelope's stories have been a catharsis for her. She writes what she knows. Lead characters deal with events and situations very familiar to her. In many ways, she feels it has liberated her from her own past traumas and taken her from being broken to being made whole again.

Music is vital to her, and she always has it as a background while writing. She affirms it gets the creative juices flowing and the imagination soaring.

Her advocacy for the protection of wild horses is near and dear to her, and you will more than likely find the struggle to prevent the extinction of those majestic creatures within her books.

Penelope met her "forever" in 2007 and lives in Scottsdale, Arizona with her husband Richard. In the summer, time is spent at their cabin up in the northern Arizona forests. Maintaining her heritage and traditions and spending time with family is very important to her. She and her husband both love to travel and have done so extensively, including most of North America, the Caribbean, and Europe, savoring the histories, cultures, and geography of those places, yet they cherish those quiet times at home, sharing each other's thoughts and dreams.

Website: www.penelopebellauthor.com
Email: AuthorPenelopeBell@Gmail.com

ALSO BY PENELOPE BELL

Phoenix Rising Series

Book 1: Hearts Rising (April 2019)

Book 2: Hearts Healing (December 2019)

Book 3: Hearts Wishing (November 2020)

Book 4: Hearts Blazing (October 2021)

Novella: Hearts Beating (TBD - Spring 2023)

Book 5: Hearts Singing (TBD)

Book 6: Hearts Dreaming (TBD)

Book 7: Hearts Reuniting (TBD)

Spring Lake Series

Book 1: Moonlight & Fireflies (December 2022)

Upcoming Stand-Alone Novels

Timeless Love (TBD)

The Cave (TBD)